The Armageddon Two-Step

early praise for **THE ARMAGEDDON TWO-STEP**

"*The Armageddon Two-Step* is a clever, witty, and frequently biting tale of unlikely fame, carved out by a genuine storyteller."
—ANTHONY SQUIERS, author of *Madness & Insanity*
Co-editor of *Philosophizing Brecht: Critical Readings on Art,
Consciousness, Social Theory and Performance*

"There's a pleasant rhythm to [Michael Loyd Gray's] sentence construction that eases you into his stories like finding relaxation in your favorite comfy chair."
—STEVE BERGSMAN, author of a dozen books; his next book is
I Put a Spell on You: The Bizarre Life of Screamin' Jay Hawkins

"Gray is at the top of his game in *The Armageddon Two-Step*. He leads the reader on a taco-fueled, rollicking good time along with his colorful cast of characters, including the unlikely hero, Shelby Albert Goddard."
—NED RANDLE, author of *Baxter's Friends, Running at Night,*
and *St. Michael Poker & Drinking Club*

"*The Armageddon Two-Step*'s humor shows the American Dream as the American-Fallacy, through Shelby's melancholic rise to fame."
—SEAN KARNS, author of *Jar of Pennies*

OTHER BOOKS BY MICHAEL LOYD GRAY

NOVELS:
Well Deserved
Exile on Kalamazoo Street
The Canary
King Biscuit
Not Famous Anymore

CREATIVE NON-FICTION:
Still Sort of Original in Unoriginal Times

THE
ARMAGEDDON
TWO-STEP

A Novel by
MICHAEL
LOYD GRAY

redbat books
2019

Printed in the United States of America

First Edition: December 3, 2019

Trade Paperback ISBN 978-1-946970-92-3

Library of Congress Control Number: 2019905799

Published by
redbat books
La Grande, OR 97850
www.redbatbooks.com

Text set in Garamond Premier Pro

Book design by
Kristin Summers, redbat design | www.redbatdesign.com

DEDICATION

This book is dedicated to all the writers snubbed by agents
and publishers because they weren't born famous.

Some other folks I'd like to mention, but in a nice way:
my personal editor Carol Burbank;
my awesome Michigander friends—Anthony Squiers and Joe Taylor;
my two outlaw cats—Suzie Lucifer and Yoda Lucifer; and of course,
Kristin Summers and Redbat Books for believing in this novel.

Once more, thanks to the two most gracious writers I've known—
Stuart Dybek, writer-in-residence at Northwestern University,
and the late novelist Monique Raphel High.

Part One

*"It has become appallingly obvious that our technology
has exceeded our humanity."*
—Albert Einstein

THE ARMAGEDDON TWO-STEP

Shelby Albert Goddard once saved the world, as in Terra Firma, Planet Earth—The Whole Damn Global Enchilada. Before that, he flipped burgers for a summer at McDonald's, but always the saving-the-world gig led his resume. Not that he needed a resume, because he got a boatload of cash from a grateful U.S. government, and the rest of the planet was awfully stoked, too: diamonds arrived from South Africa. Switzerland dispatched a ton of cheese and a banking representative. More vodka than Shelby could ever want came from Russia. He was even relieved of ever having to pay taxes. A very official card in his wallet attested to that privilege.

But tribute didn't stop there—Congress enacted Shelby Goddard Saved the World Day, though the Tea Party cabal voted no, of course. Shelby's Boise, Idaho hometown made him honorary mayor. The CIA and FBI gave gold badges, but emphasized he had no real authority and not to arrest anyone or attempt espionage. NASA named a shuttle after him and offered a ride, which Shelby declined—fear of heights. Even a moderate roller coaster scared the bejesus out of him. The president's wife kissed Shelby on the mouth, which irked the president, but Shelby had saved the world, and so the president gracefully looked the other way.

Shelby's likeness was chiseled onto Mt. Rushmore, which made it crowded, his face pinched, and he looked like he was whispering impertinently in Lincoln's ear. But *Dancing with the Stars* promised to pair him with one or more Kardashians. And Miley Cyrus gave him an energetic hand job in the back of her limo, though her tongue creeped him out and he kept his eyes shut. Keith Richards taught him guitar chords and shared a joint and mild hallucinations. Shelby also got beachfront property in Malibu, a lifetime pass to a Nevada brothel, and a pass for ten-cent tacos—the Bell Grande with extra sour cream—from any Taco Bell for twenty years. Nutrition experts concluded that twenty years was more than enough for Shelby to ruin his health. Publicly, he praised Taco Bell but privately felt it was rather petty to charge him even a dime for a taco, because after all—he had saved the world.

How Shelby had saved the world remained vague and murky because of national security and global geopolitics and plain old selfishness, too. It involved thingamabobs and thingamajigs and doohickeys and timing and fate and even some luck. It was quite secret and very mysterious, and of course the specific details couldn't be divulged. Not ever. It had been all so improbable and yet it somehow happened and certainly it had to do with the potential for big damn explosions and global devastation—like in any good Hollywood action film minus the clever, pithy dialogue. All of Shelby's colleagues agreed that there had been the imminent opportunity for one thing to lead to another and then an unstoppable conflagration. Gotterdammerung. Armageddon. The Last Roundup.

What the public was told was vague, but inspiring. Heroic, but unclear. Amazing, but confusing. At a really dangerous moment, Shelby displayed great presence of mind and everyone should certainly be very proud of him, but it was now over and classified, and really, most Americans sank back into their sofas under the spell of reality TV a few days after Shelby had saved the world, what with most Americans having the attention span of a gnat. Nothing to see here, folks—move along!

But Shelby could not move along, nor could he definitely move past it because at the time of critical mass, at the time of wondrous magic from thingamabobs, thingamajigs, and doohickeys, he had been plunked on the head by something—or someone?—and though not incapacitated, not rendered unconscious, he had witnessed approaching, impending, insistent and howling critical mass and its providential reversal through hazy, languid, heavy eyes, and it was all a jumble of noise and a whirr of color, and afterward he went down heavily to his knees, barking them both, and then he crumpled to the floor. That blurry sequence of events played at least once a day in his head, especially after the government assured Shelby he'd lose his freebies and have to pay taxes again if he endangered national security by spilling the beans about some really sensitive shit that wasn't supposed to exist and that it certainly didn't want anyone else to have. Taco Bell said they expected him to always be an upright and moral citizen since he now was sort of a roving ambassador for them. And Shelby had to admit that ten cents for a Bell Grande with extra sour cream was a smoking deal.

Shelby hadn't started off to save the world. Who does? Who even thinks of it? Who expects the opportunity? Certainly not Shelby, who as a child exhibited no traits that suggested eventual heroism or even presence of mind. He was actually quite the lethargic baby. A lump of pink flesh. Big blue eyes that always seemed on the verge of snapping shut. He often stared off at nothing. His parents, Louise and George Goddard, had at first worried he might be retarded because Shelby seemed more than just slow. He made shrill, high-pitched sounds that they didn't believe were entirely human. But a child psychologist assured them that Shelby was quite normal and just a baby and to be patient with his lethargy. It was a phase—an interlude that would give way to something more animated. And it did.

In high school, Shelby ran on the track team—low hurdles—and excelled in the sciences and joined the model building club, which was nerdy, but he liked building model cars and World War II airplanes. He acquired a girlfriend named Tulia, who was Goth at a time when Goth had been over for quite a while. Tulia was short and dark and Shelby had grown into a lanky lad of almost six-three with an angular face and longish brown hair. But since Shelby didn't fit into any specific school clique—even the Science Club didn't quite know what to make of him—he and Tulia seemed to fit at first. Both of them were a bit isolated and searching for their tribes.

But it wasn't a match made in heaven and Tulia abruptly changed and became a blonde again and went off to college at UCLA and joined a sorority, while Shelby went to Stanford and dressed for comfort rather than style—he owned a dozen flannel shirts—and graduated with degrees in the sort of sciences his parents had trouble understanding despite Shelby's efforts to explain them.

Because Shelby was quite brilliant in sciences he could not explain to his parents or anyone else, he got a job crunching data and working with thingamabobs and thingamajigs and doohickeys at a secret government agency out in the middle of nowhere, and on April 1, 2013, quite unexpectedly, in a blinding flash of presence of mind, Shelby Albert Goddard saved the world, and his old, predictable life ended and a new life in uncharted waters began.

Shelby ate his first ten-cent taco in Tucumcari, New Mexico. He drove a spiffy new Mercedes from a Phoenix car dealer in exchange for TV commercial appearances and a Saving the World Sale offering Shelby's autograph for each car sold. The dealer did very well and then Shelby was on his way in a new black 500 SL with a tank of gas and special plates—SAVWLRD.

He bought only three tacos, despite the low price—two for his dinner and one for the road. He had rolls of dimes just for the trip. The Taco Bell manager had thrown in a large Pepsi and extra extra sour cream on the house. It went predictably: Shelby flashed the special credit card issued him by the president of Taco Bell and someone produced a camera phone to have a group shot with the man who had saved the world and had extended their glorious fast-food careers. Shelby signed autographs and a reporter from the Tucumcari paper showed up with a photographer and Shelby graciously posed and provided some interesting but vague quotes about saving the world, remembering to mention thingamabobs, thingamajigs, and doohickeys.

A few miles down the road from Tucumcari, Shelby felt sleepy and pulled into a rest stop. He had been driving aimlessly since Phoenix, just lazily inspecting some of the world he had saved and keeping to the interstate and thinking too much and feeling unsure about the future. He was tired but didn't feel he would fall asleep right away and so to calm himself he masturbated in the car, which of course pretty much busted the whole Taco Bell morality clause. It dawned on him afterwards that when he was getting all the freebies for saving the world, that he should have also asked to be allowed to masturbate in public when the urge struck—not, like, while walking down a street. Certainly not anywhere where children played. Not, like, while walking in the St. Pat's Day parade in Chicago, or while on a street corner at Mardi Gras; but in his car, discretely parked at the quiet end of a rest area, for example, it ought to be okay if he was always careful. Or if he parked along a quiet city side street. And if a cop came along and caught him, sausage in hand, he would then produce another government card—like his no taxes ever again government card—and the cop would leave him alone and thank him for saving the world, but remind him to keep a low profile—maybe find a deserted country road—while whacking the old kielbasa.

Shelby had a number to call if things got weird. He understood weird to mean when he was having issues coping with his new life as a fabulously rich hero who had saved the world, but who also had to decide what to do with himself. After all, how does one top saving the world? Save the galaxy? Save the universe? Even saving the whales seemed pedestrian. The phone number was there for him for just such a dilemma, though it was also there for him—he had been clearly told multiple times—in case he was in danger of spilling any super secret secrets, and until he got used to the notion of staying mum about the specific events of April 1, 2013.

He was urged to rely on the phone number during times of stress. Or when he was drunk. Think of it as a lifeline, like on that TV show, he was told. And try not to drink too much and talk too long to strangers in bars, especially if the strangers have names such as Vladimir or Sergey or Boris, thick accents, and can drink lots of vodka. The number connected him to a government agent he had never met in person and at an agency so secret that almost no one in the government knew much about it except that it was super super secret and did good and important things, but vague things. Secret things—but good things. Men in Black times two—or three.

But the agency had a sense of humor, too, because when Shelby called the number from the rest area outside Tucumcari, the new ring tone was the distinctive ring tone from phones on *The Man from U.N.C.L.E.*, a show Shelby had discovered on a reruns channel while he was at Stanford. He had even tried to get his hair cut like Illya Kuryakin's, but it didn't quite turn out to have the desired effect, and so he was in the process of growing his hair long again and sort of resembled Illya Kuryakin needing a good haircut.

The agent assigned to Shelby was named Valkyrie.

"I love the new ring tone," Shelby said.

"Thought you might," Valkyrie said. "Napoleon Solo was a cool dude."

"What about his sidekick, Illya?"

"Can't trust those Russkies," Valkyrie said. "But that's just me. How's that Illya haircut working for you? I saw you on *Oprah*."

"It's getting there," Shelby said. "I've been meaning to ask—your name isn't really Valkyrie, right?"

"Who would be named Valkyrie?" Valkyrie said. "C'mon, Shelby, you graduated from Stanford, for God's sake."

"And I saved the world."

"That's the rumor," Valkyrie said.

"You don't believe it?"

"I'm fucking with you, son," Valkyrie said. "If it wasn't true, would we be talking right now?"

"I suppose not," Shelby said. "I suppose you're in a really secret location in Washington—maybe underground, right? A bunker?"

"I'm sitting on the can, at home," Valkyrie said. "In Maryland. My wife is waiting on me so we can go to dinner. What's up, Shelby?"

Shelby explained that he had been on the road for a while, out in the great wide open, as it were—an urban cowboy of sorts in his new Benz—to examine the country he had saved. Examining the entire world, he felt, would take too long. But he hadn't quite counted on becoming lonely so soon, and feeling adrift, despite his new mountain of cash. He was eating pretty damn well, thanks to Taco Bell, and had even added a few pounds his lanky frame could use, but he felt like it should be easier to know where to go, and what to do. Otherwise, what good was it to have saved the world? Other than having the opportunity to still pose the question, of course.

"How's the new Mercedes, kid?" Valkyrie said. "I hear it's a black 500 SL."

"How'd you know that?"

"I'm a guy with the code name Valkyrie—how do you think I know?"

Shelby looked up, into the night sky full of twinkling stars.

"Is there a satellite watching me?"

"God, no," Valkyrie said. "We have better uses for satellites—like watching that nutcase who runs North Korea scratch his fat ass."

"You really watch stuff like that?" Shelby said.

"I'm fucking with you again, kid," Valkyrie said. "Besides, another agency keeps track of that wacko."

"Oh," Shelby said. "I'll have to get better at recognizing bullshit."

"You'll get the hang of it—we're just starting out together."

"So how'd you know about my car?"

"One of our agents saw your TV commercial and gave me a call. Sometimes that's how it goes. The cloak-and-dagger shit is overrated and overblown. You okay, kid?"

Shelby hesitated. It felt odd to open up to a secret agent named Valkyrie who was sitting on a toilet halfway across the country.

"Are you really a secret agent, Valkyrie?"

"Good question, Shel. I'm not James Bond. Or Jason Bourne. Or even Inspector Clouseau, though my wife sometimes thinks I am. I don't think I resemble Agent Smith in *The Matrix*, either. Been told that a couple times. Does that help or make it worse?"

"Worse, actually—but that's okay, I suppose."

"Look at it this way, Shel—almost nobody knows what I do, and even my wife knows very little, and so I suppose I am a secret agent of sorts. But I don't topple governments or assassinate anyone."

"How'd you get the job of babysitting me?"

"We drew straws."

"Sorry."

"Don't apologize, kid. This beats getting horny foreign diplomats out of messes their dicks created."

For a moment, Shelby recalled whacking his kielbasa back in Tucumcari. It had been quite impulsive. He was convinced he didn't have an actual whacking off issue requiring embarrassing time on a couch with a doctor, that it was mostly a response to stress. That had to be it. And stress had to be combated strenuously so things didn't get bottled up and pop a gasket or two. Gaskets had to be maintained. Masturbation was normal, healthy—if it wasn't, why did God give men hands? He was very glad to know Valkyrie didn't keep tabs on him with satellites, but he did glance nervously into the sky again and thought he saw something moving. It was very faint, microscopic. He had to look several times to believe he truly was seeing something and not just a floater in his eyes, for example. But there *was* something there. And it *moved*. Stars didn't move as far as he knew. Though, that was just a reassuring misconception of sorts that people needed—everything in the sky, throughout the universe, was *moving*. Especially the portion of the sky he was gazing at.

"There's something moving in the sky, Valkyrie."

"A commercial airliner, kid. Probably headed to LA. Which way's it going?"

"East."

"New York, then," Valkyrie said. "Did you hear me on not letting your dick lead you around, Shel?"

"Don't worry. I'll try and avoid that."

"Good call, Shel. Keep it in your pants—unless you use your pass out at that Nevada whorehouse."

"I'm thinking of giving that back."

"Why?" Valkyrie said. "If I were a single man—well, never mind, but you get my drift."

"I was thinking," Shelby said. "Does a guy with lots of money who saved the world really need a whorehouse pass to get laid?"

"Good point. I would hope not. Saving the world has got to be the ultimate aphrodisiac. Maybe you should start thinking of yourself as a potential babe magnet."

"Really?"

"Sure, kid. That's a great bar pickup line—I saved the world. That and your lifetime Taco Bell pass. Just flash it to the ladies. Try the bar at any TGI Friday's, for example."

Shelby let his mind wander and imagined himself sitting at the bar in a TGI Friday's, maybe the one in Amarillo—no, maybe Chicago, or Los Angeles, or Seattle, though those cities would have much better places than a TGI. But the city didn't really matter, he concluded. It wasn't like real estate, where location was everything. Like Valkyrie said, it was the line, the saving the world line—yes, the ultimate aphrodisiac. He would merely have to cozy up to an attractive woman and mention that he was Shelby Albert Goddard, in the flesh, the man who had saved the world and talked about it on Oprah and Letterman and Leno. And maybe she would already know that, would have recognized him, and slid over to the stool next to him to seductively introduce herself and coo in his ear. Cooing sounded very good.

"Good idea," Shelby said. "And it wouldn't really enhance my image to frequent a whorehouse."

"And there's that, too, kid. Though it sounds like fun."

"So, can I trade it back in for something else?

"Trade it with who, Shel?"

"With you guys, with your agency—the government."

"Hold on, kid. The government isn't in the business of whorehouse passes, Shel. The government does not endorse whorehouses. The owner volunteered that. He's a former Marine, pretty patriotic, but likely let his patriotism override his business sense a bit there. All we did was sort of broker the deal for him. A courtesy to a veteran. But we'd deny that if it came out."

"Then what do I do with the pass?" Shelby said.

"Advertise it on eBay, kid. Or maybe Craigslist."

"Do you think the whorehouse owner would go along with that?"

"Doubtful. I wouldn't. The whole idea is to provide services to the guy who saved the world. Anyone else coming through their door with that pass is just another swinging dick eating into profits, so to speak."

"Thanks for that image, Valkyrie."

"Don't mention it. Listen, kid—my wife's knocking on the bathroom door again. We've got reservations at a place that's hard to get in—is this an emergency, for example?"

Shelby wasn't sure and hesitated.

"Kid—you still there?"

"Yeah. I'm here."

"Are you suicidal or anything like that?"

"God no. I guess I'm—lonely. I keep driving around to avoid people and questions."

"Tell you what," Valkyrie said. "I can tell you need someone to talk to, but I'm sort of tied up. I really need to score some points with the wife. So, I want you to drive to Amarillo and wait there. I'll grab a plane to Dallas in the morning and chopper over to Amarillo. I'll call you when I'm in the chopper and we'll pick a place to meet—how's that?"

"Will it be a black helicopter?"

"There are no black helicopters. That's just more Tea Party and Fox News horseshit. Our choppers are usually white, and rentals, I think."

"Why Amarillo?" Shelby said.

"I've never been to Amarillo, but I always liked the name. It really rolls off the tongue nicely—Am-O-rillo. Sounds like a tasty dessert, like something with lots of whipped cream. And it's on your way. We kill two birds with one stone."

"I think I can be in Amarillo in about an hour or so," Shelby said.

"Good. Go get a nice hotel and have a drink in the bar. Maybe two drinks. Have you had dinner?"

"I had some ten-cent tacos."

"That's a hell of a deal you got from Taco Bell, kid."

"I guess so," Shelby said, but Valkyrie had already hung up.

Shelby leaned back on a pile of pillows in his room at the Holiday Inn, just off the interstate on the east side of Amarillo. He began to masturbate, not even bothering to completely slip off his jeans and underwear; but his heart wasn't in it, and apparently neither was his pecker, which refused to cooperate. After a few minutes it was just boring labor to work his arm and hand and so he buttoned up and placed his hands behind his head on the pillow. He stared at the ceiling for a while and listened to the gentle hum of the air conditioning, but he was too restless. He jumped up and turned on the TV and surfed all the channels three times, stopping only at a movie about silly Samurai making grunting noises, running around chaotically with swords and colorful uniforms and helmets with horns that made them look sort of like giant beetles hacking each other to pieces.

Nothing on TV appealed to him, not the fake wrestling, not the vacuous Kardashians, not *Naked Island Survivor*, not Nancy Grace moaning about something or somebody, not even the porn available on the adult channel for a fee, with titles such as *Womb Raider*, *Edward Penishands*, and *Assablanca*. He was actually tempted for a moment by the potential of porn, the distracting allure of porn, thinking it might jumpstart the old kielbasa—but what was the point in the end, after the messy finish? It would all be over quickly enough and he'd be left with a wet hand, the dubious accomplishment of ejaculation minus actual sex, and the knowledge that hotel desk clerks could look at his account and chalk him up as just another weenie-whacker who'd pulled in off the interstate to watch *Assablanca*.

And what if Roger Valkyrie had pulled his leg—had flat-out lied—and there really was a satellite tracking his every move, watching him like a duck eyeing a June bug, just waiting to nail him zoning out to *Assablanca* while choking the chicken on his Holiday Inn bed, head propped up nice and comfy on pillows, the soft purr of air conditioning in the background. Could satellites even do that if he closed the drapes and got under the covers? What if he turned off the lights? He even switched them off, to see how dark it would get. But even with the drapes closed too, there was light streaming into the room through the thin fabric of the drapes from a huge neon sign on the building next door.

He opened the drapes again, deciding that drapes and darkness probably weren't much deterrence to spy satellites that could monitor flies kissing a camel's ass in Iraq, so he had heard, and they probably could penetrate anything and everything and had some sort of X-ray ability to probe every nook and cranny of a life; and that even if he was under the covers beating his meat, the satellite could nonetheless transmit a secret feed to some secret place and to some secret someone, in a secret bunker, whose secret job was to watch people who pretended to watch TV with their hand going up and down under the covers.

He slid off the bed and pulled the balcony door open. It was heavy and he really had to put some elbow grease into it. It was a warm night and a single moth circled the balcony light crazily. What did moths do with themselves before lights? Shelby could hear traffic out on the interstate, a combination of rushing and clacking sounds, but could not see it. Somewhere nearby a car horn suddenly went off for a few seconds and then ceased. He looked down into the parking lot for a moment when two men started arguing, their conversation growing into shouts about a woman named Clarise, who was definitely a bitch according to one of them, and then something even worse and more graphic, he added; but apparently she was much more admired by the second man, who shouted just as loud nonetheless, and made some colorful references to the first man's mother.

The two angry men quickly disappeared into a room, the door slamming so loud that Shelby wondered if it came off its hinges, but he didn't hear it fall. He also wondered whether Clarise was in the room, and what that might mean to the two men as well as to Clarise, and whether she truly was a bitch, or just generally misunderstood. She must at least be pretty, he believed, to have inspired such a ruckus to begin with. All in all, he felt that the satellites, if they really were on the prowl, ought to take a peek into Clarise's room. Maybe, despite all the venom spewed between the two men, and at Clarise, there was about to be an Amarillo threesome version of *Assablanca*—*Amablanca* was his choice for a porn title.

It was quiet again for a few minutes, just the soothing sound of flowing but unseen traffic on the nearby interstate, and then a dog barked for a while, apparently from a row of houses just behind the hotel. It was a sudden, disturbing sound—insistent, mournful, a wailing, a pleading. He could see a few of the houses, but not the dog, which stopped after a couple minutes. It was pretty dark over that way, with just solitary yellow porch lights on at the few houses he could see. A pickup truck pulled into a space in the parking lot below, and three boys in cowboy hats got out, two of them carrying large coolers that Shelby figured were filled with beer. They disappeared into a room, and while the door was open, blue cigarette smoke and country and western music poured out the door, and so did many boisterous voices, both male and female. Up in the sky the stars glittered and preened. He waited for something to move in the night sky and wondered just how much he should trust Valkyrie.

The next afternoon, Valkyrie landed a bit ostentatiously in a white helicopter and a cloud of brown dust in a field east of Amarillo. Shelby had watched the chopper approach from a quite a ways off, at first just a tiny, noiseless dot growing larger, like an approaching, droning gnat from the corner of an eye. Then it became a shape and the sound of its beating rotors could be heard clearly, then quite loudly. It landed with a bit of a thud and bounced up a few feet once, before staying put on the surface of the field. The pilot wore a black helmet with a dark visor covering his face, and he looked over at Shelby. The chopper rotors churned madly. Shelby was reminded of a giant, angry dragonfly.

Valkyrie jumped out and nearly slipped and fell, but caught himself with a hand on the ground, looked like someone trying to kneel to pray, mindful not to stand all the way up until clear of the swirling blades. He moved away from the giant dragonfly nearly on his hands and knees, through a brown cloud of dust, and then once clear, he stood slowly and seemed perhaps momentarily uncertain, perhaps tasting already the swirling brown dust kicked up by the chopper as it drenched his suit and hair.

For a long moment, he looked over at Shelby and his car, shielding his eyes from the swirling dust clouds, which rose into the sky high enough that Shelby figured it might trigger a report from some curious citizen, maybe someone speeding by on the interstate, that the field had somehow caught fire, or a plane had crashed—or that it was a brown dust tornado. There really were great clouds of dust erupting into the air. Shelby glanced up at the rising clouds. It must have been quite a sight if any satellites were peeking. Maybe they were flying past too quickly to notice and instead hell-bent on catching up to the latest chicanery in the Middle East.

Shelby was sitting on the hood of his Mercedes finishing a ten-cent taco and tasting brown dust. To Shelby, Valkyrie looked to be about forty or so, but in his dark suit, close-cropped blond hair, and athletic gait, he did actually sort of resemble Agent Smith from *The Matrix*. Valkyrie was a hair taller than Shelby, and a good hundred yards away, but his long legs chewed up distance pretty fast as he looked around at the field of stubble and weeds punctuated by a few anemic green bushes, and then up into the sky momentarily, a quick glance, and Shelby looked up suddenly too, followed Valkyrie's gaze toward the heavens, at the cloudless, blue sky—was this accidental proof that there *were* satellites calibrated to shadow Shelby, and was Valkyrie sort of instinctively, erroneously, tipping his hand and looking up in acknowledgment? In the daytime, satellites could float above without fear of detection by the naked eye, but Shelby looked up anyway, and even shielded his eyes with a hand, nearly dropping his taco. Grated cheese spilled into his lap.

"Think you'll ever get tired of those tacos?" Valkyrie said, brushing brown dust off his shoulders and shaking some out of his hair.

"Not in this lifetime," Shelby said warily, still thinking of satellites.

"How many dimes do you carry, Shelby?"

"I've got rolls of them."

Valkyrie looked up and down Shelby's car.

"You're my ride now, kid. How are you—not thinking of harming yourself are you?"

"When did you become Dr. Phil?"

"Protocol, Shel. I have to ask."

"That's okay," Shelby said. "It's nice to have someone ask. What do you mean I'm your ride?"

"You're driving me back to Dallas," Valkyrie said. "That gives us plenty of time to chat—let's get cracking."

By the time they reached Oklahoma City and turned south on I-35 toward Dallas, Shelby had pretty much told Valkyrie his life story.

"And remember, Shel—never tell anyone specific details about what happened, and what you saw, what you know—all that shit."

"When I saved the world, you mean."

"Maybe stop calling it that, too. Maybe call it the event, to make it less dramatic."

"The event? That makes it sound like a Bar Mitzvah. Saving the world is pretty dramatic, Valkyrie."

"Sure it is, kid. It's stupendous. Intergalactic. Winning, as that crazy Charlie Sheen would say. But we're post-event now. That's old news—everyone is back to watching Duck Dynasty and those pudgy Kardashians."

Had America truly gotten over almost being vaporized?

Shelby felt there ought to be more of a grace period, a much longer time of transition from awesome and heroic back to interesting trivia question and eventual obscurity. It was true that he got boatloads of money for his efforts. It was true that the first lady had kissed him. Oprah, too. And Letterman, come to think of it. Oh, okay—Jay Leno did, too. Both onstage and backstage. After all, the guy has a huge car collection and a lot to lose if everything just goes crispy fried. So, yeah, there had been no shortage of kissing at the time. But was that what he was now—trivia? And so soon?

"I'm old news?" Shelby said sadly.

"Sorry to burst your bubble, Shel. Of course, you're still rich, don't have to ever pay taxes, and can eat yourself to death at Taco Bell—or at that Nevada whorehouse."

"Another disturbing image. You make the possibilities seem endless, Valkyrie."

"You can do anything you want, kid—as long as you use certain words when you talk about the event."

"What words?"

"You know—thingamabobs, thingamajigs, and doohickeys."

"Right. So, if I can do anything I want, can I call you something other than Valkyrie? It feels like we're in a Tom Cruise movie."

"You can call me Roger."

"Cool. Is Roger your real name?"

"No. But you can call me that if you like."

"So, it's not your real name is what you're saying?"

"Not even close."

An awkward silence settled between them for a few seconds.

"Okay, Roger—so tell me the truth about the satellites. Are they tracking me?"

"I think you'd actually be happier if they did, kid. But no, they don't. We could probably keep tabs on you just as well by bugging Taco Bell."

"Really? You would do that?"

Valkyrie smirked happily.

"I'm joking, kid. We don't bug Taco Bell. They're bigger than the government and have more money."

Shelby drove south out of Oklahoma City, the interstate now offering curves and rises and dips, and actual vegetation of all sizes and shapes—real trees with green leaves—after the faded yellow and tan scrub brush along level plains of near-nothingness and the straight-as-an-arrow interstate of the Texas Panhandle. He was faintly thinking about the notion of Taco Bell as somehow more than just a chain of artery-clogging depots and teenage re-education centers, and instead as sort of a shadow government of sorts, capable of running the country from behind the disguise of grease-belching cholesterol franchises and sending men like Valkyrie out to keep tabs on him. They could certainly use some satellites if that was what they were really up to. Fast-food joints made for a wonderful cover story. Who would suspect Taco Bell of stealth oligarchy? After all, they could barely assemble acceptable tacos.

But could Taco Bell actually afford satellites, which cost gazillions of dollars? He guessed they could, given that the appetite of the average American teenage kid for corn shells filled with beef and cheese cholesterol was likely insatiable and created a revenue stream rolling like a tsunami into Taco Bell accounts. If they had satellites, though, they certainly wouldn't admit it. He knew that many corporations were capable of just about anything to make a buck, including moving their offices overseas for cheap labor and to avoid taxes, what with selfish business practices at the heart of capitalism. But satellites might come in handy, and even prove to be sort of cost-effective. They could spy on Burger King and Arby's and McDonald's, too, though it wasn't clear to Shelby what they would be spying *on*, since anyone could just go into Arby's and buy something. But, after all, it was a war—a war for profit to control the most damage that could be done to the American diet. Any tool, any weapon, no matter how pricey, was fair game in a war for domination.

It all made him wonder about his "reward" from Taco Bell, his deal. Was it actually just a cynical capitalist mechanism to keep him frequenting Taco Bells all over the nation, and thus driving herds of other customers along in the wake of his fame? Well, certainly Taco bell was grateful, of course—to a point, and in their own corporate way, which was one way of saying that what they were thankful for was a long time ago. Shelby had saved the world for sour-cream slathered tacos, ringing cash registers, and teenage indentured servitude, and so Taco Bell had cut him a deal, a break, but still insisted on some sort of return, even if it was a lousy dime per taco. They got oodles of free advertising and much goodwill just being associated with Shelby. It was a public relations bonanza for them, and Shelby had done all the heavy lifting. And if Taco Bell really was bigger than the government, then thanks to Shelby, they could afford satellites. Shelby was helping pay for them. Would they be shaped like a taco, for example? Or maybe an enchilada?

They didn't talk all that much until Oklahoma City, where Shelby poured out his life, beginning with old and crotchety Mrs. Connors in the second grade, who had thwacked him on the hands and rump with a ruler a few times when he got out of sorts with the other kids, followed by the high school tale about model-building club, which turned out to be a front for kids like Jack Hutchinson, who liked to sniff model airplane glue while pretending to assemble Messerschmitt 109 kits. Jack had removed swastika decals ostensibly provided to realistically decorate the 109s, and instead secretly stuck them on Shelby's English class notebook, which caused an uproar that deposited him in the principal's office after Mr. Palmer, his fidgety English teacher, had spotted the swastikas during an exam.

And then there was the time right after high school, the summer before college. Shelby regaled Valkyrie with how he got a job delivering eggs in his neighborhood from an area farmer, and so he got his old bicycle out of storage, the one with the long, leopard-skin-pattern banana seat, and playing cards pinned to the spokes with clothespins and a little basket attached behind the seat, on the rear bumper. He carefully loaded dozens of cartons into the basket, checking the contents of each carton carefully before pedaling slowly throughout the neighborhood, rain or shine, and never broke a single egg—not even when he would abruptly stop in front of his girlfriend Tulia's house, which was sort of a very sad and dangerously close to pathetic act, as he recounted, because Tulia was no longer his girlfriend, and there was no possibility she would be again. That story actually compelled Valkyrie to roll down the window and allow the rushing hot air to brush across his face for a while before he pulled himself back in and imposed a strict rule requiring all Shelby stories to have occurred within the past year.

The life and times of the pre-Armageddon Shelby Albert Goddard had been such an abrupt revelation to Valkyrie that he sunk into a coma-like nap rather suddenly, and his head lolled a bit, part of his forehead resting against the glass of the window. It didn't look comfortable, but Shelby reminded himself that Valkyrie was some sort of secret agent and must be tough, or at least resourceful, and have great powers of perseverance beyond the capacity of average people. But even he could succumb to pressure and boring stories and need a nap. For a while, the scenery was merely unbroken hills of various shades of brown, splashed occasionally with a dab of green or yellow or orange, and windmills suddenly popping up here and there like the masts of a ship rising above the horizon, out of the jaws of the curvature of the earth. The earth that Shelby had saved. He looked over at the napping Valkyrie, then back at the countryside. He had to admit that he felt pretty damn good about somehow becoming the glue that had kept the planet together, but if he thought about it too long, which was easy to do and happened all too often, it became overpowering, overwhelming—way too cosmic. It was a hell of a thing to live up to.

As Shelby dropped Valkyrie off at the Dallas airport, Valkyrie took a call on his cell phone, reluctantly muttered "I understand" several times, said "shit" at least three times, made several sour faces, and hung up.

"Really got to run, Shel, and get back to DC. Some numbnuts poked his dick in the wrong place—again—and I have to help clean it up."

"Really?" Shelby said. "You have to clean up where he stuck it?"

Valkyrie stared at Shelby a moment, then grinned.

"Shel—you're getting a sense of humor. Good for you, kid. There's hope for you yet."

"Thanks, Roger. I guess you're rubbing off on me a little."

"Worse things could happen. So, you good to go?"

"I think so. I can still call you Roger when I call?"

"Sure. And when you get tired of Roger—pick another name you like."

"What about Mortimer?"

"I'm going to pass on Mortimer, Shel."

"Can I call you Roger Valkyrie?"

Valkyrie cocked his head and assessed it for a few seconds.

"Why not. It has a good ring to it. I like it."

"And how often can I call?"

"As often as you need, Shel—but I can't always grab a plane to see you."

"I know. I appreciate it."

"So, where you headed now, kid?"

Shelby thought a moment.

"Stonehenge, ideally. Except I don't like to fly, and so that also leaves out the Plain of Nazca, down in Peru."

Roger Valkyrie nodded.

"Unless this Benz is waterproof and has a periscope, you might shoot for some place in America, where it's certainly easier for me to get to you."

"Duly noted," Shelby said, and then it occurred to him:

"Sedona."

"Arizona? What the hell is in Sedona, kid, except all those dandy red rocks?"

"Vortexes," Shelby said. "Spiraling vortexes, fueled by spiritual energy."

"Where'd you hear that?"

Shelby explained that he'd recently seen a show on TV describing how Sedona was sort of a place where spiritual and psychic power converged somehow. That part was awfully vague and very much reminiscent of thingamajigs, thingamabobs, and doohickeys, but the upshot was that all that converging was heap big medicine and could affect the earth in ways he couldn't quite recall because he had been in and out of a nap when the show was on, and really, what he mostly remembered, was a manic Shirley MacLaine droning on and on about some hippie event there in the 80s that prevented the earth from spinning off its axis, or some such equally apocalyptic affair not destined to end well but definitely in a huge puff of smoke accompanied by the sound of thunder. Shelby certainly knew the territory. Shirley MacLaine had nothing on him.

"Sounds like a plan, my man," Valkyrie said. "But remember—thingamabobs, thingamajigs, and doohickeys."

"And don't let my dick do the thinking."

"That's right, Shel. I think you'll be fine, but call when you need me. I'm your eye in the sky."

"Wait—does that mean satellites *are* watching me?"

"Fucking with you, kid."

They shook hands.

"I'm still a sucker for that," Shelby said.

"You'll catch on. Just a matter of time."

"Can I call sometimes just to talk, Roger Valkyrie?"

"Isn't that what we've been doing?" Valkyrie said as he got out and waved goodbye. "Don't take any wooden nickels, kid."

Shelby waved back and pulled away, but when he glanced back, Roger Valkyrie had already disappeared into the crowd. There were times, Shelby had to admit, when he wondered if he was delusional, but perhaps not aware that he was, and that Valkyrie was a highly imaginative figment of his delusion. But, if he actually was delusional, would he be able to question Valkyrie's existence? And if he wasn't delusional, which he hoped for very much, would that then confirm that Valkyrie was real, and not just a character in his delusion, and that it was okay to fret about being delusional as just natural questioning of his own existence?

More people were disgorged from shuttle buses, cars, and taxis as he sat there a moment, watching the sea of people hauling various methods and sizes of luggage as they surged toward the automatic doors to the terminal like scads of bees swarming a honeyed hive. Was it all just a grand simulation? And could someone viewing—experiencing—a grand simulation be able to realize it was a simulation? Did having the option of simulation as just one of the explanations for everything he saw, confirm that it was *not* a simulation at all and thus real? But if simulation was ruled out, there was still the possibility of delusion, since he was not aware of ever digesting LSD or peyote or any other wacky drug, for example, as a potential explanation for what was happening. And the problem with settling on delusion as the best explanation was that if he really was delusional, would he have the ability to analyze a variety of possible explanations and select the right one?

Shelby left the airport with his head feeling like it could explode, or implode—or both, though he briefly debated the feasibility of simultaneous explosion/implosion. He decided that either option was as good a way to describe his headache as any, and he abruptly felt the irresistible tractor beam of sudden inertia, garnished with dollops of apathy and anxiety, and he was unsure of what to do next. He pulled into a parking lot next to the interstate and just watched traffic zip by in both directions, listening absently to some tunes on the radio, but all he could find was mostly country and western jingoistic nationalism. He sat there, just gripping the wheel of his awesome black Mercedes 500 SL with both hands, looking ahead at the cars, but not really focusing well enough to see individual cars, or to make out the various brands.

What would all those people in all those cars and trucks think if they knew that he, Shelby Albert Goddard, the unlikely architect of global preservation, was sitting there absently, watching them hurtle by as though they were all just worker ants scurrying back to the ant farm? If everyone knew he was there, would traffic grind to a halt, people ejaculating out of their vehicles, arms waving wildly toward the sky, to pay homage to the poobah of their resurrections? It all devolved into colors and shapes whizzing by, left and right, and he felt he might sit there for hours, gravity gluing him in place, in his torpor—unless he had to pee, of course, or felt the taco urge drawing him to the nearest Taco Bell like a bee to a flower.

But then a dog appeared on the far side of the interstate, on the shoulder of the far lane going toward Amarillo. It peeked out from under the guardrail. It was a white dog, a mutt, maybe a cross between a Schnauzer and Yorkie, perhaps, or one or the other, maybe, but he wasn't sure exactly what those breeds looked like, and he really didn't know dog breeds at all because there were always cats in his family's house. Big, heavy, sleepy, orange cats. The dog tried to cross the lanes, but scampered back to the shoulder just in time, narrowly escaping being vaporized by a tractor-trailer rig hauling gargantuan yellow bulldozers on a long trailer. The dog sat on its haunches, nervously eyeing the traffic. Shelby regretted that he'd parked there with a front row seat to how to create road kill. Several cars honked their horns at the dog as they flew by. The dog would get up and start forward, then think better of it and sit down again.

Shelby could see that the dog was inadvertently on a canine suicide mission and it was just a matter of time, perhaps only minutes, or even less, until the road kill demonstration would reach bloody climax and be over, leaving smeared dog guts, broken, shattered dog bones, and a long red dog-blood slick, which was a hell of a way to start the day. So he jumped out and ran over to the interstate, hoping the dog would stay put, but not at all confident it would, fearing he was only accomplishing a better view of the impending dog-meets-truck-bumper massacre. The traffic was brutal, unrelenting—a real Roman Coliseum chariot race slowing down for nothing. Shelby felt as dwarfed by it all, as surely the dog did, too. It seemed very unnatural as a way of life, and it was very much like chariots spinning around a circular track, everyone chasing their tails and never quite catching up, always chasing but never quite *reaching*, and the race could not end until everyone had been chopped up by the chariots' spokes.

Shelby crossed the railing and scurried across the eastbound lanes. The dog saw Shelby and suddenly sprinted forward, in front of a black SUV, which swerved just enough so that it was a slight glancing blow and not a head-on squishing of Fido the Kamikaze Dog, which was spun around several times and left disoriented and howling in the center of the lanes, unsure what to do when Shelby got there and scooped it up. Just in time, Shelby dove across the railing between the eastbound and westbound lanes and into the ditch, cradling the terrified and howling dog in his arms. Traffic roared by in both directions like it was the Indianapolis 500, but Shelby managed to get across the eastbound lanes and back to his car.

He looked back across the interstate, cradling the terrified dog. Didn't anyone in those cars realize that the savior had appeared once more among them, had risen among the people, his flock, once more, and demonstrated his savior chops by snatching a mutt of a mangy white dog away from the sudden impact of a semi-truck's massive radiator? Of course not—they were well past Shelby saving the world and back deep into their dronish lives of blind allegiance/servitude, going from Blindly Serving Corporations Point A to Blindly Serving Corporations Point B like hamsters on crack cocaine in treadmills, too focused on getting nowhere in a hurry, to notice that the savior had indeed come calling again to ply his trade.

And this time—without thingamabobs, thingamajigs, and doohickeys.

The savior had come bareback, without tricks or magic.

Oh, the audacity of it all!

The dog whimpered and shook, but there was not much blood, just a red smear on one flank, and there seemed to be no real damage done to its leg and backside, which functioned quite well. Shelby examined its collar and found a tag with an address. He got directions to the house from an attendant at a Shell station. Fido the Kamikaze Dog could stand gingerly on the back seat of Shelby's car, which Shelby took as a good sign, until trembling Fido pissed on his seat, which was very un-Kamikaze-like behavior. Or, maybe the real Kamikazes did in fact piss their pants—and mess their pants, too!—all the way down in that lonely dive onto an American ship to honor their emperor, who got to piss in a proper urinal back at the palace.

The dog's name was Sparky. He was neither a Yorkie or a Schnauzer or a Kamikaze—not even close—and was instead just a white mutt who'd run off to find the greener grass—presumably to pee on it—but his people loved him and evidently Sparky had gotten loose just that morning. How he managed to drift way over by the interstate was a mystery to the grateful couple, a Mr. and Mrs. Whiting, average middle-aged folks living in a small, Tudor style house. Mr. Whiting sported a turquoise bola tie and white shirt. Mrs. Whiting wore a simple blue blouse and dark pants. Shelby handed Sparky over to a grateful Mrs. Whiting, who hugged the still-whimpering Sparky, while Mr. Whiting hovered in the background. Shelby had saved the world and now he saved a white mutt named Sparky from becoming a hood ornament named Fido the Kamikaze Dog.

The Whitings, so overcome by the return of Sparky the mutt, either didn't recognize Shelby, or were too emotional to care. His name appeared to bounce off their foreheads. They were so emotional over their little furry baby that Shelby was convinced they could not describe who he was or what he looked like at all just ten minutes later if asked. Had he become invisible? A wraith? Was saving Fido from inevitable flatness too small a deed to rekindle the embers of gratitude? Were only the grand deeds, the cosmic ones, deeds at all? There must be some meaning to it all, some sense of perspective to be gleaned, Shelby thought as he bounded down the Whitings' brick walk to his car, but he was damned if he knew what it was, other than that he now needed to buy Lysol and paper towels to nuke the smell of dog piss coming from his backseat. The savior was relegated to cleansing the makeshift toilet of a mutt dog. Then he drove straight through to Sedona, Arizona, stopping only for tacos, gas, and pee breaks.

Sedona was a bloody red disappointment. It was geology on an epic scale, but sort of just deader than a doornail. One gargantuan red rock looked pretty much like all the other gargantuan red rocks, but collectively they were one of many great excuses for inflating the value of local real estate. He arrived exhausted, ate some tacos drenched in sour cream, and felt a semblance of rejuvenation. And then he hiked out into red rock country after the obligatory tourist visit to Oak Creek Canyon and its pleasant creek. But if there *were* any vortexes around—spiraling or otherwise—he couldn't see them, hear them, or sense them—or even smell them, though he wasn't sure vortexes could be smelled, and that was just his imagination lunging for something to grab onto. Were spiraling vortexes actually spiritual tornadoes? Were they invisible but there nonetheless? Did they exist in an alternate universe existing parallel, or perhaps even within, the known universe? Sometimes Shelby felt as though he lived in an alternate universe, with the ability to travel from it to the known universe and back, to be invisible one moment, and quite noticeable another.

But none of that explained Sedona and spiraling vortexes, and he noted that had the world actually been saved in some fashion at Sedona, by collective spiritual energy fed into spiraling vortexes by hippies, New Age goofballs, and Shirley MacLaine, there was no evidence of it—just as now, post-Armageddon, post-Shelby and his magic, his thingamajigs, thingamabobs, and doohickeys, there was no evidence anything had happened at all except for some profane graffiti on some of the red rocks.

And on one of the rocks, someone had spray-painted Shelby Lives! He was glad to hear that he lived but on another rock, Shirley MacLaine's name was much larger than Shelby's. He sat for a long time, staring at his name on the red rock. Then at Shirley's. He existed but was he truly living? After a while he couldn't hold back exhaustion any longer and his imagination crashed as prelude to physical collapse, and he fell into a nap for several hours and then found a motel in Sedona and slept until 10 a.m. the next morning before hitting the road again, this time east, this time quite at random, just selecting roads and stopping for tacos, and then selecting more roads and stopping for more tacos, napping here and there, sometimes in the car, sometimes under a tree off the road, shaving and showering at a nearly deserted campground he stumbled across, until he wandered into a Taco Bell in Argus, Illinois. He stopped in Argus because he liked the name and saw the Taco Bell sign. His mother had a rock-and-roll collection and he remembered an album he liked called Argus by Wishbone Ash. Maybe it was a providential move.

As a quite impulsive experiment, he had bought his tacos without flashing his pass and for full price, too. He wasn't sure why he did it and no one recognized him or made a fuss. No reporters or photographers showed up. He felt—daring. Even a little—naughty. He made eye contact with several teenage girls at the next table, who smiled and went back to their conversation. A middle-aged woman in a navy business suit smiled at him, too, but did not seem to know who he was—or care. When he asked for extra sour cream on his Bell Grandes, he was politely told it was against the rules. He offered to pay extra, but the boy behind the counter diplomatically refused. For a moment he started to dig into a pocket for his pass, but then stopped, unsure as to why. It was as though his hand declined further movement toward his pass without any notion of orders from his brain. Shelby ate quietly at a table in a corner, digesting anonymity for the first time in months. It digested very well and he felt like a schoolboy who had gotten away with something. But he wasn't sure what he had gotten away with.

After he ate, and still no one had made a fuss over him, he drove around Argus, a tiny Norman Rockwell burg with a town square and a water tower and a grain elevator and not much else. It was quiet and life there moved slowly and Shelby liked that. He discovered there was a Lake Argus and he drove out to it, crossing a very long causeway splitting the lake in half. It was early September, before fall would drop hints it would arrive, and the day was warm but not hot. Subtle expectation seemed to linger in the air. The surface of the lake was a sheet of glass. Ducks quacked and sailed happily. Cardinals flitted about in tree branches above Shelby. He had parked the Mercedes so he could sit on the hood close to shore and survey the lake. The air smelled sweet.

Had he really saved the world? It wasn't that long ago. It was in all the papers. He had been on CNN and MSNBC and all the other pretentious acronyms. He was grilled by everyone in the yapping pack of ravenous talking heads, but always he stuck with what he had been told: thingamabobs, thingamajigs, and doohickeys. He was friendly but vague. Inspiring but elusive. Audiences were awestruck but confused. He had been coached well by Roger Valkyrie.

But in Argus, and now by the lake, it suddenly seemed unreal. Shelby tried to recall the day it happened—the event, as Roger Valkyrie suggested he call it—but it was a fuzzy memory. The event? Was that now all it was? He remembered the notion of thingamabobs and thingamajigs and doohickeys, but not much of the rest of it was very clear to him. There had been a building. A very large building. Football stadiums could fit within it. A ceiling so high it seemed a plane could fly around, and once, for reasons he could not recall, a helicopter did fly inside the building, sort of like an angry wasp. There had been a row of—machines. Tall and squat. Bulky. Massive. Lots of lights on them—flashing lights, flickering lights. Red and green and yellow and orange lights. Purple and even lavender lights, too. Then there was—commotion. Confusion. Chaos. People running around. Shouts and yelps and cries and even screeching. Then there was a flash—what sort of flash was unclear to him. Maybe like a camera flash, but bigger, more kinetic. Then he had been somehow plunked on the head and the lights went out in his mind. It was like scenes in a bad movie. Only he had been assured it was no movie.

Desiring distraction, he called Roger Valkyrie.

"Konnichiwa, Shel. How's it hanging?"

"Konnichiwa?"

"That's hello in Japanese, kid. I was in Japan yesterday."

"Konnichiwa to you, too," Shelby said. "It's hanging, I guess. How about you?"

"I've got jet lag and my wife is giving me grief to mow the lawn, but otherwise I'm fit as a fiddle. Where are you, Shel?"

Shelby pondered it a moment. Fractured images sprinted across his mind so fast that all he comprehended was a sliver of a notion of himself, before thingamajigs, thingamabobs, and doohickeys, fiddling with dials and switches and controls and levers, and it all seemed to be about space, and about looking at things and people from space, but not like looking through telescopes. And why things were being watched from space, and his part in that, was unclear.

"Roger Valkyrie, are you sure you haven't been messing with me and you really do use satellites to watch me?"

"Shel, I've got your phone number—I could just call and ask where you are."

"Okay, that's true. That's logical. But if you aren't tracking me, then I could lie and you wouldn't know."

"Why would you lie, Shel? Do you have something to hide? This is your government speaking, even though I'm lying on my couch with a beer. But I am wearing pants, so it's an official call."

"And if you weren't wearing pants, would it still be official?"

"That's a judgment call, I suppose. And it would depend on where I was at without pants. But seriously, kid—do you have something to hide?"

"What would I hide?" Shelby said. "My life is on display to the world."

"Welcome to the world of notoriety and heroism, kid. Now you're as big as J-Lo's ass."

"I've truly arrived, I guess."

"But you're not as much fun to look at as her ass, kid. So, where are you?"

"Seriously, Roger Valkyrie—you're really sure you don't already know?"

"Shel, I'm not the Amazing Kreskin. Are you seeing things moving in the sky again?"

Shelby instinctively looked up at the blue sky.

"Not in the daytime, no."

"Listen carefully," RogerValkyrie said. "No satellite is tracking you. We're not even tracking J-Lo's ass, as much fun as that would be. Do you know how much it would cost to watch you eat Bell Grandes at Taco Bell from outer space?"

Shelby looked up again. There wasn't even a cloud that he could see.

"Okay, Roger Valkyrie. Good to know. And I'm in Illinois. Argus, Illinois."

"Never heard of it. I'll Google it later, though."

"Don't you just push some button in a hush-hush secret room and everything you need to know about anything pops up instantly?"

"You just described Google, Shel. And we've had some budget cuts. So, what's up?"

"Something weird happened."

"You in trouble, Shel? Did you remember to give vague answers and stick with thingamabobs, thingamajigs, and doohickeys?"

"I'm not in trouble, Roger Valkyrie."

"Lonely again?"

"Well, yeah—sort of. But that's not why I called."

"Do we need another sit-down, kid? What's the nearest airport?"

Shelby thought a moment.

"Bloomington, I guess. Or maybe Peoria. Or Champaign. But I'm okay to just chat on the phone."

"Good. I've been on too many airplanes lately, my friend. And the lawn won't cut itself. Hey—hold on for a minute, Shel."

Evidently Roger Valkyrie was somewhere with other people, maybe his co-agents. Did they all sometimes go out together, maybe sit at a bar in a tavern, a long line of secret agents taking calls from various hotspots around the globe? He wondered what the other agents looked like, how they dressed. Did they all sort of look like they had been cloned from Roger Valkyrie? He made a mental note to never watch *The Matrix* again.

Shelby could hear voices in the background while he waited but couldn't make out any words. It was all just a hum, a buzzing. It was the sound, only more subdued, of course, that he often heard while strolling through a crowded mall, or in an airport terminal. Sometimes, Shelby felt like going to a mall, any mall, and maybe buying an Orange Julius, a hot pretzel with mustard on it, maybe, or some sort of chili dog drenched in sauce and onions, and just drifting around from storefront to storefront. But he knew that going to the mall was now very problematic. He could easily be recognized. Maybe draw crowds. Be expected to give speeches. Be harassed to explain thingamabobs, thingamajigs, and doohickeys, which were things he simply could not explain. Roger Valkyrie had endlessly made that quite clear.

"Do you use a push mower or riding?" Shelby said when Roger Valkyrie came back on the line.

"Still on the mowing, kid? I've got a snazzy rider, Shel. I don't have all day and we've got the Ponderosa of lawns. So, my friend—how can I help you today?"

"I just went to Taco Bell."

"Amazing—should I alert the media, Shel?"

"Funny. But that's sort of part of it. Nobody at Taco Bell recognized me. I even paid full price for tacos."

"Did they give you extra sour cream?"

"Nope. I offered to pay extra, but they wouldn't allow it."

"Where's the love?" Roger Valkyrie said. "What's a Bell Grande without extra sour cream? After all, you saved the world. Go back and flash your pass for perpetual artery-clogging and get ten-cent tacos and your picture in the local paper, kid. Business as usual."

"Maybe I really am old news."

That's how it went in America, he reminded himself—that was how it was probably anywhere. What have you done for us lately? Today's hero is just tomorrow's goat if he or she can't find a way to go with the flow of a capitalistic life of corrosive consumption and instant gratification as it quickly forgets the events that allow it to keep flowing toward—what? There was a mystery worth solving.

"It's a tough world, Shel—and you saved it. Seems unfair, I know. But it is what it is."

"I hate that expression. What does it even mean?"

"Somebody once said there's no second act in America," Roger Valkyrie said. "And your first one was a doozy. Welcome to reality."

"Did I really save the world?"

"Well, if you didn't, then you're dreaming and I'm somehow in your dream, but maybe that would mean I don't have to actually go mow the lawn. Or, if it's a dream, maybe I can get *you* to mow the lawn. Seriously, kid, the report I read certainly says you saved the whole damn world. Pretty heavy reading, my friend. It would make you sober as a judge."

"Maybe it's made up."

"It was quite specific. Spooky shit. Dark as a witch's soul. Cold as a witch's tit."

"Where's all this witch stuff coming from?"

"My wife's nagging me to get after the lawn. But back to the report—cold and dark, my friend."

"Did the report say thingamabobs, thingamajigs, and doohickeys?"

"No, but as far as you're concerned, that's what they were. Vagueness is your friend."

"Who are we protecting?" Shelby said.

"The public, Shel. And the folks who make thingamabobs, thingamajigs, and doohickeys. They run the world."

"Which I saved."

"And they're grateful, in their way."

"Are they really?"

"As much as they can be," Valkyrie said. "Certainly they were on the actual day you saved the world. That's why you're doing slow death by taco in a badass Mercedes and don't pay taxes anymore."

"So I'm not hallucinating?"

"Is Keith Richards with you, kid?"

"Nope."

"Then you're fine. Hey—hold on again, kid. Back in a flash."

Shelby smiled as he recalled the day he spent with Keith Richards, who had abruptly tried to present him with a very expensive Les Paul guitar as tribute for saving the world and extending his career as the most unlikely survivor of decades of heroin-laced rock and roll. Shelby was touched, but kept declining it, kept pushing it back toward Keith—kept protesting politely that he didn't even know how to play before Keith finally relented, shrugged, and fumbled for a cigarette, Shelby noticing the famous death's-head ring as Keith lit up.

Keith seemed quite pleasant, very talkative, and way more articulate than legend had led Shelby to believe. It wasn't really true, for example, that Keith always sounded unintelligible, like he was talking with pebbles in his mouth—or that he even sounded a bit retarded. But Shelby had never seen anyone smoke so many cigarettes, or so quickly. Keith seemed to perpetually have a cig dangling from his grinning mouth, which was a bit hard to distinguish from all the other surface-of-the-moon potholes and wrinkles decorating his face, until he smiled or frowned or wiggled his lips. Keith suggested he roll them a joint, and Shelby nodded, thought—why the fuck not? It's

Keith Fucking Richards for God's sake. How much longer could the guy really last? But people had been saying that forever. How many American presidents had Keith Richards outlasted?

As they smoked, Shelby was distracted by something resembling a fishing lure, minus the treble hooks, hanging out of Keith's wiry hair. When he moved his head at all, which was often, the shiny lure thingie jiggled and jumped. Shelby half-expected a trout to rise from somewhere and snatch the object. They spent most of the afternoon in a room Keith referred to as his library, and it did indeed have books, as well as various guitars of many shapes and colors. Once again, Keith tried to give him a pricey old guitar, but when Shelby tried to strum it, oblivious to the concept of recognizable chords, Keith quickly took it back.

After a while, one of the daughters brought them food and pints of Guinness. The rest of the family was down at the Richards hacienda in Jamaica and Keith and daughter were headed there the next day. The highlight of the afternoon was when Keith impulsively picked up an acoustic guitar and played "You've Got the Silver," promising to dedicate the song to him the next time the Stones played, which he explained was uncertain and hard to arrange because Mick Jagger could often be a bit squirrelly—but keep that under your hat and don't mention it next time on Letterman. And for God's sake, don't tell Oprah he said it. Then Keith gleefully rolled another joint and Shelby's memory of the rest of the day remained permanently hazy.

As the memory evaporated, Shelby noticed a man had come out of the trees farther down the lake shore. The man was too far away for Shelby to get a clear picture of what he looked like, how old he was, but he wore a cowboy hat and carried a fishing rod and at the shore he cast a lure out into the water and slowly retrieved it. But Shelby was sure that the man periodically glanced his way. He was equally sure that it wasn't Keith Richards in a cowboy hat.

Was the man watching him? Who wanted to watch him? Why? Shelby was just stopping by a lake to relax. Was the man actually an agent—one of Valkyrie's men? Shelby waved to the man, who waved back, and then continued to cast and retrieve. Shelby felt the hairs on his neck stand up and he retreated to his vehicle and locked the doors.

When Roger Valkyrie was back on the line and sounding a little distracted, he sheepishly asked Shelby what they had been discussing and Shelby told him, "slow death by taco."

Shelby looked around, to see whether the fisherman in a cowboy hat had suddenly appeared, but he seemed to be alone.

"Right," Roger Valkyrie said. "Well, shit, kid—I can't imagine all those Bell Grandes with extra sour cream are good for your blood pressure."

"There's a guy here, fishing," Shelby said. "Do you know anything about that?"

"Why would I know about some jamoke fishing out in the boonies, Shel?"

"Because maybe he's one of your—you know, people, agents. He's wearing a big cowboy hat, jeans, and a brown sweatshirt."

"He doesn't sound like much of a dresser, kid. We wouldn't send anyone out into the field looking like that. We'd at least hand him a copy of GQ first."

Shelby got out of the vehicle and crept through the trees for a view of the lake: the man had disappeared. He immediately felt like someone was behind him, but no one was there. Everywhere he looked, he was sure the man was lurking, but no one was around. He felt pretty vulnerable

"I guess he's gone," Shelby said, not convinced. "Anyway, I don't see him around."

"He probably got embarrassed by his get-up and went home, kid. Or maybe the fish aren't biting—or, maybe they got a glimpse at his get-up and swam to the other side of the lake. Fish can see people on the shore, you know."

"Really?" Shelby said. "I'm being shadowed out here by God knows who and you're talking about fish who can see people?"

"Just being educational, Shel. And sometimes a fisherman is just a fisherman. You paranoid, kid?"

"No more than your average guy who saved the world. But just what the hell did I save, Roger Valkyrie?"

"You saved the farm, kid. Planet Knucklehead. Capitalism and all the other self-righteous isms. You kept life safe for outrageous consumerism and more wars and so oil companies can finally suck the last bit of juice out of the planet and it dries up and whizzes away like a balloon losing air."

"You drunk, Roger Valkyrie?"

"I had some sake on the flight from Japan, but I've had a nap since then. Watch out for that sake. It sneaks up on you."

"Maybe *I* should get drunk."

"Well, if you do, Shel, remember—thingamabobs, thingamajigs, and doohickeys."

"I know, I know—be vague and avoid long conversations with strangers."

"And wash your hands often in public, kid. There's a flu bug going around."

"You know, Roger Valkyrie—in a way, saving the world's over-rated."

"Not to me, Shel. Not to everyone else."

"So, you're grateful?"

"I owe you my life, Shel. So does my wife. So do those wacky Cajun clowns on Duck Dynasty. And those ridiculous Kardashians. So does everyone on the planet and everyone about to be born and folks not yet even conceived. I wouldn't miss mowing the lawn, but I'm certainly glad you fixed it so I still have to."

"Jesus—no pressure at all, Roger Valkyrie."

"Pressure's what you make of it, Shel. Pressure creates diamonds."

"That's another of those vague pearls of wisdom—like it is what it is. That's as bad as thingamabobs, thingamajigs, and doohickeys."

"They are what they are," Roger Valkyrie said. "Where you headed next, kid?"

Shelby thought a few seconds.

"To see the country, Roger Valkyrie. To see just what the hell it is that I saved."

The world that Shelby had saved had moved on from being saved. It was definitely post-event. Selective amnesia. Selective gratitude. Selective lucidity. There would always be folks who marveled that it had been saved, and that Shelby Albert Goddard had had the presence of mind to do it—even though they had no idea at all how he had done it. But, almost no one outside the super super secret secret site in Nevada—so super secret it didn't even have a number, like Area 51—had even known the world had *needed* saving until they were told that the need had arisen and the deed had been accomplished. It became popular to re-litigate a tired old saying: If a tree falls in the forest and no one is around to hear it, does it make a sound?

And when the world was told it had been saved, most people couldn't relate to a murky event that was over before they even knew it had happened. There was no time to be afraid and panic and become discombobulated. No aimless zombies shuffling about. No apocalyptic landscape. And they had already seen Bruce Willis save the world on the silver screen with his trademark smirk and lots of explosions and improbable science and dubious dialogue—now that was how to save the world! A lesson for Shelby in case the opportunity arises again! Shelby Rides Again—the sequel!

Fox News insinuated that the whole saving-the-world escapade was made up by liberals and the president and al-Qaeda to distract from his health care law. Rush Limbaugh wondered whether Shelby might be Muslim, and certainly communist, since he hadn't saved the world just for the rich. A growing number of people, like the folks who still didn't believe a man landed on the moon in 1969, and that shots came from The Grassy Knoll, didn't really believe the world had been saved at all. Or had even been in danger. Like global warming, it was just more liberal hokum. A new bumper sticker sold like hotcakes: But What Have You Done For Us Lately, Shelby Albert Goddard?

Soon, a second bumper sticker became incredibly popular: I Brake for Thingamabobs, Thingamajigs, and Doohickeys!!!!

A few days after leaving Argus, Shelby finished a Bell Grande at a Taco Bell in Colorado Springs. Once again, he had paid full price and remained anonymous, though several people in line had eyed him a bit more than was comfortable to him, and they had whispered to each other. Shelby had taken his pass out of his pocket as he entered and stared at it a moment but stuck it back in a pocket and stood in line submissively. He had taken to wearing sunglasses and a green John Deere cap he got in Illinois, pulled down tight on his head, and so when he bought his Bell Grandes, he didn't ask for extra sour cream, for example. He avoided eye contact. He slouched a bit and shoved his hands deep into his pockets while he waited. No one behind the counter appeared to suspect who he might be, though one nervous girl seemed to regard him as capable of robbing the place, or maybe exposing himself.

The next morning, just south of Cheyenne, Wyoming, Shelby tossed his Taco Bell pass out the car window while doing 85 and soon stopped at a Burger King for cheeseburgers and fries and a chocolate shake. He felt he was finally done with Taco Bell, finally through with Bell Grandes, finally through with extra sour cream, and though he had never told Roger Valkyrie, he had kept count—867 tacos in just a couple months.

Untold amounts of sour cream.

A white river of sour cream.

Barrels of taco sauce.

From Cheyenne, he impulsively called Roger Valkyrie.

"Salam keif alhal, kid," Roger Valkyrie said.

"What?"

"That's Sudanese for hello, Shel. Quite a mouthful, ain't it? I just got back from Sudan."

"Sudan? Really—Africa?"

"Some people call it *The* Sudan," Roger Valkyrie said. "And officially, it's the Republic of the Sudan. But plain old Sudan works well enough."

"Isn't it pretty dangerous there?" Shelby said.

"Worse than a porcupine in your underwear," Roger Valkyrie said. "I'm glad to be home and even looking forward to mowing the lawn again.

"You just mowed it a few days ago," Shelby said.

"I know, but I earn major points with the wife if I do it without being asked. And we had some rain. And it's a lot easier to mow when the grass doesn't actually need to be cut."

"Doesn't she notice stuff like that?"

"Not really, Shel. It's just me, a cold beer, and my riding mower. Just another urban cowboy pretending to round up the cattle."

"Awesome," Shelby said. "Maybe it'll rain some more and she'll let you off the hook."

"If we get more rain, she'll bug me to get up on the roof and see how the gutters are doing. And they probably aren't doing well. That means digging the ladder out of the garage, which needs cleaning. And it's pretty slick up on the roof. I'd rather mow, kid."

"Does she know you were in Sudan?"

"She knows not to ask anymore. Sudan or Sausalito—all the same to her now. I can tell you there's not much to mow in Sudan, Shel, though they mow each other down pretty well."

"Do you suppose the Sudanese are pretty pleased I saved the world, Roger Valkyrie?"

"They're too busy hacking each other up, kid. But if I go back, I can ask around."

"Don't bother. I'm sure they're pretty much post-event, too."

"Many of them are post-sanity, kid, and post-morality, but that's another story."

"One you can't tell."

"Correctomundo—like with you and thingamabobs, thingama-jigs, and doohickeys."

"I suppose you've seen the bumper stickers," Shelby said.

"My wife has one on her Honda—sorry, Shel."

"Which one?"

"I brake for thingamabobs, thingamajigs, and doohickeys."

"Well, that's not as snarky as the other one, I guess."

"Kid, I got to put you on hold a minute—there's a toll booth ahead, and damned if I know where I have some change."

"Take your time," Shelby said.

He drove steadily on toward Cheyenne and tried to recall as many Taco Bells as he could from the past months, but they all looked the same, smelled the same, and had blurred together. But he was certain he had been recognized at the last one, in Colorado Springs. Well, so what. It didn't matter anymore. Fuck it. He was finally done with Taco Bell. His arteries, veins, and—what was the next one? Capillaries? Whatever. All of his blood vessels were done with Taco Bell. He was done being their roving shill of an ambassador.

There were plenty of other places to get the fast-food gorp fix coursing through his blood system and back to the task of making fat deposits on his stomach. It was the American Way, after all, to overeat and to overeat with the wrong foods, and he had guaranteed that fast-food America would live on to belch out more gorp for more people endlessly on a merry-go-round of capitalism, driving from homes to jobs to stores to banks to malls to gas stations to fast food outlets, and then starting all over the next day, endlessly in a circuit, a maze, trapped like rats, waking everyday in a cage that followed them every step of the day, sitting through endless traffic lights desperately trying to find a song on the radio from the good old days to remind them of what freedom used to be before they accepted the chains and shackles; then driving mindlessly to more banks and to more malls and to more stores with gorp stops in an endless array of fast food depots lining streets and guarding entrances to malls.

Gorp?

Where did that one come from, he thought.

He had saved the world for gorp.

And a new anthem: Welcome to the land of the gorp eaters, and the home of the gorp eaters.

Hallelujah.

"I threw my pass away," Shelby told Roger Valkyrie when he was back on the phone. "No more tacos. From now on, I'll find a McDonald's. Then Arby's. And maybe KFC, too."

"No shit? Damn, kid. When that gets out, they'll want you on Good Morning America, or Leno or Letterman—or both—to explain why, and Taco Bell might get sore and take offense over it, too."

"Fuck Taco Bell," Shelby said. "Fuck Bell Grandes. Fuck extra sour cream. I tossed the pass on the interstate outside Cheyenne."

"That's where you are now—Cheyenne?"

"For now. Soon I'll be somewhere else, I reckon."

"Did you toss the pass onto the road, or into a ditch, Shel?"

Shelby wasn't sure.

"Does it matter?"

"Well, yeah, Shel. If it's in a ditch, maybe no one will find it. But on the road—that sucker might turn up pretty quick, and then you're in the limelight again, and maybe Taco Bell gets pissy."

"I tossed it into a ditch," Shelby said. "I can always claim I lost it."

"You saw it *land* in the ditch?"

"I was going way too fast for that. But I'm sure it landed in the ditch. I whipped that sucker pretty good. And it was windy."

"That means you have no fucking idea," Roger Valkyrie said. "Just saying, my friend. Just saying."

"Well, I'm not going back for it. So that's that."

"I guess so, Shel. The die is cast and all that Julius Caesar shit."

"I don't need no fucking Taco Bell pass."

"No, you really don't, kid. And now you're adding some variety to your artery-clogging mission."

"Are you going to start nagging me to eat more vegetables, Roger Valkyrie?"

"It wouldn't hurt, Shel. You're still young, but that's when good health starts."

"I'll look for a Pizza Hut and get a pie with artichokes on it," Shelby said. "How's that?"

"Sounds like an improvement over all those damn tacos. You've eaten a shitload of Bell Grandes, my friend. And enough sour cream to fill a swimming pool, I guess."

"Almost 900," Shelby said. "I kept count—867 tacos."

"Leapin' lizards!" Roger Valkyrie said. "Good Lord and General Jackson. Have you had your blood pressure checked lately?"

"I'll be sure to put that on my list."

"I think there are blood pressure machines at Kmart, or Wal-Mart—Walgreen's, maybe. You should stop and check, kid."

"Goes on my list, Roger Valkyrie."

"Good, Shel. And, the good news is, you don't have to carry rolls of dimes anymore."

"There's that. I'll mark it off my list."

"What else is on your list, kid?"

"Enlightenment."

"You're ambitious," Roger Valkyrie said. "Where do you think you'll find it?"

"I don't know. Maybe I'll know it when I see it."

"What if you don't see it?"

"Then I'll keep looking."

"Good luck with *that*."

The Exalted Church of the Intergalactic Moment

Of course, there were those folks who believed fervently that the world had indeed been gloriously saved, and quite magnificently, by Shelby Albert Goddard. Ray Spurlock, a trucker in Parsons Grove, Arkansas—the Rev. Spurlock thanks to an internet divinity course—was so grateful that Shelby had saved the world that he started a church in Parsons Grove devoted to the event, which he called the Intergalactic Moment, and so the Exalted Church of the Intergalactic Moment was born. So far, the church only had eleven members and met at the American Legion Hall, but Rev. Spurlock was in his heart a hopeful man, a cautious optimist of sorts, and he always began his "presentations" with, "My friends—let us never forget thingamabobs, thingamajigs, and doohickeys."

Shelby heard about the Rev. Spurlock and his church while surfing the internet at a Starbucks in Gillette, Wyoming. He got acquainted with Rev. Spurlock by email, and without really knowing why or thinking much about it at all, Shelby put himself on the road to Parsons Grove. A decision from the gut. He was hoping for enlightenment, but tried not to expect too much. Perspective, for example, seemed like a less lofty and more attainable goal. He promised himself to try and avoid actually using the word enlightenment because it sounded pretentious and seemed a bit desperate.

In Dallas, Shelby ditched the Mercedes at a dealership and headed for Arkansas in a used red Ford F150 pickup, quite to the dealer's amazement. But searching for enlightenment in a black Mercedes

Benz 500 SL with SAVWRLD plates seemed not only unlikely to Shelby, but a tad ludicrous. The dealer knew who Shelby was and gladly offered to give him some extra cash for saving the world on top of the difference between the Benz and F150, which was quite a lot, but Shelby told him to keep the money, which flabbergasted the man, who then insisted on at least filling the truck up with gas. As an added touch, Shelby stopped in Texarkana and bought the appropriate sticker and slapped it on a bumper:

I Brake for Thingamabobs, Thingamajigs, and Doohickeys!!!!

Shelby stopped to pee and drink a Grape Nehi at a country store southwest of Hot Springs just off I-30. The store clerk eyed Shelby suspiciously, but didn't say anything. The store was apparently a monument to bottle caps because the parking lot was a sea of them. A bottle cap ocean. Every conceivable bottle cap was represented, it seemed—Dr. Pepper, RC Cola, Mountain Dew, and also many beer bottle caps, too. Shelby had to slosh through bottle caps to enter the sore. He had been tempted to complete his rolling disguise as just another redneck cruising the back roads by buying a Confederate battle flag decal for the truck, but decided against it. The truck had Texas plates and that was redneck enough for him.

Parsons Grove was still hours away on up the interstate and well north of Little Rock, and so Shelby decided to stay in Hot Springs for the night, at a Holiday Inn. He was beginning to think he should have made some sort of sweetheart deal with Holiday Inn, like the one with Taco Bell. But he didn't want that. He could afford any hotel, and Hot Springs had some pretty snazzy ones, he knew, but he opted for average and continued anonymity. Holiday Inn was just fine. It was quintessentially American. It was late September and the nights were slowly cooling and no one was sitting around the hotel pool.

He leaned back into a chaise lounge and exhaled slowly. It had been a long day on the road. It felt awesome to stretch out, to not be sitting and clutching a steering wheel. To be like a cat stretching its full length out on a bed, luxuriating in the stretching, the freeing of tension from a body. He kicked off his tennis shoes. Stars littered the sky. But he forced himself not to focus, not to see if anything moved. He was looking up at the sky, and if the sky was looking back at him—so be it. He was thinking he ought to make peace with the sky and stars and any lurking satellites. A treaty.

The I Don't Give a Fuck About Satellites Treaty.

He decided to call Roger Valkyrie.

"Greuzi, kid," Roger Valkyrie said.

"Greuzi?"

"Or, Greuzi Mitenad, which would be hello in the Alemannic dialect to a group of people. But to just one person—Greuzi."

"Where are you, Roger Valkyrie?"

"Home, Shel. On the couch again—and wearing pants. We're all official here and good to go."

"What's the Alemannic dialect?" Shelby said.

"It's what they speak in Liechtenstein, kid."

"I don't think I could even find Liechtenstein on a map," Shelby said.

"I'll send you a globe, kid. Actually, the official language in Liechtenstein is German. But they also have this Alemannic dialect thingie, too. For example, to say good evening does sound pretty German—Guten Abig."

"Danke Schoen," Shelby said. "But that's all I know besides sauerkraut and wiener schnitzel."

"That's good enough, kid. I love a good schnitzel. Just don't say Heil Hitler or Hermann Goering or Nazi or anything like that in public. Did you know there's only about 40,000 people in Liechtenstein? Maybe it's even less than that. It's like going to Muncie, Indiana, with better food and a better view."

"You've been to Muncie, Roger Valkyrie?"

"I was born there, Shel. But we moved to Pennsylvania when I was just a kid."

"Is that true?"

"Does it need to be, Shel?"

"I guess not. How's the lawn looking?"

"Snazzy, kid. I just mowed it—earning those important points with the wife. But fall's creeping in and I won't have to deal with it much longer."

"But when the leaves fall, you'll have another problem."

"That's true. But I think I can pay the wife's nephew to rake and bag them. That way I dodge the work and get points for helping the kid. See how that works? I can drink a beer on the couch and watch the Redskins."

"Until they send you someplace else."

"Keeps me on my toes, kid. And besides, the Redskins suck. How the hell are you? *Where* are you?"

"Hot Springs, Arkansas."

"You're putting the miles on that Benz."

"I traded the Benz."

"Yeah? What'd you get, a Maserati?"

"A Ford F150. Red."

"No shit?" Roger Valkyrie said.

"Used, too, but in good shape."

"You must have got a buttload of cash out of that deal, kid."

"I gave it to the dealer."

"Really? Interesting. Shel—is this part of the whole enlighten-ment thingaroo?"

"It's part of something. I don't know what."

"I believe you. Why are you in Arkansas, kid?"

"I'm on my to a way to a town called Parsons Grove, on up north of Little Rock in the boonies."

"Boonies—I love that word, Shel. Not sure why, but I do. Shit—gotta call coming in. Hold on, kid."

"Holding."

The submerged pool lights glowed and a faint haze, a subtle mist, coiled and floated just above the pool, giving the impression that the blue water might start boiling at any moment. It was a long and narrow pool. It would show up easily to a satellite, he mused. A satellite couldn't miss it. And if a girl were in the pool, wearing, say, a tiny red bikini, just leisurely doing the breast stroke, or the butterfly, the satellite could zoom in and catch every splash, every stroke, could zoom in so close it could count the moles on her forearms, or scan the muscles of her thighs.

But there was no girl, no red bikini, just Shelby stretched out, his body no longer glowing and tight from the rigors of the day, but getting tired of holding a cell phone to his ear.

Then Roger Valkyrie's urgent voice was in his ear.

"Shel, let me call you back in a flash."

"Trouble?"

"There's always trouble."

Then he was gone and Shelby sat the phone on a table next to the chaise and looked back at the sky, hands behind his head. The sky and stars no longer appealed to him and he went into the hotel bar and got a beer, a cold Pabst, and when he got back to the pool, there actually was a girl in it, not in a red bikini, but a blue one-piece. She was pretty, athletic, long-legged, had long blond hair, an oval face and a sort of upturned nose that qualified as both cute and sexy. She slipped a swimming cap on, a red one, and slipped into the pool as effortlessly as a seal or penguin gliding off a rock into water.

Shelby sipped the cold Pabst and watched the girl first swim underwater nearly halfway to the other end of the long pool, which seemed to him a pretty far distance. She emerged, slipping into a breast stroke until she touched the far end and then kicked back immediately with a tall splash, swimming with determination to the far end without stopping. She briskly swam full laps a number of times that Shelby failed to keep track of, but he watched closely as she swam and kicked, noting her hard arm muscles whenever an arm emerged before digging back into the blue glowing water.

He finished his beer and she swam even more laps. He got up into a sitting position for a better look. Then she was done, resting for a moment, her back against the edge of the shallow end, half out of water. She didn't seem out of breath. She was a swimmer, for sure. Her suit revealed a hint of cleavage and Shelby admired her large breasts. She had a deep, caramel tan. The girl was maybe nineteen. Maybe older, but also maybe younger.

She pulled the cap off and pulled at her hair, letting it stream down on her shoulders. She shook it and water flew in several directions, drops striking the dry poolside surface. She turned to the steps and walked up and out if the pool, shaking her hair more. The girl dried herself carefully with a large red and blue striped towel. Then she wrapped the towel around her, slipped into yellow flip flops, and opened the pool gate, turning as she went through it, smiling briefly toward Shelby, and then she was gone down a walk-way toward the hotel.

The show over, the phone rang.

"So, what the hell is up in Parsons Grove," Roger Valkyrie said.

"Maybe not as much as here," Shelby said, looking over at the gate again, hoping the girl forgot something and would re-appear.

"Are you going to have to change your name to Bubba or Lee Roy or Billy Bob, Shel?"

"Maybe I should," Shelby said. "Maybe I should legally change my name to avoid being Mr. Saved the World."

"I don't know, kid. People would still recognize you. You'd still be you, no matter the name. What would you change your name to?"

"Could I change it to Roger Valkyrie?"

"Sure you could. But why?"

"I don't know," Shelby said. "What if I change my name to Billy Bob Thingamabob?"

"Or, Billy Bob Thingamajig—both have pizzazz and good ca-dence. Maybe avoid Billy Bob Doohickey, though. Give it more thought, kid. It has to feel right. So, what's in Parsons Grove besides guys dating their sisters?"

"I'm going to see the Exalted Church of the Intergalactic Moment."

"Really? That's a mouthful of a title, Shel. Is that some kind of Dogpatch religious play?"

"It's an actual church, Roger Valkyrie—I think."

"What's this intergalactic moment?"

"The day I saved the world."

"Oh, I see, Shel—it's a cult."

"That's harsh, Roger Valkyrie. And I hope not since it's all about me. Or starts with me—something like that."

"Sounds way beyond Mormon, Shel. Are you sure about this?"

"I've come this far. I might as well go see it. What's the real harm?"

"What if it's about a circle jerk with you in the middle, kid?"

"Reverend Spurlock seemed okay by email. I even chatted with him on the phone. He sounds nice enough—sane enough."

"That's the head holy roller, this Spurlock?"

"Raymond Spurlock."

"I don't know, Shel. Maybe it's time I actually do some official agency shit on this, using sophisticated agency resources."

"You mean Google Raymond Spurlock?"

"That's right. Give me a second."

"Take your time, Roger Valkyrie. I'm just sitting around the Holiday Inn pool. It's a pretty nice night."

"Okay," Roger Valkyrie said. "I'm not seeing anything on Spurlock. But check Facebook. See if he has a page for his wacko church. If he does, and it looks like his flock is The Addams Family at summer camp, you might want to bypass Parsons Grove, kid."

"Roger that, Roger."

"Oops," Roger Valkyrie said. "Another damn call, kid—you know the routine."

"Right—holding."

Shelby put the phone down and looked over at the gate, but the girl didn't re-appear, dripping wet or otherwise. He got another beer from the bar and sat at the shallow end of the pool, his feet dangling into the warm water. He checked the phone after a couple of minutes and Roger Valkyrie had hung up, but Shelby was confident he'd yet return the call. Shelby may have saved the world, but it seemed to be Roger Valkyrie's job to trot around the globe putting out fires before the whole damn globe went up in flames like a colossal cherry bomb. They were sort of in the same business, one apparently by choice, the other completely by chance and accident. Shelby went on up to his room and finished his beer sitting on the balcony, which had a view of a field and a grove of trees. From one of the branches high up a tree, he saw a pair of eyes, which he presumed belonged to an owl, or maybe a raccoon. Or maybe it was Roger Valkyrie. Shelby's ability to be surprised by events had steadily eroded to almost zero.

The phone rang and startled Shelby, who glanced again at the eyes in the tree. They sure looked to be staring right at him. It was Roger Valkyrie on the phone.

"Roger, there's no chance you're actually sitting in a tree by the balcony of my room, is there?"

"Good gravy, Shel. Why would I be sitting in a tree down in Dogpatch USA? I'm not an owl, or a raccoon, you know."

"No reason. Never mind."

"Where were we, kid?"

"You had to go do—whatever it is you do," Shelby said. "What *were* you doing?"

"You'd rather not know. Me, either. But I have no choice. So, kid, I think we were talking about your latest road trip. I'm concerned about this circle-jerk cult up in Parsons Grove."

"I'll be okay, Roger Valkyrie. Are you actually worried about me? Do you actually care?"

"Do you mean, are you just an assignment? Just a job?"

"That's right. Am I? Am I just the short straw you drew?"

After a long pause, Roger Valkyrie said, "There weren't any straws, kid. We didn't draw straws. I volunteered."

"Really? Why?"

"I saw you on TV, Shel. Right after the big old intergalactic moment. You looked a little lost, and a little scared, too. The old deer-caught-in-the-headlights moment. I guess I just figured maybe I could help. The assignment sounded more promising than the rest of the muck I have to wade though."

"I'm still lost, Roger Valkyrie. Scared, too."

"I know. But you have to find your way, Shelby. We all do. Life ain't easy, but it beats the alternative. Life is about looking for home, I suppose. Go see the cult, kid. It helps to know what *won't* work for you in order to know what will."

"Maybe I'll like it, Roger Valkyrie."

"Maybe you will, kid. Maybe you need to go hear what these people have to say about it all. But remember, Shelby—*you* decide who you are, and what you are. Not them."

"I'll keep that in mind, for sure."

"And if it is a big wingnut circle jerk, get your ass out of there pronto."

"I was on the track team in high school, Roger Valkyrie."

"And you once saved the world."

"That's the rumor."

"A rumor can become perception, Shel, and perception becomes truth."

"Even if the rumor isn't true?"

"It's true enough when people choose to believe it."

Shelby started off from Hot Springs early the next morning after gassing up the truck and scoring a breakfast cache of tacos and extra sour cream at the closest Taco Bell, a relapse of sorts that he vowed not to repeat, but this time from the relative anonymity of the drive-through. He wore sunglasses to try and avoid recognition, which seemed to work, though the skinny teenage girl eyed him oddly a couple of times as she handed over his sack.

A half-hour up the interstate, he got off at an exit to pee and spotted a rolling country lane lined with trees and meandering off into the distance. He impulsively decided to take it and look for a place to eat his taco breakfast. The lane took him out into a forest and then past a clearing and small pond. There was a picnic table and he sat and munched tacos, applying liberal doses of taco sauce. After eating, he watched a turtle swim across the pond and climb onto a large piece of wood floating in the water. He lifted his Mountain Dew in salute to the turtle and was convinced that it turned its head slightly toward him.

For the first time in days, Shelby felt a sense of calm. Not complete calm, not complete relaxation, not complete peace, but a smidgeon of all those things, a sliver, and perhaps something to build on if he could. Saving the world had seemed to take much of the starch out of him and he needed to figure out how to get it back. He backed the truck toward the pond and dropped the tailgate and sat on it. The sky was clear and he glanced around it a moment. Did the satellites know where he was? He raised his Mountain Dew to the sky and then gulped the rest of it. He thought of Roger Valkyrie and raised his empty can in salute to Roger, too. Fuck the satellites, he thought. Fuck them very much. Part of him figured they might be real, and the other part of him seemed to know better. Both parts were who he was, and so he decided to try and make peace with both selves and push on.

Shelby drove on straight through to Little Rock, stopping only to pee again, and then headed up another highway north, crossing the White River at Batesville. The towns were all small, and life in them looked to be very slow and modest as he passed through each one slowly, curious about everything and everyone that he saw. He stopped for coffee in Cave City, which claimed to produce the world's best—sweetest—watermelons in addition to the annual watermelon festival, which he had just missed, and a mysterious cave somewhere in downtown, with a mysterious underground river of unknown origins, according to the chatty waitress who poured his coffee at Cave City Café.

He had saved the waitress and the Cave City Café with its stained Formica counter, and the famous mysterious cave and its famous, mysterious underground river, and all of tiny, sleepy Cave City. It was a hell of a thing to carry around inside, like an internal anvil, an unmovable object to juggle—like a tumor. Or even a mysterious underground river coursing through him. He sipped his coffee and looked around the café at the faces of calm people not looking at him.

It was time to keep moving forward, to push on—once more unto the breach—and Shelby decided against having a gander at the cave, figuring one cave was pretty much all caves, just as once you've saved the world you've saved the world and it's time to move on. Nothing to see here folks—move along. The world had clearly arrived at that conclusion. But move on to what? That was the dilemma he was no closer to solving. But at least he knew what the dilemma was.

The leaves in northern Arkansas had not yet started turning colors, but there was something in the air, a hint of cooling, transition. Parsons Grove was a sleepy hamlet nestled in the green hills straddling a river valley. Swift, cold water rushed and created many rapids as the river meandered aggressively through town. Just outside the city limits a very large and very black crow picked at a possum carcass on the road and declined to move aside. Shelby had to swerve to avoid it. When he looked back, the crow puffed itself up and spread its wings menacingly.

Shelby called Reverend Spurlock as he cruised along the town square, and when he pulled into the reverend's driveway, the reverend was sitting in a porch swing smoking a cigarette. He flipped the cigarette into the yard and hurried down the steps to greet Shelby with a smile.

"As I live and breathe, it's Shelby Albert Goddard in the flesh," he said. "You look taller in person, son, and TV does not do you justice—why, you're a colossus."

Shelby processed the notion of being a colossus as they shook hands. He figured he seemed taller because the reverend was quite short, rather almost-dwarfish, perhaps only five-four, and quite stocky with a large forehead and a rich black beard and was a man who seemed wider than he was tall. A bowling ball with hair. With a cowboy hat and six-shooters, Ray might have resembled Yosemite Sam. The reverend had a grip like a vise and the handshake lingered to Shelby's dismay.

"That's some grip you've got," Shelby said, hoping to get his hand back intact pretty soon. "Do you work out?"

"Lordy, I'm sure sorry about that," Ray said, releasing Shelby's hand. "Driving a truck for twenty years gives a man strong hands. I forget that sometimes. And I'm excited to meet you, son."

"That's okay, Rev. Spurlock. No harm done."

"No need to call me reverend, Mr. Goddard. That's only for the church. And even there, no one calls me reverend. I go by Ray just fine. And I'm your humble servant."

"And I'm just Shelby."

"But so much more, my friend—a messiah, really, some say" Ray said. "I should bow in your presence." Ray got down on one knee with some difficulty and looked up, hands clasped together as though to pray.

Shelby was dumfounded, horrified—creeped out. He glanced around to see if anyone was looking, but saw no one. Maybe Roger Valkyrie was right and this was a wingnut circle jerk after all. He pulled on Ray's arms and helped him to his feet.

"Please, Ray—no bowing. Please, please, please. We really can't have any bowing. And I'm not a messiah. That's—unrealistic. I'm just Shelby, from Boise, Idaho."

"No, no, no—so much more, son."

"No, no, no—not at all," Shelby said. "I'm just a man. Promise me there won't be any more bowing, Ray. Or I'll have to leave right away. We just can't have any bowing."

"Well, okay," Ray said reluctantly and frowning, too. "I promise. But we owe you so much, Shelby. We're so grateful. Thank God you had the presence of mind to do what you did, whatever that was, and even though we don't understand it."

Shelby was beginning to think he might actually prefer the people who didn't believe he had saved the world.

"Promise me you won't call me a messiah, Ray. Never again. And savior's out, too."

Ray bit his lip slightly. He looked as subdued as a scolded puppy. "I promise."

"And just call me Shelby—or Shel."

"Would you like some iced tea, Shelby?"

"I'd love some iced tea, Ray. I really would. You're a savior."

Ray chuckled.

"And that from a man who would know."

Over iced tea on the porch—Shelby was accorded the honor of swinging in the swing—he discovered that Ray Spurlock really wasn't a wacko at all, just strident at times, and well short of Mormon, as Roger Valkyrie might say. And his church really wasn't a cult or even a wingnut circle jerk. Shelby made a mental note to let Roger Valkyrie know that when he had a chance. Ray appeared to be quite normal and had a wife, Mitzi, who was at work that day as a secretary at the middle school.

Ray was between trucking runs. He didn't work as steady as he was used to, but they managed living paycheck to paycheck. Ray and Mitzi had grown up Baptists, but had become a tad more liberal than the rest of Parsons Grove thanks to a few years in Chicago when they were first married. The Baptist fire and brimstone no longer suited them and it made them uncomfortable. They even stopped going to church and read from the Bible together at home sometimes. They were convinced that Christianity was being hijacked by folks who were decidedly un-Christian and with a lot of help from Fox News.

As Shelby sipped his tea, Ray went into the house and came back with a pint bottle of Old Crow whiskey.

"How about I spice up your tea, Shelby? You game?"

"That's a plan. Let the spicing commence."

Shelby raised his glass and Ray poured a hearty dose of whiskey.

"You might want to stir her with a finger," Ray said. "To water down the bite a bit at first. Old Crow has sharp teeth."

"I saw a crow as I came into town. A tough-looking customer." Shelby stirred his drink and licked his fingers. "You're not a teetotaler sort of reverend, I take it, Ray."

"Lordy no. Self-righteousness kind of bunches my panties. And I like a good snort. No sin in it."

Shelby made a face after his first gulp of whiskeyed tea.

"Whoa," Shelby said. "That's got a kick. I think it stripped the enamel off my teeth."

"Too strong, son?"

"No—just right. I can spare some enamel. And I'm in good shape on brain cells, I figure."

Ray raised his glass.

"What do we toast—saving the world?" Ray said.

"No, no, no," Shelby said, raising his glass. "That's old news, Ray. Let's toast enlightenment."

"Enlightenment," Ray said flatly and appearing to ponder the concept with a deep furrow across his brow. "Well, I can drink to that, son. I just don't know what it is."

"It is what it is," Shelby said. "That's what a friend of mine likes to say."

By his second sip, Shelby was used to the whiskey and liking the warm glow as it erupted in his stomach.

"I have to ask, Ray—why'd you start your church?"

Ray shrugged. "Just an impulse. Mitzi and I watched all the news coverage at the time. We saw you on all the shows. You seemed humble."

"I was drunk on some of those shows. All the networks put me up in fancy hotels. After a while, I'd ask for a room without a mini-bar. Too tempting. Too many hangovers."

"A man has to keep the lid tight on drinking, Shelby. Keep it medicinal. Maybe that's part of being enlightened."

"Couldn't hurt. But why start a church, Ray?"

"Mitzi and I went to the Baptist church here. For years. But after your, your—your accomplishment, we soured on how political it got. We're fed up with all this nonsense about the president being Muslim and not American. And that only certain folks can be truly American, and only some folks can truly be Christian and all that hooey. We knew better. So, I decided to start my own gathering. On a whim, we called it a church. Maybe it's more of a social club with a faith component. Plus, I figured the name would rankle the Baptist preacher."

"Did it?"

"We bunched his panties, for sure. He calls us heathens. Not very Christian, if you ask me. In his book, you're only Christian if you follow along blindly. But then, the man gets his ideas from Fox News, so there you go."

"And how many members are there now, Ray?"

"Up to an even dozen. But I've got a question for *you*. Just what *are* thingamabobs, thingamajigs, and doohickeys?"

Shelby sipped his whiskeyed tea and looked at daisies growing from a planter on the porch railing. A bee pollinated one of the flowers.

"They're things that don't exist, Ray."

Ray nodded solemnly and watched the bee, too.

Shelby spent a few nights at a rustic bed and breakfast overlooking the river. He woke to soothing gurgles from rapids just below the deck to his bedroom. The bed and breakfast was owned by Ray's cousin, Viola Atteberry, and her husband, Virgil, and both were members of Ray's gathering—his "flock of skeptical individualists," as he termed it. Shelby elected to take up residence in Parsons Grove for as long as it seemed like a good idea and no longer than when it became boring. That was as precise as he cared to be about it.

He rented a house along the river with a dandy view of rapids and a sandbar popular with vocal white gulls. The far bank held back a pasture. One day, a cow stepped out into the river and stood mutely in the rapids, staring expectantly at Shelby. The cow really eyed him like he was a long lost relative.

"Oh for God's sake, cow—you're welcome," Shelby finally said. "I saved the world for you, too."

Then Shelby called Roger Valkyrie.

"Anyoung haseyo, Shel. How's it hanging?"

"I won't even try and pronounce that, Roger Valkyrie. What country are you in now?"

"The one you saved, kid."

"I saved them all."

"Good point. And a clear sign you don't show favoritism. An admirable quality."

"It was sort of an all or nothing deal, Roger Valkyrie. There was no time to pick and choose."

"That's certainly the nature of thingamabobs, thingamajigs, and doohickeys, kid. And I'm at home, Shel—on my trusty couch. But I just got back from Korea."

"Which one?"

"There's only one you can go to and have a decent meal, kid—unless you're Dennis Rodman, of course."

"Did you see Dennis?"

"I did have a word or two with him, kid. The only thing stranger than how you saved the world is a conversation with Dennis Rodman."

"And how's your lawn looking, Roger Valkyrie?"

"Like a putting green at the Masters. Greener than guacamole. My wife's nephew does a crackerjack job of it."

Shelby imagined Roger Valkyrie at home, maybe sitting in a rocker on a wraparound porch of an old, stately, Victorian house with tall columns reaching to the overhanging roof. Roger would sit in his chair and rock, smoking a pipe maybe, sipping a scotch, the already scanned *New York Times* in his lap, his cell phone resting dormant on the paper but ready to erupt and demand his attention to some political global brushfire about to ignite; until then, he imagined Roger Valkyrie as content to sip his drink and cheer on his nephew mowing a green lawn that stretched on out of sight—all the way to the distant horizon.

"How about the gutters?" Shelby asked.

"That boy is a workhorse, Shel. I'm getting my money's worth, believe you me. He has those gutters as clean as a whistle and flowing like Old Faithful."

"Doesn't Old Faithful erupt rather than flow?"

"Good point, kid. I stand corrected. Those gutters flow like shit through a goose—how's that?"

"Colorful."

"So, where are you, Shel?"

"Still in Parsons Grove."

"Still in Dogpatch? How's Lil Abner and Baby Yoakum? How's the circle jerk cult going—getting a firm grip on that?"

"You should do stand up comedy, Roger Valkyrie."

"I would, but I'm lying down on the couch."

"But not lying down on the job, right? Are we official, Roger Valkyrie? Are you wearing pants?"

"Indeed I am—corduroy. Thin wale, not wide wale. Wide wale is for rubes. Or maybe someone stuck in the 60s. It's almost fall, you know. Fall is for corduroy. Or maybe it's the other way around. The wife frowns on me lounging about just in my boxers."

"Sounds like she wears the pants in the family."

"There's that new sense of humor, kid. I'm loving it. Makes me worry less about you."

"But you still worry."

"I'm paid to worry. I'm trained to worry."

"I thought you were paid to clean up messes, Roger Valkyrie."

"I'm paid to worry and *then* clean up the mess, kid. Are you in any messes today?"

"Naw—just checking in. Things are pretty smooth here, I'd say. I speak to the church tomorrow. It should be a hoot."

"Just remember, kid—"

"I know, I know—thingamabobs, thingamajigs, and doohickeys. I even got that bumper sticker for my truck."

"Good for you, kid. You're embracing what life doles out. I'm proud of you. How long you plan to be in Dogpatch?"

"As long as it's interesting, but not a day past boring."

"There you go, Shel. A man with a plan. Avoid boredom, for sure. What do you figure to do while you're there, besides a sit-down with the cult?"

But he was not a man with a plan at all. He wished he had one. There ought to be some government issue manual for heroes. Or for reluctant saviors. Everywhere he had been so far, he looked for signs of what to do. Or maybe he missed them. Maybe he wasn't looking hard enough. Or he couldn't see what was right in front of him. What *was* right in front of him? A cow, making cow eyes toward him. A moocow, which he vaguely knew was something out of James Joyce. He knew just enough about Joyce to know that his own life was currently like a page from *Finnegan's Wake*. Any page. Upside down or right side up.

But he did know what would be very nice to have: "Enlightenment," he said to Roger Valkyrie. "Enlightenment's my new thing. My raison d'etre."

"Sounds French, kid. Watch out for the French—great food, but they can be as slippery as an eel."

"It's the only French I know, Roger Valkyrie. It means my reason for existing. I ran across it on the internet. And I'm going to pursue it. Find it. Define it. I think I'll pull it all together, what I find, and call it a manual. Maybe sort of a user's manual for living."

"You'll need a spiffy name for it, Shel. How about, Saving the World Before Noon. Or, Saving the World and How to Live In It on $25 a Day. People are always looking for a good guide book. Be sure to include lots of color photos."

"Photos of what?"

"Doesn't matter," Roger Valkyrie said. "People love lots of color photos—any photos."

"Photos of thingamabobs, thingamajigs, and doohickeys?"

"There's that sense of humor again, kid."

"I'm calling it The Manual for Complete Enlightenment," Shelby said confidently. "How's that?"

"Ambitious, Shel. Not just enlightenment, but *complete* enlightenment. Aim high, I always say."

"I'm shooting for the stars, Roger Valkyrie. The heavens."

"Inspiring, kid. You may end up the cosmonaut of enlightenment."

"Cosmonaut? Why not astronaut?"

"That, too, Shel. I just like saying cosmonaut. It sounds like an emotion, or a mood. Like someone might say, gee, today I'm feeling pretty cosmonaut, for sure."

"Or, that's so cosmonaut," Shelby said.

"Exactly, kid. It might work in almost any situation."

"Do you want me to call you Roger Cosmonaut?"

"It does have a nice ring to it. I'm tempted. But let's stick with Valkyrie. If we actually change my code name, even a modification, I'd have to fill out a form 1050D-89. And that booger sucks up the time. And I'd have to explain it to my boss—he's no picnic. Worse than a day at the DMV, believe you me. Worse than watching my wife's nephew clean gutters on a Saturday."

"Sounds too cosmonaut."

"Right, kid. As usual, you're exactly cosmonaut."

"Feeling it, Roger Valkyrie. I'm feeling pretty cosmonaut today."

"Are you feeling regular cosmonaut, Shel, or extra?"

"Oh, extra, Roger Valkyrie. Definitely extra cosmonaut."

The twelve members of the Exalted Church of the Intergalactic Moment—actually thirteen counting Ray, but that seemed unlucky and so they were calling it twelve until a new member was on board—agreed that a gulf was widening between democracy and Christianity. Or at least Christianity as practiced in many parts of America. Specifically the South. They agreed that Fox News existed to misinform viewers and solidify power and wealth for the extremist goons running the Religious Right. Beyond that, they mostly had gravitated to each other because they believed in tolerance, facts, honest elections, and didn't care to have a self-righteous Baptist preacher—rumored to have cheated on his wife—tell them what was moral and what wasn't. And they all enjoyed a good argument over a snort on Wednesday evenings at the American Legion Hall.

In addition to Ray and Mitzi Spurlock, the group consisted of Viola and Virgil Atteberry, Tom Mitzdorfer, Hera Thompson, Oceanna Cooper, Sam Crittenden, Harry Longabaugh, Robert Leroy Parker, and Martin and Susan Cummings.

Ray began the evening in the usual manner—once their drinks had arrived, that is:

"My friends—let us never forget thingamabobs, thingamajigs, and doohickeys," he said enthusiastically.

"Absolutely," Mitzi Spurlock said.

"Where's Shelby?" Hera Thompson said impatiently. "We want to meet Shelby."

"He's on the way," Ray said. "He called to say he had a flat tire."

"A flat tire?" Oceanna Cooper said. "He saved the world and now he has a flat tire? Mercy me! What if he had had a flat tire on that fateful day?"

"We wouldn't be drinking good whiskey," Sam Crittenden said with a chuckle.

"I'm having a margarita," Oceanna Cooper said.

"And this is a vodka gimlet," Hera Thompson said, holding it up.

"I'll revise my statement," Sam Crittenden said. "If he had had a flat tire that day, we wouldn't be here with various types of booze."

"That's all well and good, but I beg to differ," Tom Mitzdorfer said. "On the fateful day, even with a flat tire, surely Shelby would have persevered—thingamabobs, thingamajigs, and doohickeys, of course."

"Yes, yes," Viola Atteberry seconded. "He would have indeed."

They all nodded approvingly and had a sip of their drinks.

"To thingamabobs, thingamajigs, and doohickeys," Oceanna said abruptly, holding her glass up, and they all had yet another sip.

"But what if Shelby had had engine trouble that day," Martin Cummings said. "A flat tire's one thing—but engine trouble is something altogether different."

"Oh it is, for sure," Tom Mitzdorfer said. "I see where you're going with this—Shelby could have called AAA for a flat tire—they're quite prompt you know—and maybe still have made it to work on time. But a blown engine—poof, there goes the world."

"Blow a head gasket, blow the world," Sam Crittenden agreed.

"Hold on a minute," Hera Thompson said tersely. "Even with engine trouble, I believe Shelby would have caught a ride to work and still made it in time. He would have improvised. It would have been close, but he would have pulled it off."

"Like on MacGyver?" Martin Cummings said.

"Shelby was destined, Martin," Hera said, patting Martin's knee. "TV's an illusion."

"That again, Hera?" Tom Mitzdorfer said. "He was destined? Born to save the world and all that? He had skills. That's how it got done. He knew how to do things and did them when they had to be done."

"Thingamabobs, thingamajigs, and doohickeys," Martin Cummings suddenly exclaimed, raising his glass and spilling whiskey on his pants. His wife hugged him and he spilled more.

"But, he had to be there to do them at all," Hera Thompson said. "That's the destiny part."

"I still say it was skills," Tom Mitzdorfer said. "Many people were destined to be there that day, but it was Shelby that had the skills to do what had to be done."

"What if it was just sort of an accident," Harry Longabaugh said. "What if Shelby had only gone to work that day because of guilt."

"What guilt?" Hera Thompson said.

"What if Shelby had temporarily wigged out and did something wrong," Harry Longabaugh said. "Something totally out of character. What if he flipped for some reason and, I don't know—robbed a bank on the way to work?"

"Why would Shelby rob a bank?" Hera Thompson said. "Where does that come from?"

"I think Harry's premise assumes Shelby had wigged and wasn't rational, Hera," Robert LeRoy Parker said. "Or was broke, of course."

"Shelby wouldn't have wigged," Hera said. "He was destined."

"Here we go again," Tom Mitzdorfer said, throwing up his hands.

"But you have to admit, it's an intriguing premise," Oceanna Cooper said. "The notion that even though Shelby saved the world, he did so only because he was broke and felt guilty over robbing a bank, and so he went to work instead of escaping with the money."

"Instead of going on the lam to Mexico with the money," Martin Cummings said. "That makes it somewhat random, I think."

"Not exactly random and more about choice and morality," Oceanna said. "He had two choices—Mexico and drinks with umbrellas in them on some beach, or go to work and return the money. Then it was time for thingamabobs, thingamajigs, and doohickeys."

"And so there goes the old destiny theory, Hera," Tom Mitzdorfer said happily, crossing his arms over his ample chest with a rather smug look.

"Not at all," Hera Thompson said. "Shelby could have been destined to rob a bank, feel guilty, then go to work, save the world, and that would be his atonement."

"Maybe," Tom Mitzdorfer said. "That's a neat package, for sure. But even if he felt guilty and showed up at work to atone—he still had to have the skills. My theory is still sound."

"It won't be after another round of drinks," Ray said and everyone laughed.

"And we can ask Shelby when he gets here," Hera Thompson said.

"One question, though," Viola Atteberry said. "Did he give the bank money back? And does saving the world automatically wipe out the robbery? I mean, if he didn't save the world, the robbery wouldn't matter, of course."

Oceanna put a hand on Viola's elbow.

"Dearie—he didn't actually rob a bank."

"That we know of," Tom Mitzdorfer said. "After all, the whole thing was hushed up—thingamabobs, thingamajigs, and doohickeys."

"That's right," Martin Cummings said. "We just don't know."

That was when Shelby walked in, and he had heard the last few comments about robbing a bank.

"I think I can clear all that up, folks," Shelby said, smiling but nervous.

All heads turned his way and all faces had expectant looks. The woman named Oceanna, though, was quite pretty. He was sure she cocked her head ever so slightly to a side to look him over, and Shelby caught himself smiling at her, thought better of it, and hoped that instead it would just seem like he smiled at everyone. He was abruptly nervous, intimidated. He swallowed hard once and sniffed. It looked to be a tough audience, judging by just the remnants of conversation he heard coming in. The kind of audience that could smell fear and pounce like a cobra. Did cobras actually pounce? No—more like lunged, he decided, which was certainly no better or less dangerous, and not at all helpful or calming information. It was a crowd of strangers before him, a crowd of lunging cobras.

"Here he is now," Ray said, taking a few steps toward Shelby and waving him on. "My friends—let me introduce Shelby Albert Goddard."

Shelby waved to the group, but then didn't know what to do with his hands, which eventually wound up in his pants pockets.

"He looks taller on TV," Hera Thompson said.

"But more handsome in person," Oceanna Cooper said, winking.

"Did you really rob a bank?" Viola Atteberry said.

"No, I did not," Shelby said, suddenly worried that he didn't sound convincing.

"You don't sound convincing," Tom Mitzdorfer said.

"He just got here," Oceanna Cooper said. "Let the man breathe. And he had a flat tire, for God's sake."

"Did you call AAA?" Tom Mitzdorfer said. "They're very prompt. I called them a few weeks back when my car wouldn't start, and they sent someone right away. Turns out it wasn't the alternator, thank goodness."

"Nobody wants to hear about your alternator," Hera Thompson said.

"We want to hear about the bank robbery," Viola Atteberry said.

"There wasn't one," Shelby said quietly as he found a seat. "I'd probably remember it."

"But Tom says it would have been hushed up," Viola said. "Since you saved the world."

"I suspect it would have," Tom Mitzdorfer said. "For the greater good."

"For the greater good of what?" Hera Thompson said.

"For the greater good of humanity," Tom Mitzdorfer said. "For the greater good of the planet. And even today's incident—a flat tire—could have been hushed up, too. National security."

"There was no robbery," Shelby said. "And I really did have a flat tire. National security wasn't involved. And it wasn't the alternator, either."

"You should have that alternator checked, though," Tom Mitzdorfer said.

"You really should," Sam Crittenden said.

"So, you didn't rob a bank, dearie?" Viola Atteberry said.

"Not at all," Shelby said, shaking his head vigorously. "Are you disappointed?"

"Well, it would be way cool to say a famous bank robber stayed at my bed and breakfast," Viola Atteberry said. "I could even put up a sign. My cousin Percy up in Missouri owns a house Jesse James stayed in, so they say."

Oceanna Cooper patted Viola's arm.

"Dearie—a famous *world saver* stayed at your bed and breakfast."

"Still, a famous outlaw—that would be pretty cool," Viola Atteberry said.

"Like Butch Cassidy—or the Sundance Kid?" Harry Longabaugh said.

"Bingo, Harry," Viola Atteberry said. "Now you're talking."

Shelby ordered a Jameson on the rocks and tried his best to smile warmly between sips.

After the meeting finally broke up amid bristling conversations still tingling with a touch of confrontation, though subsiding some as everyone realized it was time to go home and become sober adults again, Shelby left the legion hall and walked along Main Street, enjoying the fresh night air and the whiskey still percolating inside him. The moon was nearly full and cast a benevolent glow. A soft breeze rose and fell, rustling the leaves in the trees.

People smiled at him as they went by. A man actually tipped his hat, something Shelby believed only existed in black and white movies and from another era altogether. He stopped and put his arms around a parking meter, hugging it for support, and just let Parsons Grove sort of soak in, sink in—wash over him—filling him up with the quiet hum of a small town in no hurry to become any larger or unduly ambitious.

Shelby walked back to his rented house and retrieved a beer from the fridge. He walked down to the river and slipped off his shoes and socks and waded in. He reached the line of rapids and sat on a large boulder and sipped beer, which on top of the whiskey was affording him a splendid little buzz. The moon glowed through an opening in the trees. Far down the river were the green and yellow lights from other houses perched on its banks.

He sipped his beer and tried to pour his thoughts out of his head and into the rushing water. After a while, he no longer noticed the cold water tickling his feet, or the pounding of water against rock, or the warm glow from the moon. He got up and walked into the river up past his knees, enjoying the sheer force of the current attempting to push him forward, and he had to resist its power with more effort than he at first had expected. Later, after he had changed out of his wet Levi's and sat on his rented sofa in his rented house along the river, which was free of charge, he called Roger Valkyrie.

"Dobry den, kid," Roger Valkyrie said.

"And to you, too, Roger Valkyrie. How's it hanging?"

"It's hanging."

"What language is Dobry den?"

"Czech, Shel. I was just in The Czech Republic—though, I always liked calling it Czechoslovakia so much better. A great cadence in that name, and so many syllables."

"Dobry den means hello?" Shelby said.

"That's the formal version, kid. But the informal is Ahoj. I had drinks in Prague the other day and ended up sounding like a drunken admiral—Ahoy!"

"We may have to call you Roger Ahoy."

"I like it, Shel—but remember, form 1050D-89. They take changing a code name pretty seriously around here."

"Do I have a code name? I've been meaning to ask."

"Shelby."

"That's it? My code name is Shelby?"

"I can get you a different one, but that means a form 1050D-90. It's quite similar to the 1050D-89, but has an extra page since you're a civilian. But I'll do it for *you*, kid. After all—you saved the world."

Shelby sighed. It was a long, flowing sigh. It took some time to clear him, his belly quite distended momentarily as the air oozed out. He breathed back in, slowly, fully, and expended that air, too. Saved the world. Ugh!

"No thanks. I'm fine with just Shelby, I guess. I know how you hate paperwork as much as mowing the lawn."

"You should see my lawn *now*, kid."

"Still greener than guacamole?"

"Nope—fading, and that's good news," Roger Valkyrie said. "Fall is creeping in. Soon I won't have to pay the wife's nephew to mow it."

"But you'll still need him to rake leaves."

"That's a one-shot deal, kid."

"What about winter and snow?"

"I'm covered there, too. I have a tricky back and a note from my doctor—my wife doesn't mess with me on snow and the driveway."

"Things sound pretty cosmonaut at your end, Roger Valkyrie."

"Ultra cosmonaut, Shel. Mega cosmonaut. What's the cosmonaut level at your end?"

"Regular cosmonaut. Not ultra."

"What's dragging it down, my friend?"

"Well, it's the folks in this church here. Some of them seem to think I robbed a bank."

"You robbed a bank, kid? That's not good, Shel—that would require a form 1050D-100, which would essentially sever our relationship. The government can't have you robbing banks. Very bad PR indeed."

Shelby wondered about that. It presented an interesting, unprecedented dilemma: Given that saving the world was the highest point by far of any totem pole of good deeds, requiring an altogether new totem, as yet perhaps not in existence, what would be done—what *could* be done—to someone who achieved universal acclaim, only to track mud all over it by robbing a bank?

It was a dilemma worthy of great philosophers. How much good credit did saving the world really earn? Should he have been just made emperor of the world for his troubles? And if so, would the world look the other way if he became a modern day Caligula?

Could he rob a bank and get away with it? Would they have to make him a deal if he did, just to make it all go away and preserve his status as savior?

"I didn't rob a bank, Roger Valkyrie."

"You're sure, kid?"

"Would I forget something like that?"

"Maybe not, though maybe it was an *accidental* robbery."

"How do you accidentally rob a bank, Roger Valkyrie?"

"It's conceivable, kid. You would go to a bank's drive-through, leave a pistol on your dashboard in plain sight, and the teller gives you all the cash. But maybe you were just putting the pistol on the dash while you fumbled for your license and a bank slip, for example."

"Have you been drinking sake again, Roger Valkyrie? Are you at home and wearing pants? Are we official here?"

"Absolutely, Shel. I'm wearing a new pair of cords—forest green. I think I may wear corduroy all winter. I love these fine wales and the feel of the fabric. But back to business—that's how someone with a gun accidentally robs a bank."

"I don't own a gun, Roger Valkyrie."

"Do you have a knife? You could put a knife on the dash—same result, an accidental robbery. A big Bowie knife would certainly do the trick. But so would one of those nasty little switchblades. Certainly a samurai sword would do the trick."

"I don't have a knife," Shelby said. "Or a samurai sword."

"How about a hammer, kid?"

"Nope."

"How about a really long nail, like a roofing nail?" Roger Valkyrie said.

"Nope."

"A spoon?"

Shelby visualized a spoon, tried to imagine how it could help rob a bank. It would certainly have to be a big spoon, at the very least. A teaspoon—waste of time. A tablespoon—not much better. How about one of those big soup ladles? Now *they* had some weight to them—and hot soup could be a weapon, too. But, if somebody threatened to hit a bank teller with a teaspoon, for example, that would be laughable. He supposed some damage could be done by *throwing* a spoon. But what if you miss?

What if a teller picked up the spoon and tossed it back?

"Nope," Shelby said. "I don't have a spoon. Not even a soup ladle."

"How about scissors?"

"Nope."

"Nail clippers?" Roger Valkyrie said.

"Nope."

"How about a pencil, kid?"

"Nope—really, a pencil?"

He had to concede that a sharpened pencil had some penetration values, was capable of some nasty scratches, and could even put out an eye, for example, but what if a bank robber showed up and had forgotten to sharpen it? He also wouldn't be able to use it to write a robbery note. A pencil seemed quite useless overall. What if it broke in two during the robbery? What if the pencil needed sharpening and there was a sharpener on the other side of the bank counter, but the teller refused to sharpen it? Bank robbers really had to think ahead.

"In the right hands, a pencil is a deadly weapon, Shel. Ever watch a Steven Seagal movie?"

"Not on purpose."

"How about a toothpick, kid? I'll bet Vin Diesel could rob a bank with a toothpick."

"Nope. I don't have any of those things, Roger Valkyrie."

"Well, at least it doesn't sound like it would be armed robbery."

"There was no robbery at all," Shelby said. "Not armed or unarmed or with a toothpick or even a wet washrag. There may be a plastic fork in the glove box of my truck."

"Leave it there, kid. Never put it on your dash. Better to be safe than sorry. And avoid bank drive-throughs."

"There was no accidental robbery, Roger Valkyrie."

"Well, I certainly found it hard to believe there was, kid. What's the back story here?"

"Some of the church members, for very odd and unexplained reasons, think it's possible I robbed a bank on the way to saving the world. And that the government is covering it up."

"We certainly would," Roger Valkyrie said. "Saving the world would far outweigh the robbery. We'd encourage you to give the money back, of course, though maybe a deal could be worked out, for sure—you saved the world, after all. The robbery money could even be a down payment on the reward for saving the world. But we certainly wouldn't tell anyone about it. And the robbery itself—we would officially be against that. That would damage the image of a heroic effort to save the world."

"What about the people at the bank I didn't actually rob?" Shelby said. "They would know about it, even though it never actually happened."

"Witness protection program, Shel. And you should see the paperwork—form 1050D-1000X."

"You'd put the bank employees in witness protection?"

"Ha—got you, kid. Just fucking with you. Some secret agent humor. We don't do witness protection."

"Nice, Roger Valkyrie. Very cosmonaut."

But Shelby was actually a bit disappointed. He had seen a lot of the movies and TV shows about witness protection and knew it meant a new life, a new identity, anonymity for those who truly embraced it, and who needed to avoid getting whacked; though, in the movies, the mafia dudes usually fucked that up royally because you can take the dude out of the mafia, but apparently not the mafia out of the dude, and witness protection was just too tame for them. He sort of half-thought that witness protection ought to be an option for himself. But if it required plastic surgery, he wasn't so sure.

"I'm *the* cosmonaut today," Roger Valkyrie said. "I may go find the wife and see if she wants to play some cosmonaut games."

"Well, you're certainly ahead on points with her, I guess."

"I've got points out the wazoo, Shel. Enough points to pull a Napoleon and crown myself God Emperor Cosmonaut. What's on *your* agenda, Shel?"

"No big plans."

"Avoid bank drive-throughs, kid."

"I use my debit card. Hey—here's something that will pop your gasket. Two of the church members are named Harry Longabaugh and Robert Leroy Parker."

"Are they nice?" Roger Valkyrie said. "Do they wear corduroy?"

"I didn't notice. I can check that when I go back. They seem nice enough—sort of quiet."

"Is there a problem with them, kid? You want me to command endless agency resources and look into them?"

Yeah—Google them."

"Googling."

"Check Facebook, too, Roger Valkyrie."

"Checking—Good Lord and General Jackson, kid. They're Butch Cassidy and The Sundance Kid."

"Thought you might appreciate that, Roger Valkyrie. I didn't realize it at first, either. Is that like ultra cosmonaut or what?"

"Off the cosmonaut charts. We may need a new category—Astrocosmonaut, maybe."

"Astrocosmonaut—I like it," Shelby said. "It was Harry Longabaugh who suggested I could have robbed a bank."

"Really—Longabaugh? Man—The Sundance Kid. Love the irony. That's very cosmonaut of him, Shel."

"There's also a woman named Hera. That's a pretty interesting name, too."

"Hera? Why does that sound familiar, kid?"

"Greek mythology, I think. Command some more endless agency resources, Roger Valkyrie."

"Googling."

"There's also a woman named Oceanna. That's a nice name, too—and she's pretty."

"Does she have big boobs, Shel?"

Shelby tried hard to recall. She wore a loose blouse, a navy blue one—it looked to be silk, maybe—but she was also sitting down, sort of leaning forward a lot, and often crossing her arms across her chest, which was no help at all, and so he really couldn't tell what the pertinent booby dimensions might be.

"I'll look closer next time," Shelby said.

"You have to pay attention to these things, kid. I would have noticed."

"Well, you're a secret agent."

"Here we go—Hera," Roger Valkyrie said. "Queen of the Gods. And goddess of women and marriage. Very cosmonaut. But keep her away from my wife, just in case."

"Just in case of what?"

"Secret agents like to say just in case, kid. A lot. It makes us feel like we're really on the ball."

"How very Astrocosmonaut, Roger Valkyrie."

"No doubt, kid. Any other wild characters in this church of yours?"

"It's not my church. And not really a church at all. Mostly a social group that rejects organized religion and embraces alcohol. Something like that."

A silence settled between them.

"You still there, Roger Valkyrie?"

"You know, kid, I'm having some thoughts here. Longabaugh and Parker—they sound like they could be in witness protection. Man, that just occurred to me. Just a gut feeling, mind you."

"Really?" Shelby said. "They seemed pretty harmless to me. Just two middle-aged guys who ought to get more exercise."

"But you just never know, Shel. Maybe I should come down there. To get a feel for the situation."

"I guess you can't just Google witness protection."

"That would certainly defeat the concept of witness protection, kid."

"Do you like to fish, Roger Valkyrie?"

"Fish?"

"Yeah—fishing poles, hooks, water, bait and fish. The river here is apparently full of trout. Is there an agency form you'd have to fill out to go fishing?"

"A 1050D-22, Shel."

"Really?"

"Ha—got you again, kid. There's no form for fishing. But there's one for hunting—1050D-14—because that would involve a gun other than what I was issued. But to go fishing would be a vacation day, and so we use a 1050D-17 for that. But, since I could include fishing as part of official business—like a cover story—there's no form at all."

"Cosmonaut, Roger Valkyrie."

"So, what's the nearest airport, Shel?"

"Little Rock, I guess. Or Memphis."

"I'll chopper in there tomorrow afternoon."

"Wouldn't a secret agent like something a little more—secret?"

"No way, Shel. The helicopters are just about the coolest part of the job."

"The cosmonaut part of the job."

"Correctomundo," Roger Valkyrie said. "Without the choppers, kid, I might as well be selling insurance. Or mowing lawns full-time with my wife's nephew."

"Definitely *not* cosmonaut."

"Not even close. So, can I fish in corduroy, kid?"

"I don't see why not. I'm sure the trout won't mind."

Thingamabobs, Thingamajigs, and Doohickeys

Roger Valkyrie's helicopter blasted leaves off trees as it landed next to the Civil War cannon on the lawn behind the Parsons Grove courthouse. People emptied out of shops on the town square to gawk with hands covering ears. Several men's hats cartwheeled along a sidewalk. A woman's skirt was blown over her head and she shrieked and tried to cover herself, much to the amusement of several geezers who had been whittling on a bench outside a barber shop.

"Quite the subtle entrance," Shelby said as he shook hands with a grinning Roger Valkyrie, who indeed wore corduroy—light brown thin-wale trousers and a darker brown corduroy shirt with lots of pockets and shoulder straps.

"Was it cosmonaut enough for you, kid?"

"I think it was *beyond* cosmonaut for just about everyone in town. Now the trees won't have to wait for fall to drop leaves."

Roger Valkyrie raised his mirrored sunglasses and looked around: the woman was still smoothing her dress and hair and the geezers were still delighted. Men recovered hats and dusted them off. Children pointed at the chopper and one of them cried. The hovering chopper was wreaking havoc on hairdos and women ducked back into shops all along the street with hands holding down hair.

"Okay," Roger Valkyrie said, nodding. "I get it. The whole landing on the courthouse lawn thing did sound a lot better on paper, I admit."

"Is there an agency form for landing on a courthouse lawn next to a Civil War cannon?" Shelby said.

"That would be 1050D-12T, kid. It's applicable with or without the Civil War cannon."

Roger Valkyrie waved to the pilot and the chopper lifted off. It sounded like a very large and very angry insect until it disappeared into the blue sky over the hills.

Leaves still floated in the air and settled slowly to earth.

"Think you used enough dynamite there, Butch?" Shelby said with a sleepy grin.

Roger Valkyrie stared at Shelby a moment.

"Of course," he said, smacking his forehead lightly with a hand. "That's the line when Butch and the Kid accidentally blow up the rail car—money floating in the air. Nice touch, Shelby."

"Thought you might appreciate it."

"Cosmonaut, kid. For sure."

A perturbed-looking fat man in his fifties in a dark suit approached them stridently from the courthouse across the lawn. The fat of his belly jiggled under his shirt as he walked, probably as fast as he had ever moved in his life. His face was red and he had a determined look on his face, which was also sweaty, heavy. His arms were rather short, stubby, and his enormous body made them seem even more like fins, like penguin fins.

"And who might this solid citizen in need of a diet be, kid?"

"That would be the mayor, Roger Valkyrie. That would be Ronald Cuppersmith."

"Oh it would, would it? Cuppersmith, you say? Not Coopersmith?"

"I'm pretty sure it's Cuppersmith."

"Well, I hope he doesn't have a stroke before he gets here."

"He does look determined," Shelby said.

"More like maniacal, Shel. I guess we're going to hear an earful."

"I don't think he plans to give you the key to the city."

"The key to Dogpatch, kid. But I believe you're probably right. Still—that would be pretty cool. I'll hope just in case."

"Is there an agency form for dealing with irate mayors, Roger Valkyrie?"

"Sure—1050D-11."

Shelby studied Roger Valkyrie's face. "No there isn't. You're fucking with me. Secret agent humor."

"Yes, I am—good for you, kid. You're really starting to get the hang of all this."

"It's easier when I can see your face."

"You're learning, Shel."

"Is there a form for accepting the key to a city?"

"That would be 1050D-13J, kid."

"Nope," Shelby said, shaking his head and grinning. Not buying that one, either. The J—didn't sound authentic."

"Two for two, Shell. I'm impressed. We don't accept gifts or keys to cities—defeats the notion of a secret agent working for a secret agency. We could only accept secret gifts, and from secret people."

"You mean, gifts so secret, you don't even know about them?"

"That would work. So, any wager on whether Mayor Ron here collapses before actually reaching us?"

Mayor Ron had actually screeched to an abrupt halt, not an easy task for a man of his mass, rolls of fat jiggling even more than before, and he leaned over, hands on knees, to catch his breath. Given how short his fins for arms were, he looked like he was coiled into a massive bowling ball as he leaned on his knees. He looked up, at Shelby and Roger Valkyrie, and then around the lawn and square to see who might be watching him. Mayor Ron pulled a handkerchief from an inside coat pocket and mopped his forehead and then blew his nose with it, too. He slipped his glasses off and wiped them with an edge of his coat and put them on again. He ran a hand through his unkempt brown hair, flecked with gray at his temples, to attempt to slick it back, but it resisted and stood up some.

"He does look gassed," Shelby said, "but he still has a head of steam. I'm betting he makes it."

"Let's hope he does, kid. There *is* a form if he dies in my presence on official business, which this is. I hate it when that happens."

Shelby studied Roger Valkyrie's face. "Okay, I believe there is on this one—right?"

"Yep—1050HD-101. The agency takes it seriously when we're around to see someone drop. We don't want the blame."

"How do you remember all the forms, Roger Valkyrie?"

"We had pop quizzes. On slow days my boss would stick his big head in my office and quiz me. If I pooched it, I got sent on a mission to some sweaty place and not one with good air conditioning. You learn fast that way. It's sink or swim, my friend."

Mayor Cuppersmith finally reached them, sweat beading on his forehead, his face crimson. He had to catch his breath and coughed several times before he could speak. He extended a fin masquerading as an arm and Roger Valkyrie grasped it.

"Easy there, Mayor Ron," Roger Valkyrie said. "No hurry—you want to sit on this bench over here?"

Roger Valkyrie steered the mayor to the bench and guided him slowly into a sitting position. Mayor Ron looked quite relieved to sit and sagged heavily against the wooden backrest of the bench, which groaned under the weight. Shelby smiled. He knew Roger Valkyrie was establishing who was in control. Roger Valkyrie had told him how he learned to do that by watching John Travolta in "Get Shorty."

"Deep breaths, Mayor Ron—you'll be fine in a few seconds," Roger Valkyrie said. "That's it—just in and out, slowly, deeply."

"My word," Mayor Cuppersmith said, his breathing finally slowing. "That lawn is a deceiving Lucifer. I believe it's actually uphill."

Shelby glanced across the green lawn, which was flat as a pancake. He could see the trampled grass turned into footprints where Mayor Ron had thundered across it.

"Some days, it might as well be Kilimanjaro," Roger Valkyrie said, patting the mayor gently on a shoulder. "Better now?"

"Much better, thank you," the mayor said. "But, sir—who are you? What is the meaning of landing your helicopter on the town square?"

Roger Valkyrie leaned close to the mayor's ear and whispered. Shelby could not hear what was said, though the mayor's eyebrows arched slightly.

"Oh, I see," the mayor said, nodding.

Roger Valkyrie paused and leaned close to him again and whispered some more.

"Oh, yes, yes—I do indeed understand," the mayor said.

Roger Valkyrie smiled and eased back against the bench. He patted the mayor's knee.

"So, about back to your old self now, mayor?" Roger Valkyrie said.

"Oh, yes I am. Thanks to you. But I believe I'll sit here a spell."

"Take your time, mayor." Roger Valkyrie stood, then leaned over close to the mayor's ear again and whispered.

"And you, too," Mayor Cuppersmith said, accepting a handshake with Roger Valkyrie. "You can certainly count on me."

Shelby cast a spinner out into the cold, swift river current toward jagged falls and reeled slowly, intermittently, to make the lure mimic a minnow. Roger Valkyrie was still tying a spinner onto his line. The river was perhaps only thirty feet across. Shelby was actually pretty adept at casting and reeling, having fished many times with his father in trout streams in Idaho.

He had been just another boy then, well before something happened inside his brain: Activity intensifying in the thalamus, the cerebellum, the basal ganglia, perhaps the reticular nucleus—he had heard the terms somewhere, somehow. Some sort of cerebral critical mass had occurred. He wasn't sure just exactly when it was or what it was or how to describe it. It was sort of like a switch getting turned on. Dark to light—*voila!*

It was all a bit murky, but the bottom line was that he suddenly awakened intellectually in ways he never had before, in ways at first quite unsettling to his parents, and speeding up his transition from scrawny, goofy, but otherwise average American kid into first a math wizard, and then someone altogether capable of thingamajigs, thingamabobs, and doohickeys.

"Are you going to tell me what you whispered to the mayor?" Shelby asked.

Roger Valkyrie cast his spinner into the current and reeled slowly. A white heron stalked slowly along the far bank.

"This is fun, kid. I'm glad you suggested it. Clean air—very bracing."

"And no pesky form to fill out, either."

"Perfectly cosmonaut, Shel. This sure beats sweating in The Sudan."

"What did you say to the mayor?"

"I suggested cooperation, Shel. I employed a tone and a vocabulary, and I utilized incentives and motivational skills honed from years of service and observation."

"You threatened him?"

"We never threaten, kid. That's ugly. Uncivilized. Unseemly. Rude. Sometimes we suggest possibilities that could come to fruition. Or, we point out alternatives with better endings than other alternatives."

"You *did* threaten him."

"I managed the situation, kid. I maintained the operational integrity of the mission."

"Like Chili Palmer in Get Shorty?"

"You have to admit, Travolta is silky smooth in that one."

"And don't forget Rene Russo," Shelby said, and after a few more casts he added, "What if Rene Russo had saved the world?"

"How could she, kid? She's an actress. A good one, and a babe, but it's all make-believe. She could save the world in a film, sure. But not in real life. Was she in Armageddon with Bruce Willis, for example?"

"I don't think so—that was Liv Tyler. If Rene Russo had saved the world, what would her code name be?"

"Hot Babe," Roger Valkyrie said. "Or, maybe Savior MILF. How about Hottie Messiah? Something like that. But of course if she asked us what her code name was, then we'd have to lie and make up something else. I doubt she'd want us calling her Hot Babe, but you never know. Actors have a lot of narcissism in them."

"You would lie, Roger Valkyrie?"

"We never lie—we sometimes massage facts to improve situations."

"Isn't that the same thing?"

"It depends on who you're talking to, and where you are at the time. And the outcome, of course. Outcome is big in these things."

"Really?" Shelby said. "That's not lying?"

"Think of it as more like managing a situation to optimize the outcome, Shel. To improve reality."

"And how's that not lying?"

"Reality is fluid, kid. Truth—also fluid. It can be shaped—even improved."

"We can improve truth?"

Shelby stopped reeling and lowered his rod. He glanced at Roger Valkyrie for a few seconds, who was happily focused on reeling in his line. Shelby was confused. He always thought truth was one of those wonderful things that couldn't be improved, like maple syrup on pancakes, or peanut butter and jelly. The soft fur of a cat. Peeing after holding it too long. Or drinking a cold beer in a Jacuzzi with a naked girl—well, with *two* naked girls, that would be improvement, for sure. But truth, actual truth, was something he always assumed couldn't be improved because it was called truth in order to identify something as absolute.

"We can minimize negative outcomes, kid," Roger Valkyrie said absently as he got into the rhythm of reeling, stopping, reeling again. "We can improve reality by re-shaping truth—improving it."

"*Improving* truth? Isn't truth either truth or not?"

"Well, that's one way to view it."

After a few minutes of casting, Shelby said, "Hottie Messiah—that's my favorite Rene Russo code name."

"I have my moments, kid. The wife says so all the time."

"What form again would that be?" Shelby said. "To change Rene Russo's code name?"

"Good old 1050D-90."

"That one's a real pain in the ass, right?"

"A monster, kid. Brutal. They all are. But for Rene Russo, the pain would become pleasure. Damn, are these fish ever going to bite?"

"I bet they would bite for Rene Russo."

Roger Valkyrie glanced at Shelby and wrinkled his nose slightly. "I could look into it, kid."

"Could you really?"

"It's a pretty tall order. Just saying."

"But I *did* save the world."

"That's a card you certainly can play," Roger Valkyrie said.

"But would that mean a form, Roger Valkyrie?"

"It's a judgment call. Certainly it sounds like a 1050D-9A, but not necessarily. There are also elements of 1050D-8, which is essentially a shorter 1050D-9A without several tiresome sections to complete. But, if I mention the idea to my boss over a beer, no need to document."

Shelby abruptly jerked his fishing rod and reeled fast. He reeled the spinner all the way in, but there was no trout. He looked out into the water but wasn't sure what he expected to see.

"I think I just had a bite." He examined the spinner's hooks. "Does that hook look bent to you, Roger Valkyrie?"

Roger Valkyrie examined it.

"Hard to say, but we could agree that it is, kid, and then it would be."

"Just, massage truth?"

"Shel, there's no real way to know whether you just had a bite, or you were temporarily snagged on a rock. But we can choose to believe it was a fish. That would be the positive choice. The positive outcome."

"And it becomes truth?"

"It certainly becomes *our* truth. It represents what we believe we saw and experienced. And it can't really be disproved. It *could* have happened, and so in a sense it *did* happen. We just decide to believe it was a fish and not a snag. The perception is the reality."

Awesome, Shelby thought. Nothing is real unless we decide it is, unless we *claim* it is. The flowing weight of the current tugged the line, perhaps, but I choose to believe it was a fish, which I couldn't see, and so I don't really know if it was there; but, if I choose to believe it really was there, then it was. And no one is the wiser. Did he really save the world, or did he just claim it and everyone bought it? But what about the money, the adulation—Oprah and Letterman? And Roger Valkyrie? Did he dream it all up? Was it all just a simulation? Was anything real at all? Was anything true?

"We choose the truth we want to believe instead of what we know to be true?" Shelby said. "Is that about it?"

"Fox News does it every day, kid. Works for them with the wingnut folks."

"Roger Valkyrie, you're starting to sound like Sarah Palin."

"She's a looker, kid, Disconnected from reality, but a looker, for sure."

"What would her code name be?"

"Mama Grizzly Fool."

"Very cosmonaut, Roger Valkyrie."

"And after all, kid, her mind does seem to be in outer space most of the time."

Shelby looked across the river at the heron, still stalking in tall reeds along the far bank. He pointed it out to Roger Valkyrie and they watched it for a few seconds.

"Roger Valkyrie, would we tell people we saw a heron, or a chicken?"

"They're both white, kid. And there are farms out here—a chicken is by no means out of the question."

"A chicken on stilts?"

"With a little imagination and creativity, that's essentially what a heron is, a chicken on stilts."

"Not even remotely close," Shelby said.

"With imagination, they look exactly alike, Shel. We see what we want to see. That explains ghosts, by the way."

"I could tell people I had a bite from a fish and saw a heron, Roger Valkyrie."

"Or, you had a snag and saw a chicken, Shel. How much difference does it make? At this distance, to someone with faulty eyesight, it could be a chicken with really long legs. The chicken of all chickens. Megachicken. A chicken that could dunk for the Celtics. Tell Mayor Cuppersmith you saw a chicken out here and he would believe you and soon all of Dogpatch knows you saw a chicken. Maybe Lil Abner himself shows up and asks if anyone has seen his missing chicken. No one can disprove it, no one would think it needed disproving, and it becomes truth."

"It becomes a possibility," Shelby said. "It becomes a potential version of truth."

"Truth has many versions, kid. It's all about knowing which one to go with."

"I'll be sure to give that some thought."

"Think of it as finding the right truth—the most *effective* truth, kid."

"Effective truth trumps actual truth?"

"Shel—if it's effective truth, then it becomes the *best* truth. Now, what did you decide on Rene Russo?"

"Pass," Shelby said. "Sounds like an arranged marriage."

"But it's Rene Russo, Shel. Didn't you see her in Tin Cup with Kevin Costner?"

"I did, but thanks anyway. It's good to know the truth about what's possible."

"You mean, what possibly might be the truth?"

"That, too."

Shelby persuaded Roger Valkyrie to spend the night in Parsons Grove, which didn't take much arm-twisting because Roger Valkyrie wanted to get a drink or two or three, and then have another healthy gander at the river. He took a room at the Marquee Motel, overlooking the river. It was just downstream from the house Shelby rented. Roger Valkyrie went to his room to freshen up and sat for a long time on the room's balcony in a chair with his feet kicked upon the railing, his suit jacket draped around the back of the chair, the river gurgling in a rush underneath him. He sat there a long time and fielded many calls. Shelby could only wonder what they were about. Shaping and improving the truth, apparently.

Shelby also persuaded him to meet Ray Spurlock's "flock," but not as Roger Valkyrie, not as a government agent with endless knowledge of government forms, not as anyone the group could worry about or even much care about. But he cautioned Roger Valkyrie to avoid any prolonged examinations on the philosophical nature of truth, given the unique debating skills he had seen from the group.

"We'll call me Joe LeFors, kid."

"Why Joe LeFors? Is that your standard undercover name?"

"I don't have a standard undercover name. I make up whatever suits me—whatever the situation demands."

"Sort of like with the truth, right?" Shelby said.

"The truth is a tool, Shel. Good tools have more than one application. Tools can do different things—like a Swiss Army Knife, for example."

"So, truth is a blade, a screwdriver, and a corkscrew all in one?"

"And fits comfortably in your pocket, out of sight. Now you're starting to get with it, kid."

"That's what worries me, Roger Valkyrie. Now tell me again—why Joe LeFors?'

"That was the sheriff who chased Butch Cassidy and the Kid."

"Oh, right," Shelby said. "And now we have to snoop around Longabaugh and Parker to—to do what, exactly?"

"To assess them, Shel. To gauge the cut of their jibs."

"What's a jib?"

"Something on old sailing ships, Shel. I can't really describe it, or explain it, or really tell you where it was on a ship. Or even what it looked like."

"Oh—sort of like thingamabobs, thingamajigs, and doohickeys."

"Very much so, kid. Anyway, it became an expression—how something looks or seems—as in, I like the cut of your jib."

"Try saying that in a men's room to a guy at the urinal next to you, Roger Valkyrie."

"Very cosmonaut, kid. Your sense of humor is really coming along."

"But how is all this jib business going to help with Longabaugh and Parker? Why don't you just ask them if they're in witness protection?"

"If they were, they'd just deny it. Then where would we be?"

"Ready to drop it and move on?"

"That's not how it works, Shel."

"So, what if they *are* in witness protection? Why do we care?"

"I have to know what sort of people are around you, kid. I can't let anyone take advantage of you."

Shelby momentarily thought about who might have taken advantage of him lately. Not the car dealer in Dallas, who got a smoking deal to take an awesome Mercedes off his hands in return for a redneck special. Certainly not the girl at the Holiday Inn pool, whose swimming had been sort of an exquisite athletic performance combining beauty and skill. But he chastised himself for not talking to her. You just never know about those things. Next time, he thought—next time.

"Really? How cool. I like the cut of your jib, Roger Valkyrie."

"Joe. Joe LeFors."

"Oh, right. So, Joe—you'll need to ditch the corduroy look and the mirrored sunglasses. Just try not to look like Agent Smith in *The Matrix*. You need to blend in and look like a local."

"You mean yokel, kid."

"Good one, Roger—I mean, Joe."

"I'll go buy some yokel apparel and meet you at the church, Shel—where *is* the church?"

"The American Legion Hall." Shelby pointed across the street.

"Give me an hour, kid. When do we have to be there?"

"In an hour, Roger—"

"Joe. Joe LeFors."

"In an hour, Joe."

The members of the Exalted Church of the Intergalactic Moment were enjoying their first round of drinks. Whiskey, as usual. Except for Hera Thompson—a vodka gimlet, as usual. And Oceanna Cooper—a margarita, as usual.

"My friends—let us never forget Thingamabobs, Thingamajigs, and Doohickeys," Ray Spurlock said, as usual.

"Where's Shelby?" Hera Thompson said, as usual.

"Probably robbing a bank," Viola Atteberry said, as usual.

"Dearie—Shelby really really didn't rob a bank," Oceanna Cooper said, as usual.

"That we know of," Tom Mitzdorfer said, as usual.

"We just don't know," Martin Cummings said, as usual.

Virgil Atteberry grinned and said nothing, as usual. Susan Cummings hugged Martin Cummings and he spilled his whiskey on his pants, as usual.

"Blow a head gasket—blow the world," Sam Crittenden said, as usual.

Harry Longabaugh and Robert Leroy Parker said very little and smiled impressively, as usual.

"Did Shelby have another flat tire, Ray?" Hera Thompson said.

"I think the boy may be accident prone," Tom Mitzdorfer said. "Two flat tires in such a short time."

"One flat tire, Tom," Ray said. "I didn't say he had another flat tire."

"Then maybe it's a blown engine again," Sam Crittenden said.

"It's one or the other," Martin Cummings said. "We just don't know."

"He blew another engine?" Viola Atteberry said. "How in the world did he ever make it to the bank to rob it?"

Oceanna Cooper rolled her eyes and sipped her margarita.

"I know a good engine man, over in Shady Glen," Martin Cummings said.

"Be sure to let Shelby know, "Oceanna Cooper said. "Mention their bank, too."

"He's going to rob the Shady Glen bank?" Viola Atteberry said.

"I'd advise against it," Sam Crittenden said. "Everybody knows who he is now."

"But if he does, that'll sure spruce up business at the bed and breakfast," Viola Atteberry said. "I might rename it the Goddard Inn."

Oceanna Cooper managed to arch her eyebrows and smirk at the same time.

"You're priceless, dearie," Oceanna Cooper said to Viola Atteberry. "Would you like a margarita?"

"I don't mind if I do."

Roger Valkyrie met Shelby outside the American Legion Hall. Roger Valkyrie didn't look like Agent Smith from *The Matrix*. He looked like Agent Smith from *The Matrix* pretending to dress as a yokel and pretending to be Joe LeFors, but actually looking like a tourist in Hawaii just off the plane from Iowa. He wore blindingly new white tennis shoes, too-tight jeans, and a light blue Hawaiian shirt with pink flamingos emblazoned across the front and back. Shelby had changed into khaki shorts and a plain white t-shirt. He was going with simplicity.

"Wow—you can see those flamingos coming a mile away," Shelby said. "Maybe even from outer space. And the shoes hurt my eyes—scuff them up a little."

"No way, kid. I'm getting a free pair of new shoes courtesy of the agency."

"You plan on keeping that shirt, too?"

"Sure—it'll be my Sunday-watching-the-Redskins getup."

"Think that'll score points with the wife?"

"No, but a man has to have his quirks."

"The mirrored sunglasses—ditch them," Shelby said. "I don't think Joe LeFors wore mirrored sunglasses."

"He wore a skimmer hat."

"You couldn't find one?"

"The options were limited. It was either redneck ball cap or redneck ball cap. They did have redneck cowboy hats—would you have preferred a redneck cowboy hat? They had plenty."

"No—a cowboy hat would be way too country for that shirt," Shelby said. "But I'm sorry we won't see a skimmer hat paired up with those flamingos. That shirt's so bright it may be radioactive."

"These sunglasses would look good with the shirt," Joe LeFors said as he put them in a pocket. "I can hide behind them and assess people—intimidate people."

"Intimidation isn't what we're going for right now," Shelby said. "And we're indoors. Slick back your hair a little."

"Remember, I'm Joe LeFors," he said as he ran his hands through his blond hair, but the result was spiky instead of slicked-back.

They walked along the street and looked into store windows, just taking their time, pretending to saunter as though they were locals with no place they had to be by a certain hour. Except that everyone they crossed paths with cast skeptical glances at Roger Valkyrie in his ridiculous neon Hawaiian shirt. One woman even burst out laughing, but quickly covered her mouth and kept going.

"No accounting for taste," Roger Valkyrie sniffed.

"No doubt," Shelby said. "So what's your cover story, Joe?"

"I'm your cousin, Joe LeFors from Memphis. I heard you were in the area and so I dropped by to visit. Howdy, cousin!"

"How'd you hear I was in the area?"

"You called me in Memphis, of course."

"We're a good three hours from Memphis, I think."

"Just a short drive, kid. No one will think anything of it—you saved the world. Remember?"

"How could I forget?"

"You can't. That's part of saving the world."

"What if Ray or one of the others saw you get out of the chopper, Joe?"

"They would have seen Roger Valkyrie. *Now* I'm Joe LeFors."

"I hate to burst your bubble, Joe, but you pretty much look the same except with spiky hair and the loudest shirt in the county."

"If we were in London, kid, I could cobble together a costume from Savile Row. We make do with what we have. A Hawaiian shirt is high fashion in Dogpatch."

"I think even Dogpatch has gotten past Hawaiian shirts, Joe. But you're the secret agent."

"I'll make people see what I want them to see, kid."

More of that perception is reality stuff, Shelby thought, shaking his head, but good-naturedly. He was certainly learning a lot. But it was difficult for him to imagine anyone who encountered Roger Valkyrie's get-up could view it as anything but the real truth of the matter—it was about equivalent to strolling downtown dressed as a circus clown. Only nudity would have been more jarring to small town, mid-South sensibilities, of which Shelby was certainly no expert, and not a secret agent, but he felt pretty confident on that one.

"And you make people hear what you want them to hear, right?" Shelby said.

"Exactly, Shel. Perception is reality."

"You mentioned that. Didn't you also once say your wife called you Inspector Clouseau?"

"I may have mentioned that."

"You did. And I can sort of see why—sorry. You're not going to attempt a southern accent, are you, Joe?"

"I'll toss a howdy and a y'all in from time to time to make it seem authentic."

"Why not just say you recently moved to Memphis from Maryland. Then no one will worry that you don't sound like a local."

"Yokel. But I actually live in Maryland and can't use that. I'll say I'm originally from Ohio."

"Is there an agency form if you use your actual state of residence, Joe?"

"The old 1050D-47A, which hardly gets used and likely gets phased out altogether pretty soon. We can only hope. But it's still active."

Shelby studied Joe's face.

"Okay—I can buy that. Am I right?"

"You're three for three, kid. I may have to get you a job with the agency."

"Let's just get through this thing for now," Shelby said. "And let's decide what you do for a living."

"Accountant. We'll go with that, Shel."

"Do you actually know anything about accounting?"

"I can balance my checkbook."

"Perception truly will be reality," Shelby said.

"We extend truth, kid. We extend it until it reaches its full potential."

"Awesome, Roger Valkyrie—I mean, Joe."

Shelby and Joe LeFors entered the Legion hall, which was cool and dark after the brilliant sunshine. As they cruised past the bar, a half-dozen grizzled old men in faded blue bib overalls—redneck clones—turned around to look at neon Roger Valkyrie, who bowed to them before moving on. It was an audacious maneuver for an American Legion post. One of the men held up his Bud Light can in skeptical salute. Shelby and Roger Valkyrie located Ray's group in a back room as it ordered a second round of drinks after developing nicely lubricated tongues from the first round.

"Here's Shelby now," Ray said, popping out of his chair to rush over. "And he's brought a friend, too."

"I'd like everyone to meet my cousin, Joe LeFors."

"Howdy, y'all," Joe LeFors said, grinning.

"He looks like a cop," Hera Thompson said.

"But do cops have spiky hair?" Tom Mitzdorfer said.

"We can't be sure," Martin Cummings said.

"I'm not a cop, y'all" Joe LeFors said. "I'm an accountant. From Memphis. Howdy."

"Maybe an accountant in Honolulu," Oceanna Cooper said, arching her eyebrows.

"Shelby, did your cousin help you rob the bank?" Viola Atteberry said.

"No, Viola. He didn't."

"Oh—then you did it by yourself?" Viola Atteberry said. "Very self-reliant."

"It always sounded like a one-man job to me," Tom Mitzdorfer said.

"But we can't be sure," Martin Cummings said.

"Sure we can," Viola Atteberry said. "Shelby just admitted he did it alone."

"Shelby didn't rob a bank, dearie," Oceanna Cooper said.

"Okay," Viola Atteberry said. "But is he still planning to rob the one over in Shady Grove?"

"I'm not going to rob the Shady Glen bank," Shelby said.

"What changed your mind?" Viola Atteberry said.

Shelby shrugged. "I don't have a getaway driver."

"What about your cousin?" Viola Atteberry said. "He's a pretty strapping fellow. Can't he drive?"

"He's an accountant, not a getaway driver," Shelby said.

"Well, at least he would be able to help you count the money," Viola Atteberry said.

"I'm an accountant, y'all," Joe LeFors said. "From Memphis."

"Memphis is a good three hours from here," Tom Mitzdorfer said.

"*About* three hours," Martin Cummings said. "We just don't know for sure. Not exactly. Traffic is definitely a factor."

"I still say Joe looks like a cop," Hera Thompson said.

"Accountant," Joe LeFors said.

Harry Longabaugh rubbed his upper lip with a finger.

"Wasn't Joe LeFors the sheriff who chased Butch Cassidy and the Sundance Kid?" Harry Longabaugh said.

"I believe that's right," Robert Leroy Parker agreed. "I'd bet my bottom dollar on it. I saw the movie."

"What does 'bet my bottom dollar' mean, anyway?" Viola Atteberry said.

"It's just an expression, dearie," Oceanna Cooper said. "How's your margarita?"

"Delightful," Viola Atteberry said.

A young brunette waitress stopped by the table.

"Could I have a bourbon on the rocks?" Shelby said.

"Me, too, y'all," Joe LeFors said. "A double."

Viola Atteberry leaned close to Shelby.

"Are you sure you aren't going to rob the Shady Glen bank?" Viola Atteberry said.

Shelby shrugged, smiled.

"I'll certainly give it some thought."

"Thanks—that's all I ask," Viola Atteberry said. "You're so considerate, Shelby."

Everyone smiled politely until the drinks arrived.

"I think Joe LeFors here was the fella that got out of that helicopter today," Hera Thompson said.

"But we can't be sure," Martin Cummings said.

"Sure we can," Hera Thompson said. "I was coming out of Pflueger's Hardware when it happened."

"I wasn't there," Tom Mitzdorfer said.

"I wasn't either," Martin Cummings said. "And so I can't be sure."

"It was him," Hera Thompson said. "Now he's wearing this Hawaiian getup and spiking his hair like one of them grungers from Seattle."

"It wasn't me," Joe LeFors said.

"Maybe it wasn't him," Ray Spurlock said. "You could be mistaken, Hera. Accountants probably don't ride around in helicopters."

"That's right," Joe LeFors said. "I'm from Memphis."

"Then who was it," Hera Thompson said. "And why did he land in Parsons Grove?"

"We just don't know," Martin Cummings said.

"It was him," Hera Thompson said quietly, sipping her vodka gimlet.

Shelby elbowed Joe LeFors lightly. "Howdy, cousin."

After the group headed home tipsy, but still endlessly talkative, their voices a rising chorus as they disappeared down the block and into the night, Shelby and Roger Valkyrie stood outside the American Legion Hall under a street lamp. The moon was full and the town square was well-lit. They could hear the group's voices even after it had crossed to the next block down. Shelby watched the group until it was another block away and then he saw individual members of it splinter off into their own directions home.

"Well, *that* went well," Shelby said.

"Okay, okay. I know sarcasm when I hear it, Shel."

"Are you still Joe LeFors, or are we back to Roger Valkyrie?"

"Which do you prefer, kid?"

"I kind of like Joe LeFors. But I guess that would mean some agency form comes into play, right?"

"One of my favorites—1050D-23H, to extend use of an undercover alias past the operational phase."

"Then we just go with Roger Valkyrie," Shelby said.

"Good call."

"And what do we conclude about Butch and the Kid?"

"Probably *not* in witness protection." Roger Valkyrie said. "Probably not ex-mafia or ex-drug traffickers. Probably just two local yokels with boner names."

"That would be my guess," Shelby said. "What did you think of the group?"

"Whacked, but lively, kid. Quite whacked. You may yet have to rob the Shady Glen bank just to satisfy them."

"What if I did?"

"Did what?"

"Rob the Shady Glen bank."

"I was kidding, kid."

"But what if I did?"

"Well, for starters, then Viola Atteberry could name her bed and breakfast after you. She seems determined to claim a famous criminal stayed there, even if she has to make one up. And that's a good marketing strategy, I suspect."

"The old improving-on-the-truth strategy, right?"

"That's the one, kid. Extending truth. Create the reality that works best. Push truth until it's really as good as it can be."

They walked down the street and stopped to watch the river rush beneath a pedestrian bridge. Roger Valkyrie leaned far over to look down into the water. Shelby was afraid he might fall in and he'd have to go in after him.

"Roger Valkyrie, if I robbed the Shady Glen bank, would the government look the other way because I saved the world?"

"Seriously?" Roger Valkyrie said, still leaning far over the bridge. "Trying to test us, Shel?"

"Just asking—just trying to understand the rules."

"The rules are as they always were, before or after saving the world, Shel. Robbing banks is a bad idea. The government does not endorse bank robbery."

"I'm not saying I would do it."

"Gee, kid—that's swell of you to refrain from becoming John Dillinger."

"Or Butch Cassidy."

"Please—no more Butch and the Kid, kid. I've had enough of those two for one night."

"They were popular," Shelby said. "So was Jesse James. And Dillinger. People liked Dillinger."

"Americans have always had a bit of a perverse affection for outlaws, Shel. I can't explain it. But that doesn't mean you should be one."

"Would people still like me if I robbed a bank? Dillinger did it and was popular, and he never saved the world. He even killed people."

"That's right, kid. He was a killer. A thief and a killer. Just remind yourself of that if you ever find yourself near the Shady Glen bank. Or any bank. What—saving the world isn't a good enough legacy?"

Now it was about a legacy. He sighed. Shelby had never ever thought much about legacies. He figured he was way too young for stuff like that. What good was a legacy? If you had one—you were dead. Or close to it, probably. Or a veggie in a wheelchair having gorp spooned into your mouth. No one needs a legacy on the way up in life. Only on the way down, at the end. He was pretty sure he wasn't on the way down, or at the end of anything. It was really all just beginning.

"I don't know what it means anymore," Shelby said. "I don't think I've ever quite known what it means."

"It means all those perks you have, Shel. No more taxes and plenty of money. Beachfront property, endless tacos if you still wanted them, and your own secret agent. Maybe even Rene Russo if you really put your mind to it. And your face is on Mt. Rushmore, for God's sake."

"I didn't ask for that. I didn't ask for any of it."

Shelby thought hard to remember if he had ever asked for anything. It had all just come down on him, a shower of good and gifts and money and the First Lady's kiss. An outpouring of gratitude. He had not asked for a dime or a handshake. Even the Taco Bell deal was their idea.

"I'm afraid it's too late on Mt. Rushmore, Shel. It's a good likeness, though. You're right there smack next to Abe Lincoln, for God's sake. The Great Emancipator, and next to him—you, the Great Taco Killer."

"I've considered sneaking up there and painting a moustache on myself," Shelby said.

"I'm afraid you're stuck with it, Shel. You've been immortalized. But just between the two of us, go for the moustache. Just leave Lincoln's face alone. And no graffiti."

"Lincoln *was* a savior. I'm *not* a savior. I'm Shelby, from Boise, Idaho."

"Well, you're getting the credit for one, Shel. Time to accept it. Time to grow into the role."

Could he actually grow into the role of savior? What an awesome job description—savior. Would he have to get used to cultivating groupies, maybe find a ring for everyone to kiss as they knelt at his feet—maybe a death's head ring like the one Keith Richards wears? And if people were going to kneel and kiss his ring, he'd need a throne. Where could you even buy a throne? Wal-Mart? Would a lawn chair work just as well?

"Grow into being a savior? Like, on-the-job training?"

"If it helps to look at it that way, look at it that way."

They walked onto the bridge and looked down into the rushing water. Moonlight twinkled off the river's surface. Up ahead they could see the Civil War cannon under the courthouse floodlights. It was pointed their way. Shelby wondered how long it had been since someone had fired it. Had it killed many people?

"What's all this outlaw crapola really about, Shel?"

"Maybe I'm just thinking out loud, Roger Valkyrie."

"You're thinking way too out loud, kid. It's nutty to think about robbing a bank. Especially for a guy who doesn't need the money."

"This isn't about money, Roger Valkyrie."

"It sure isn't. It's about what's been established and isn't going to change. The saving the world genie can't be shoved back into the bottle. If you robbed a bank, someone would have to order workmen up Mt. Rushmore to jackhammer your face off. You don't want that, now do you? One of the workmen could fall while obliterating your nose, which might then be the most tragic nose-picking in recorded history. Worse even than that Seinfeld episode."

"I can live without Mt. Rushmore," Shelby said, trying for a moment to recall the Seinfeld episode and then remembering it.

"Well, I could forget about it, too, kid. But that's not the point. The whole world would be watching as your face was blown off the granite. Not a pretty site. Not a pretty memory, my friend. Not a pretty legacy."

"I didn't ask for the legacy, Roger Valkyrie. I just went to work one day and then everything was a blur and when it was all over *something* had happened and *something* had been prevented, but to this day, I'm not at all sure what."

Shelby tried very hard to remember. He closed his eyes and tried to relax and make something about that day come into focus, but all he got was the same memory he had in Sedona—the immense building, the rows of massive machines, the banks of flickering lights, the screeches and yelps of people running around, the flash, the plunk on the noggin, and then nothingness. As before, he was left with only the image of thingamajigs, thingamabobs, and doohickeys, but this time, emblazoned in huge red letters on a highway billboard, the paint dripping below each letter, like blood.

"That's where thingamabobs, thingamajigs, and doohickeys come in, kid. They are what they are. And it's best to just forget them and move on."

"Could you?"

"I would certainly try."

"Just like that?"

"No—not just like that, Shelby. But in time. And sooner rather than later. An amazing set of circumstances have been handed to you. Now you must live with them."

"I don't know what it means."

"It means whatever you want it to mean, kid."

"Just make my own truth—right? Extend truth to its fullest potential?"

"Why not? You get to do what you want with your life with fewer restrictions than almost anyone in the freaking galaxy. Even the president has to kiss more ass than you do. You're not even thirty and the IRS can't ever touch you."

"Will that be on my tombstone—the IRS couldn't touch him?"

"More likely it will say, he ate 867 tacos and now he's here."

"Even better, Roger Valkyrie. I'd be known as the man who saved the world and then ate all the tacos in it."

"What if your tombstone said simply, he saved the world. Just fucking saved the whole damn enchilada. Not bad, eh, kid? Short but awesome. Very cosmonaut. Who could top that one? I suspect you have a long life ahead, Shel. Though all those tacos likely shaved off a few years."

"Care to give me some sort of guarantee, Roger Valkyrie?"

"I'd have to fill out a form if I did."

"Which one?"

"That would be 1050D-66A."

"There's actually a form for predicting the future?"

"For promising something tangible, kid, and the future isn't really tangible. It sounds wonderful, but it's fleeting, really. The future doesn't exist until it becomes the present, and then it's no longer the future and quickly becomes the past. No form applies to that."

And once everything is in the past, it can never again be in the future, Shelby deduced, and so as long as we ignore the past, who can say it truly happened? Nothing's real but the present, and the present becomes the past in mere seconds. Everything we do that seems real is fleeting and quickly becomes the past, which is a dead zone. Saving the world was now in the dead zone.

But Shelby still lived in the present, would always exist in the present because the future didn't exist until it became the present, and the past could never be accessed. He was getting a headache, but somewhere in all those mental gymnastics he was sensing that saving the world, and thingamajigs, thingamabobs, and doohickeys, had existed for mere seconds and then had disintegrated into the dead zone past, which was not a real place and existed only in the minds of people. And minds were just a lot of goo and neurons.

"Makes perfect sense to me, amazingly," Shelby said. "And I don't really care if that form's real or not."

"And it doesn't really matter."

"It's all the truth we need right now," Shelby said.

"Exactly, Shel. Sometimes there's just enough truth and you don't need any more than what you have. Until you need more, of course."

"Of course."

They looked down into the rushing water for a long moment.

"When do you leave?" Shelby said.

"In the morning, kid."

"Planning another dramatic and leaf-shattering chopper flight off the courthouse lawn?"

"I promised Mayor Ron that was a one-time deal."

"Good choice. And it's not like there's that many leaves left to blow off the trees."

"There you go, kid—that growing sense of humor. You'll be just fine. I know it."

"I'll do my best."

"Keep busy, Shel. Focus on something. What about that book you want to write on enlightenment?"

"I'm still waiting to get some—some enlightenment."

"It's not going to fall out of the sky on you, like chunks of an asteroid. Or yellow ice from an airliner."

"I'll watch out for that yellow ice, Roger Valkyrie."

"You do that, Shel. But don't stare all the time into the sky. Enlightenment is all around you. It's in the trees and in the wind. It's flowing in this river underneath us. It's beneath your shoes every step you take. You just have to look and listen."

"Listen for what?"

"Truth," Roger Valkyrie said as he strolled off the bridge toward the town square.

"Hey," Shelby called. "I've made a decision. Just this second."

Roger Valkyrie stopped and turned around.

"What have you decided, Shelby?"

"To call you Roger from now on. Just Roger."

"Works for me," Roger said and he turned and walked toward town. "Call me whenever you need me, kid."

Shelby watched Roger until he was out of sight. Then he walked back to his rented house along the river and didn't see a single soul on the streets the entire way.

Part Two

"With our love, we could save the world."
—George Harrison

SPONTANEOUS COMBUSTION

The amount of money bestowed on Shelby by a grateful government was judged commensurate to saving the world without breaking the bank because gratitude loses steam exponentially each day after an event requiring a tangible expression of gratitude.

It was an amount of money less than any run-of-the mill defense contract supplying, say, toilet paper, soft drinks, and soft-core pornography for military bases. But it was more money than Shelby ever dreamed of and far more than he knew what to do with. So he did very little with it other than to occasionally check the balance online and whistle at the amount from the house he rented along the river in Parsons Grove.

He sold the Malibu beachfront property and watched the account grow more, his whistling growing louder, shriller. He mustered the courage to tell Taco Bell he had "lost" his taco pass, shamed them for thinking ten-cent tacos were enough for saving the world, and negotiated a settlement to give the pass back. In addition to the settlement, Taco Bell agreed to give all Bell Grande customers extra extra sour cream for a month. Shelby's bank account grew even more. Whistling no longer seemed an adequate expression of amazement.

The brothel owner in Nevada simply didn't have the means of a Taco Bell, of course, but as a former Marine with medals, he was still patriotic and grateful to Shelby and negotiated to take *his* pass back in return for Shelby's request of a dandy (but necessarily anonymous) contribution to a home for wayward boys. Shelby enjoyed the irony but the idea of actually visiting the brothel made him sometimes wonder if he should have at least sampled the goods before making his deal.

Shelby wrote thank-you notes: first to Keith Richards for the guitar lesson and sharing some powerful Jamaican ganja and those moderate and fascinating hallucinations; then to Miley Cyrus, complimenting her on her very strong grip and general earnestness as an entertainer; and finally he sent a note to the president, apologizing for considering a thrust with his tongue when the First Lady had kissed him on the mouth. Shelby knew he could have just kept that desire to himself but felt that honesty befitted someone who had saved the world. The president called and said think nothing of it and even hinted that he had French-kissed her once or twice in public, which created an onerous week in which he had to fend off Tea Party attacks accusing him of being French as well as Muslim.

His amends made, Shelby concluded that since he had done good, he must do more good. Lots of good. Mega good. Good, good, good. He felt that the answer to the dilemma of having done galactic good, and the resulting eternal public scrutiny, was more good. As long as he continually did good, he could somehow live up to the good of saving the world. But what was good enough? After saving the world, he had often fretted that he had nothing left but a rush to the bottom rather than the top. Could there be a top that was attainable after saving the world? Or was saving the world and living his life two different things not to be confused? He certainly knew good from bad and would not suddenly go bad—would not rob the Shady Glen bank, would not imitate John Dillinger. He had saved the world, which was good, good, good—so good there really were no good words to adequately describe its goodness. Calling it awesome, stupendous, and marvelous was good, but also like trying to toss bricks across the Grand Canyon. It was just no good.

For a while he stopped attending meetings of the Exalted Church of the Intergalactic Moment. Once he even drove over to Shady Glen and walked around in their bank just to see what it would look like to someone robbing it. Just to get a rise out of Viola Atteberry, he stopped by her bed and breakfast and revealed that he had "cased" the Shady Glen Bank. Over tea, she wanted to hear all the details, what the bank security was like, how many guards there were, whether his cousin the accountant from Memphis would drive the getaway car, and how soon after the robbery she should erect a sign announcing he had once slept at her inn. He left her place hoping she just liked to pull his leg, but he wasn't entirely sure.

One day after practicing yoga in the nude on the deck of the modest house he rented, Shelby dressed and bought a six-pack of Dixie beer and some sandwiches—roast beef and Swiss on hoagie buns with honey mustard—at the Piggly-Wiggly and climbed on top of the Porter Newhouse Bridge over the river at the north end of town. He didn't think much about it and why he was doing it and just nimbly hustled up there like a monkey. He settled in among the trusses and girders with a splendid view upriver and downriver. An eagle floated above him for a time before moving upriver. It was a Saturday in late October and cooling off, trees dropping red and yellow leaves—even the trees blasted by Roger's helicopter had a pitiful few leaves left to drop—but he wore a jacket and the sun was out and the wind was absent, making it seem warmer than it was.

Soon word got around that Shelby was drinking Dixie beer atop the Porter Newhouse Bridge. Mayor Ron concluded that it ostensibly wasn't his concern because the bridge was county and not city; but certainly Shelby's antics were ill-advised, dangerous, and counter to a positive image for Parsons Grove—even for someone who had saved the world. Mayor Ron didn't want the man who saved the world killed on his watch by tumbling off the Porter Newhouse Bridge in a drunken stupor. He knew that tragic celebrity deaths ought to more appropriately happen in expensive Los Angeles and New York City hotel rooms, for example.

Shelby wasn't yet drunk, but he was working on it, and had already tossed his shoes into the river to see how long they would float. He was disappointed by their efforts and so he tried his socks, too, and while the socks fared much better, he was contemplating tossing his pants and underwear when Mayor Ron walked out to the bridge with the town police chief, Horace Winchester, and hollered up to Shelby that tossing his shoes and socks in the river technically was littering and thus illegal. Horace quietly explained to Mayor Ron that he didn't care to arrest the man who saved the world for being a litterbug. About that time, Viola Atteberry drove by and stopped to wave up at Shelby, who waved back enthusiastically, and when Viola heard Horace repeat that arresting the man who saved the world for being a litterbug from atop the Porter Newhouse Bridge was not the sort of career move he had in mind, Viola mentioned that Shelby was plotting to rob the Shady Glen bank, which was certainly more serious than tossing shoes and socks off the Porter Newhouse Bridge.

After two bottles of Dixie beer, the inevitable arrived and Shelby needed to pee. With awkward hand gestures, he managed to make Horace and Mayor Ron understand his urgency and so Horace escorted Viola away from the bridge under the pretense of wanting to grill her about the Shady Glen bank. Shelby stood and peed a long, steady yellow stream into the river far below and Mayor Ron was thankful he was witnessing a number one and not a number two, but he knew that number two had to eventually plop into the world. It all made Mayor Ron suddenly need to pee, too, and so he delivered a steady yellow stream into the river, checking over his shoulder to make sure Horace and Viola were out of sight. Above, Shelby grinned and gave him a thumbs-up.

Soon a crowd gathered at the Porter Newhouse Bridge. Ray Spurlock was there, waving up at Shelby. So were Oceanna Cooper and Hera Thompson. And Tom Mitzdorfer and Sam Cummings. Pretty soon all the members of the Exalted Church of the Galactic Moment had showed up, as did much of the town, as the rumor spread that the man who saved the world was drunk on the Porter Newhouse Bridge and planned to jump. It was the second most exciting thing in recent Parsons Grove memory, right after the helicopter that blasted leaves from trees when it landed on the lawn behind the courthouse next to the Civil War cannon. The helicopter escapade had generated much buzz and a front page story in the Parsons Grove Daily Bugle. Some townsfolk claimed it was one of those sinister and mysterious black helicopters they heard about on Fox News, but Mayor Ron assured the town that the helicopter had merely lost its way and carried an accountant from Memphis, which prompted a second story and a headline that read, "Chopper Delivers Memphis Accountant to Perform Emergency Tax Return."

By this time, Shelby had worked his way through Dixie beer number four. Peeing had again vaulted to the head of his short to-do list, but there was quite a crowd below. Mayor Ron could clearly see there were now four empty Dixie beer bottles sitting on a girder and he became very nervous because he knew that not only would Shelby need to pee again, but so would he. And Shelby could clearly see the large crowd below as he tried not to piss his pants. Arch Morgan, editor of the Daily Bugle, arrived and asked Shelby if he really planned to jump and whether that helicopter and accountant from Memphis would be making an appearance. Shelby assured Arch that jumping had never entered his mind, but he wasn't sure what the accountant was up to. There was a collective sigh from the crowd, which now numbered several hundred. A TV crew from Little Rock arrived, thanks to a call from Viola Atteberry that Shelby might jump off the Porter Newhouse Bridge because he robbed the Shady Glen bank.

Viola had not actually said he had robbed the Shady Glen bank, even though she still held out hope he might some day do so, but, the station manager in Little Rock *thought* that was what she had said, and he also thought she had said Shelby planned to jump off the bridge, and so not only did he dispatch his crew in the field, he sent another team by helicopter. By the time the chopper from Little Rock was circling over the Porter Newhouse Bridge and blowing hats off of heads, Shelby had worked his way through Dixie beer number five and the need to pee had become a necessity for short-term survival. He made some even more awkward hand gestures—because now he really was drunk—to Mayor Ron below, who suddenly had a look of horror on his face because he misinterpreted Shelby and assumed it was now time for a number two. The notion of Shelby taking a dump off the Porter Newhouse Bridge with half the town below, and an incessant Little Rock TV station helicopter circling above like a giant dragonfly, so freaked out Mayor Ron that he peed in his pants, waddled off to his office, and was not seen for several days.

Meanwhile, Shelby was confused as to why Mayor Ron had abruptly waddled off and his need to pee was now about to reach a critical mass, and so he wedged himself into a small corner-like space that seemed shielded from the crowd below and he peed into a Dixie Beer bottle. He in fact needed two Dixie beer bottles to get the job done, leaving three empties and one bottle of actual Dixie beer. He arranged all the bottles so that he didn't accidentally mix the real bottle of beer with the two full of urine. He felt good to see that he still had three empties he could fill when the urge struck again, which would be soon enough, because he had started drinking the last bottle of Dixie beer.

After a second gulp of the last Dixie beer, he called Roger Valkyrie.

"Bon bini, kid," Roger Valkyrie said.

"Boner what?" Shelby said drunkenly.

"That's welcome in Papiamento, Shel. I'm in Aruba."

"Aruba?"

"The island, kid. In the Caribbean."

"What the hell are you doing *there,* Roger?"

"I'm on vacation. I promised the wife years ago we'd go to Aruba and so we finally made it. It's pretty swell, kid. Beats watching her nephew clean gutters, believe you me. And I'm wearing the Hawaiian shirt. What are *you* up to?"

"Oh, not so much, Roger. Just hanging out."

Shelby looked down at the hundreds of people and then up at the helicopter, which now hovered next to him a few yards away. The female reporter smiled and waved to him. It was an awesome crowd on an awesome day overlooking an awesome river.

"Is that a helicopter I hear, kid? It sounds awfully close."

"Oh—it is. Very close."

"What's it doing, Shel?"

"What's what doing?"

"The chopper."

"It's hovering."

"What's it hovering over?"

"Me."

Shelby again gauged the distance to the chopper and even reached a hand out like he could touch it.

"How close, Shel?"

"Pretty close, Roger. I can practically touch it. The lady inside's waving—she's pretty hot-looking, too."

"What? Where are you at, kid?"

"On the Porter Newhouse Bridge."

"In Parsons Grove?"

"Just outside of town."

"But on the bridge?"

Shelby looked around.

"Yep. I'm definitely on the bridge."

"What *part* of the bridge, kid?"

"The very top, Roger. I'm up in the girders."

Shelby heard Roger speak to someone else but couldn't make out what he said. And he was too giddy to care all that much. He had a splendid view of the crowd and the river. It was exciting, like going to a fair and riding the Ferris Wheel and Tilt-a-Whirl and eating cotton candy. Only he had beer, which was more fun than cotton candy.

"Shelby—so that I understand completely, you're on the very top of that bridge and not down where normal people would usually decide to be?"

"I guess that sums it up, Roger."

"And there's a chopper hovering right next to you, kid?"

"So close I could practically pee on it, Roger."

"I see. Whose chopper is it, Shel?"

WTVK, in Little Rock. That's what it says on the helicopter."

"And it's so close you could pee on it? Are you *planning* to pee on it, kid?"

"No way, Roger—I still have some empty Dixie beer bottles. I already peed in two of them—got three left."

"Oh, good, kid—you're drunk *and* sitting on top of a bridge with a hovering chopper."

"Not just any bridge, Roger. The Porter Newhouse Bridge."

Shelby gazed down at the crowd again. People waved and smiled, and he waved and smiled back.

"And that's significant for what reason?"

"How the hell do I know? But it's a snazzy name and everyone below seems to think pretty well of it."

"Who's below, kid?"

"People from town."

"How many?"

Shelby looked down, made a quick assessment.

"All of them."

"I see," Roger said, sounding as though he did not at all. "I suppose Mayor Ron is there, too."

"He was. But he left. Not sure why. But the police chief is still here. I just waved to him."

"That's just outstanding, kid. Give him a wave for me, too."

Shelby waved to the chief, who happened to look up just at that moment and returned a salute to Shelby.

"Just did. He seems nice enough, Roger. His name is Horace Winchester."

"As fine a Dogpatch name as I've ever heard, Shel. Who else is there?"

"There's Arch Morgan. He runs the newspaper. And there's Ray Spurlock—he's waving to me again. You remember Ray, don't you?"

Shelby waved at Ray and Arch, but they were busy chatting and didn't look up.

"Oh, sure, kid. How does Ray look?"

"Confused. They all look a little confused."

"I can't imagine why, Shel."

"I see Viola Atteberry. She's been talking to Chief Winchester a lot."

Shelby waved to Viola, who crossed her arms across her chest and then noticed Shelby and waved back. Everyone seemed to enjoy all the waving.

"For God's sake," Roger said. "Is Viola Atteberry telling the chief you plan to rob the Shady Glen bank?"

"I don't know, Roger. But I did go over there."

"Where?"

"Shady Glen. I went over and looked at the bank, just for the fuck of it."

"Kid—tell me you didn't somehow rob the Shady Glen Bank. Please, please tell me that didn't somehow happen."

"You mean accidentally? Like, leaving a knife or a fork or a pencil on the dash in the drive-through?"

"That's exactly what I mean, Shelby."

"They don't have a drive-through."

"But you went inside the bank?"

"I did."

"Well, what happened?"

Shelby stood up for a moment and stretched his legs, looked beyond the crowd, glanced down the river.

"What? Oh, nothing happened, Roger. The manager asked if I wanted to open an account. I said maybe later and went to Burger King for lunch."

"Thank God," Roger said. "That's really all that happened?"

"That's it. I had cheeseburgers at Burger King. Shady Glen has a Taco Bell but Bell Grandes no longer appeal to me."

"That's pretty valuable knowledge, kid. Thanks for sharing. But why are you on top of a bridge?"

"Not just any bridge, Roger. The Porter Newhouse Bridge. The view is awesome."

"That's great, kid, but why the fuck are you on that bridge, Shelby?"

"I just am."

"How drunk are you?"

Shelby pondered that. He wasn't really an experienced beer drinker. He figured his tolerance was probably fairly low. But he had a damn nice buzz.

"Just finished my sixth Dixie beer."

"That's god-awful beer, kid. I had one in New Orleans. How much more do you have?"

"I just had the six pack, from Piggly-Wiggly. You're right—it's shitty beer, but the empties are great for pissing."

"Kid—are you pissing in Dixie beer bottles with that chopper sitting there right next to you?"

Shelby instinctively glanced at the buzzing chopper. The reporter was still trying to get his attention. He smiled and waved.

"Don't worry—I peed once before it showed up. But I'll need to go again pretty soon."

"Well, something to look forward to," Roger said absently. "What's the chopper doing now?"

"The lady keeps waving. Oh, now it's moving away, Roger. It's looking for a place to land, I guess."

"Kid, I'm not there to help you. I—"

"Don't sweat it, Roger. I didn't call to ask for help. All this is just what it is. I just called to say hello. I imagine I'll be down pretty soon, actually. Like, real soon."

Shelby looked down at events developing on the ground. The crowd had parted and a red fire truck arrived.

"Why do you say that, Shelby?"

"The town fire truck just pulled up. They're getting ladders off it."

"Good," Roger said. "Will you cooperate with them, kid?"

"Sure. Why not? I just climbed up here to drink some beers, eat lunch, and see the view. I don't know why everybody's having a cow."

"Because you saved the world, Shel. Everybody's got an investment in you. Everyone has a piece of you, kid."

"How about I relieve everyone of their investments, Roger? How about I just stand up and declare us all even and the past is past and all that shit. A clean slate, brother."

Shelby did stand up, but lost his balance for a second and regained it, though there were plenty of ooohs and aaahhs from the crowd below.

"Sounds spiffy, kid. But that's a fantasy for another day. Now it's about getting you off that bridge and containing the fallout."

"What fallout?"

"The fallout of climbing on a bridge in front of an entire damn town and TV camera crew, Shel. That fallout."

"Oh," Shelby said. "*That* fallout."

"Shel—listen to me. I'll get there. I will. But not right away."

"Don't pop a gasket, Roger. You're on vacation. Tell the wife hello for me."

"I will. But I have to know you're okay."

"I'm just dandy. Drunk, but dandy. Dandy drunk, if you need me to sum it up."

"I can make a call, Shel. There's an agent designated to respond to you when I'm on vacation."

Shelby pondered it a few seconds as he scanned the crowd of expectant faces. He felt everything had sort of gotten blown way out of proportion, but he got it that a huge crowd, fire fighters, and a TV chopper flitting about like a pissed off bumblebee had escalated lunch among the girders into some sort of social conflagration. And he didn't care to speak to some agent he didn't know.

"Naw. I don't want to break in a new guy, Roger. And there's probably a form for that, right?"

"Right—1050D-122. But it's no trouble, kid. It's one of the newer, streamlined forms. It practically writes itself."

"That's okay," Shelby said. "I'm fine. Really. There's a fireman coming up the ladder now."

"Are you sure you'll be okay, Shelby?"

Shelby glanced at the fire fighters manhandling ladders below.

"I'm sure. A little drunk, but sure."

"Don't sugarcoat it, kid. Are you really okay?"

"I am, Roger. It's time I handled things myself. You make the wife happy and stay in Aruba."

"Okay, kid. But once you're down and talking to people, don't forget—thingamabobs, thingamajigs, and doohickeys. Be pleasant, but vague."

"I was born vague, Roger."

Once Shelby was down off the bridge—and had posed for photos for Arch Morgan and the Daily Bugle with the fire fighters who had "rescued" him—he assured the crowd he had just climbed up there for lunch and an awesome view. Horace Winchester quickly and loudly declared to the crowd pressing close that no laws had really been broken, though he fudged on the littering law by explaining that Shelby's shoes and socks did not seem to him to qualify as litter or harmful to the environment, and that besides, a fisherman might eventually catch the shoes and so problem solved—not that it was a problem at all, he quickly added.

Horace simply did not want his record blemished with the arrest of the man who saved the world unless it was for something juicy that would get him interviewed on CNN or MSNBC—or maybe a guest appearance on *Duck Dynasty*, for example. As for the whole Shady Glen bank business, Horace knew that Viola loved to exaggerate and exploit even the most innocuous notions from other people, and he had called the bank to make sure no one had actually robbed it.

Someone in the crowd said it was all fine and dandy about Shelby's shoes probably sinking to the river bottom, and thus not posing some sort of navigational hazard, but what about his socks? Someone else pointed out that the socks would likely float and wouldn't they become a hazard to a boat motor's propeller? Horace said that he agreed the socks likely would float, but there just wasn't that much boat traffic in the river in the fall, and he felt sure they'd drift unimpeded downriver and eventually become part of a heron's nest, for example, or wash up on a sandbar. Several men in the crowd ran to their trucks and raced off, hoping to find the socks as souvenirs to sell on Craigslist or eBay.

Meanwhile, the WTVK chopper from Little Rock had landed and reporter/celebrity in waiting Sally Davenport made her way toward Shelby, who was still posing for photos with firemen. Sally was pretty and tall—five-ten flat-footed—but in impossibly high, high heels, she was a giant woman with Medusa-like blond curls cascading down her shoulders. Her heels clanked loudly and even ominously on the metal flooring of the Porter Newhouse Bridge as she crossed it to reach Shelby, who needed to pee again but had no Dixie beer bottles handy. As Sally approached, looming taller with each determined step and clank of her heels, Shelby could no longer pretend he could ignore his bladder and he ran off toward town and finally into the courthouse men's room to relieve himself, which took quite some time but was more pleasurable than a dozen Bell Grandes had ever been.

After that, Shelby poked around inside the courthouse for a few minutes because it was empty, or so he thought, until he looked in an office window and saw Mayor Ron looking out a window just in his shirt and socks—his pants draped over a chair. Mayor Ron had drawn the blinds down over the window and peeked carefully through them. Mayor Ron's phone rang and he glanced over at it on his desk as though it was something mysterious he didn't understand, but he ignored the rings until they stopped and he just kept staring out through a crack in the blinds. Shelby watched as Mayor Ron finally took a heavy blanket from a closet and sat in an easy chair in the corner, pulled the blanket up to his chin, leaned back, and fell asleep. Seeing that, plus the six Dixie beers, made Shelby suddenly feel sleepy, too.

Shelby was halfway down the courthouse steps when he saw reporter/celebrity-in-waiting Sally Davenport and her videographer, a skinny young man with a beard and long hair lugging a video camera, just a block away and advancing on him like Pickett at Gettysburg, or how he imagined Pickett must have advanced at Gettysburg, which would have surely been determined and resolute before the shit really hit the fan. Sally just kept coming at him like Pickett's Virginians, her rather mannish square jaw set firmly, those blond curls bouncing and gyrating, a now-apparent ample bosom heaving beneath the navy blazer with each aggressive step. Shelby, still drunk enough to make perspective and lucidity pretty slippery, suddenly recalled an old movie from TV he'd recently seen—*Attack of the 50-Foot Woman*, and so he ran again, down the rest of the courthouse steps and across the town square.

By now, the crowd that had gathered at the Porter Newhouse Bridge had wandered back into town, and when it spotted Shelby running across the town square, and then saw Sally and her videographer running after him, the crowd started running, too. It was a spontaneous combustion of people transformed into mob. Tom Mitzdorfer and Sam Cummings from the Exalted Church of the Intergalactic Moment were in the vanguard of the sprinting mob.

"Why are we running?" Tom yelled to Sam as they ran even faster.

"We just don't know," Sam yelled back.

Shelby rounded a corner and dove into a stand of bushes in front of the library. Sally and her videographer made the corner seconds later and by this time Sally was carrying her heels and putting some distance between herself and the videographer. She had been a track star at Vanderbilt—the hurdles—before becoming a reporter/celebrity-in-waiting. Shelby hunkered down in the bushes like a rabbit hiding from a fox as Sally and her videographer, now puffing heavily and losing steam fast, disappeared down the block and around another corner. Then the crowd swept by right after them like a flashflood filling a dry gulch. A horde on the hunt with no idea whatsoever what it was hunting. A posse of regimental size primed by boredom and fueled by adrenaline. A town shedding inhibitions and a bit of sanity.

Shelby saw Tom Mitzdorfer and Sam Cummings leading the way and admired their dedication but wondered what the crowd would do when it discovered it wasn't chasing anyone at all except reporter/celebrity-in-waiting Sally and her out-of-shape videographer. And if the horde were to catch up to someone, anyone—what then? It was shaping up as a fine day for Arch Morgan and the *Daily Bugle*, and WTVK in Little Rock. Someone would call Fox News and *that* wingnut circus would show up eventually, too.

After the crowd went by, a few stragglers, breathing hard but somehow determined to push on and be part of something they didn't understand at all, and which could not be articulated, Shelby heard a car door slam across the street. When he peeked out from the bushes, he saw a smiling Oceanna Cooper headed toward him. She stopped in the middle of the street, hands on her hips, and looked both ways. Shelby had always thought she was pretty, with her long straight blond hair down well past her shoulders, and large, lively eyes—sort of a blond Cher—and now, with the advantage of the upward angle, he could see she filled out her jeans nicely, too.

"They're all gone, Shelby," she called, looking again in both directions to make sure. "C'mon out."

Shelby awkwardly climbed out of the bushes and brushed leaves from his hair and batted them off his shirt, which had a long tear along a sleeve.

"You should see the look on your face," Oceanna said, chuckling. The look on *her* face was amusement.

Shelby brushed dirt from his jeans and realized he was barefoot. Then he recalled tossing his shoes and socks in the river.

"Yeah?" he said. "How do I look?"

"You look like a fox sitting under a porch as the hounds fly by."

Shelby was still catching his breath but had sobered up some.

"I feel more like a turkey than a fox. But I'll take fox. Do you think it's over by now?"

"Reckon so," Oceanna said. "I'm betting they've all collapsed in a heap on the other side of the block. And that reporter is probably interviewing them. What a field day for TV cameras."

"What do they want?" he said.

Oceanna shrugged. "They don't have the faintest damn idea. Why did *you* start running?"

"I don't know, either. I just did."

"You did, they did—a spontaneous eruption. This old burg needed the excitement, if you ask me. Maybe it blows the carbon out, so to speak."

"They were like—rabid dogs," Shelby said. "A pack of dogs."

"People are always just a hair short of exploding into a mob," she said. "They just need something to light the fuse."

"You a pessimist, Oceanna?"

"A realist," she said. "And the reality now is that your face needs to disappear for a while. That isn't pessimism or optimism—that's necessity."

"I can't go home. People will be there."

"I could hide you at my place for now," she said tentatively.

"Why?"

"Why not? Do you have better options?"

"Where do you live?"

"Not far. Just outside town. But we better go right *now*."

Oceanna drove him out past the Porter Newhouse Bridge and he slumped down in his seat because there were still a few people milling about the bridge and another camera crew from WTVK had shown up. Her house nicely sat a rise up a lane lined by thick pines. It was a roomy old farmhouse, but well-maintained, and the back porch had a splendid view of a bend in the river below. Shelby splashed cold water on his face in the bathroom and when he joined Oceanna on the back porch, she had poured two glasses of merlot.

"I figured you've sobered up enough to have another drink," she said. "Or do you just want water?"

He didn't tell her that he had slurped water from the bathroom sink.

"How about wine *and* a glass of water?" he said.

"Deal. And spirited for a man who just escaped a mob."

Shelby sipped his wine. "I don't understand what happened, exactly. It was surreal, for sure."

"Do you *need* to understand?" she said.

"Human nature demands understanding." He wondered if he was remembering that from a book. It certainly didn't sound like anything from a conversation with Roger.

"And there's a lot best left unknown, too," she countered.

"Like how I saved the world," Shelby said absently.

"Now *there's* an interesting topic," she said playfully. "That's not one we want to leave unknown."

"But it *has* to be left unknown."

After all, Shelby reminded himself, saving the world—even saving Sparky the Kamikaze Dog in Dallas, were now non-events, lacking matter and form in the dead zone. They had to remain unknown—forgotten—because they didn't exist anymore.

"Who told you that? You're accountant cousin from Memphis? Who is he *really*, Shelby? FBI? CIA? Some acronym we've never even heard of?"

"He's Joe LeFors. From Memphis."

"My money's on CIA," she said. "And did you notice that he kind of looks like Agent Smith from *The Matrix*?"

"Agent Smith didn't wear Hawaiian shirts."

"And Agent Smith was, like, a computer virus. Is your cousin a computer virus, Shelby? A hologram?"

She kicked his shin lightly and Shelby grinned. He sipped more wine. But he liked that bit about Roger as a hologram.

"He's an accountant. From Memphis."

"You're well-trained—I'll give you that, Shelby."

"Saving the world comes with certain guidelines."

"I'll bet it does," she said.

"You can't imagine."

"Try me."

Shelby looked around the living room. Lots of books lined shelves that almost covered an entire wall.

"Have you read all these books?" he said.

"Some of them twice."

Shelby realized he had no idea how Oceanna made a living.

"I just realized I have no idea how you make a living, Oceanna."

"Well, I never saved the world," she said. "I live quietly."

"Except when you meet with the church."

"We don't call it that. That's a misconception. I don't believe in organized religion."

"Then how'd you end up with the group?" Shelby said.

"They're the only liberals in town. No choice, really, if you want a drink and something resembling intelligent conversation."

"The group has intelligent conversations?" he said.

She smiled, looked away for a moment.

"You caught us on a couple bad days, I guess. Usually it goes a lot better."

He couldn't imagine it actually getting much crazier or more manic.

"Do you have a job, Oceanna?"

"I used to. But I don't need one anymore."

"Can't find one?"

"Don't *need* one," she said.

"Where does the money come from?"

"You're blunt, cowboy—where does *your* money come from, Shelby?"

"You know where my money comes from—it was in every paper and magazine and on every TV show. Everyone on the planet knows where my money comes from."

In his head he quickly re-capped just how much dough had accumulated from various governments.

"You're accountant cousin from Memphis arranged all that? Will he be doing your taxes, too?"

"I don't have to pay taxes. Ever."

"That's right. I forgot. Sweet."

"Yeah, for sure. Have to admit."

They both sipped wine. Shelby glanced at the bookshelves again.

"Not needing a job—is that part of all these books?"

"Not needing a job paid for all those books."

"Okay—that's mysterious enough."

"Not as mysterious as saving the world and not having to pay taxes, and having a cousin who's an accountant from Memphis who looks like Agent Smith in *The Matrix*."

"There's plenty of more mysterious things," he said.

"Name one."

Shelby gave it some thought and sipped more wine. He was feeling a little buzzed again.

"Just one," she said. "I'm waiting."

"Okay—who killed JFK, for example," Shelby said smugly.

"That's a good one. It probably had something to do with whomever your accountant cousin from Memphis works for. I'll bet he's been to the grassy knoll and loved it."

"Well before his time, Oceanna. And he doesn't work for the CIA. Or FBI. That's all I can say."

She sniffed.

"He probably works for the *secret* CIA, or the *secret* FBI. The shadow government."

"I wouldn't know about that."

"Oh, *right*. I'm sure you *don't*."

"He's mostly just a good family man," Shelby said. "A guy who mows his lawn and pays his wife's nephew to clean the gutters. He just took his wife to Aruba."

"If he was a true family man," she said, "he'd clean his own gutters."

Shelby had an abrupt visual of Roger in his suit—no, in his Hawaiian shirt—on his roof cleaning leaves from gutters while his wife oversaw things from the ground..

"Doesn't Aruba count for something?"

"Some," she said. "But anyone can spend money. Climbing up on the roof to clean gutters shows character and resolve. And the common touch."

"Well, you got me there. So, tell me again why you don't need a job?"

"I inherited money," she said.

"From who?"

"My father. He owned much of the farmland around here and other places, and several large industries down in Little Rock."

"A lot of money?"

"Enough to be having this conversation."

"I know the territory," Shelby said. "Did you have a job before that?"

"I was a psychologist."

"In Parsons Grove?"

"Boston."

"Really, Boston?" Shelby said.

He couldn't quite picture Oceanna in Boston. It seemed like it would be too confined for her. And maybe too cold.

"You don't think I could have lived in Boston just because I'm from Parsons Grove?"

"I didn't mean it quite that way."

"*How* did you mean it? I'll have you know I got my master's from Michigan and a PhD from Northwestern, Mr. Savior."

"And I went to Stanford," Shelby said. "Yet here we are in Parsons Grove."

"It's home," she said. "And it used to be quiet—before you got here, that is."

After an awkward silence, Shelby said, "So, a psychologist. I guess you really *have* read all these books."

"Twice."

"Impressive."

"And a necessity."

"How much of all that reading do you remember," Shelby said.

"All of it."

"Sweet."

"How much of saving the world do you remember, Shelby?"

"None of it."

That was pretty much the truth, he admitted. It was all now in the dead zone of the past, which had no form, no matter. He kept telling himself that.

"They probably wiped your memory clean."

"No way—I'd remember if they did something like that."

Oceanna laughed.

"If you could remember it, then it wouldn't have worked."

"Then what am I remembering?"

"What they *want* you to remember."

"Or, they didn't do anything at all."

"It's your delusion, Shelby."

Shelby spent the night at Oceanna's—in one of the roomy spare bedrooms with a huge canopied bed and prints of Monet and Seurat on the walls. He recognized Monet's Water Lillies, but that was the only one. The bedroom—the whole house—smelled of cedar. The next evening it was cool enough for a fire in the living room fireplace. The fire glowed orange and blue and popped and cracked pleasantly while Oceanna made delicious lasagna washed down with more merlot. She had gone into town on a recon mission to gauge the mood, which had improved, calmed, slowed, but there were still minor tremors of nerves as people struggled to understand just what the hell had happened. Reporter/celebrity-in-waiting Sally Davenport still skulked about town towering over people but was losing interest fast, people said. The rest of the media had pulled out, assuming Shelby had skipped town for good. The search was on elsewhere!

Shelby had spent part of the day rummaging through the bookshelves and found a novel to read—*Catch-22*. He had read it once before. Well, he had mostly *skimmed* it in college. A friend had suggested it. Back then it didn't really get his attention.

"I can relate to the guy—Yossarian," he told her after he had read a good portion of it.

"How so?" she said as she re-filled their glasses with merlot.

"He's living in a crazy world. The Germans are trying to kill him, but, in a way, so is his own side. He's just trying to survive."

"I loved the conversations with Milo," she said. "Milo and Colonel Cathcart—priceless nonsense. And effective psychology."

"I know someone a little like Milo, in a way," he said. "But different, too. Different in ways that count."

Shelby realized that despite all the antics, he rather liked Roger Valkyrie.

"The famous helicopter accountant from Memphis?" she said.

"Let's call him Joe—Joe LeFors."

"Let's *not* call him the sheriff who chased Butch Cassidy," Oceanna said. "We're not in grade school."

"What do you *want* to call him?"

"What's his real name—James Bond? Or maybe just 007 for short?"

"I don't know his real name."

"How often do you see him?"

"I call him, usually. When I need to talk."

"What do you talk about?"

"He travels a lot," Shelby said. "We talk about that."

"I'll just *bet* he gets around—starting revolutions and such."

"He doesn't do that stuff," Shelby said.

"Is that what he told you?"

He had to concede that Roger told him a lot, was often quite candid about everything, despite the cynicism masquerading as bravado and even detachment. He was learning a lot about Roger. And maybe life, too. He was also learning to avoid the dead zone of the past.

"I believe him," Shelby said.

"Why?"

"I just do. I can't explain it."

"Really?" she said. "And did you know the Porter Newhouse Bridge is really the Brooklyn Bridge? I can get you a smoking hot deal on it."

"I could afford the Porter Newhouse Bridge," Shelby said.

"What about the Brooklyn Bridge?"

Shelby shrugged, cocked his head to a side.

"I don't know. I don't know what it's worth. I wonder if I could get it renamed the Shelby Albert Goddard Bridge."

"Ask James Bond."

"Let's not call him that."

"And cheat ourselves of so much fun? So, what do *you* call him?"

"Roger Valkyrie."

"His name is Roger *Valkyrie?*"

"No—his *code* name is Valkyrie."

"Is he living some Tom Cruise fantasy when he's not doing taxes in Memphis?"

Shelby got up and went to a window. He could see the river. The sight of it always seemed to begin a sense of calm in him. Roger had seemed pretty impressed with the river, too. There was a lot more to know about Roger Valkyrie.

"It's just how they—he—does things. They have plenty of forms to fill out, I can tell you that."

"Why do you call him *Roger* Valkyrie?"

Shelby sipped wine.

"I guess I wanted to humanize him. At first I only knew him over the phone. Now he's *Roger* Valkyrie so he seems more like a real person.

"The name Roger Valkyrie doesn't make me think of a real person, Shelby."

"Call me Shel. Roger does."

"Yeah? Okay—Shel."

"He also calls me kid. A lot."

"Does it bother you?"

"Not anymore. I know he means well. He says his wife calls him Inspector Clouseau."

"I like her already," Oceanna said. "That was certainly a Clouseau performance he gave the group."

"He wanted to check on Parker and Longabaugh. Because of their names, he thought they could be in witness protection."

"Harry and Bob? I've known them for years. They're harmless, Shel."

"Well, Roger wanted to judge the cut of their jibs—his words."

"What a douche. He talks like that?"

"Roger's—colorful," Shelby said. "But it's no crazier than Viola and her nutty obsession with getting me to rob the Shady Glen bank, you have to admit."

"Okay, I'll grant you that one. But not by much."

Over breakfast the next morning, Oceanna suggested that maybe Shelby might want to find a job, or at least a serious hobby. Something that interested him enough to focus his energies, avoid getting drunk on top of bridges, and prevent riots. He promised to look into it and when he checked his email he found a message that intrigued him. Oceanna drove him to his rented house and the coast seemed clear. No one lingered outside. The media had cleared out of town. News reports began to spin it all as a misunderstanding not worth the trouble, and the media quickly moved on to the next pretend crisis. Parsons Grove seemed its old, quiet, slow self again.

WE ARE GOBITEK!

With the dust settled after what would officially be called Shelby Mob Day, and Shelby had made amends by donating a library wing and statue of Porter Newhouse, a Civil War officer from Parsons Grove, a private jet with a large G on its tail landed at an airstrip outside town and whisked Shelby away to Chicago. In posh Michigan Avenue offices, Shelby was the guest of Bern Brindlestickler, founder of Gobitek, a German firm with offices all over the world that Shelby had saved.

We Are Gobitek! was lettered above every door at Gobitek-Chicago. We Are Gobitek! was on every piece of letter, on every envelope, and even on the nameplates worn by Gobitek employees. We Are Gobitek! was how Gobitek employees greeted each other every morning and how they said good-bye at the end of every day. We Are Gobitek! was what secretaries said when they answered phones. We Are Gobitek! was handwritten above the signature to every piece of Gobitek correspondence and in email, too.

There even used to be a little hand/arm gesture that went along with the morning and evening We Are Gobitek! salutations, but that was quickly squelched when someone pointed out that it was a German company and that the hand/arm gesture, combined with, We Are Gobitek!, looked a little too much like Nazis exclaiming, "Seig Heil."

Gobitek was in the "synergies" business.

And the "results" business.

And the "visions" business.

Gobitek was all about process and marketing and partnerships. Gobitek was a self-proclaimed world leader in helping other companies help themselves by utilizing how Gobitek could help them. Gobitek was the cat's meow when it came to platforms and systems and realignment and product definitions. In short, Gobitek did stuff that no one could really explain or easily understand, but they were really good at it, and apparently made a lot of money from it.

"Visions, Synergies, and Realignments" was the Gobitek motto.

And in a very indirect and rather mysterious fashion, Gobitek supplied the government with thingamajigs, thingamabobs, and doohickeys, Shelby had learned, though Gobitek didn't actually *make* those items and instead merely *packaged* them—enabled them to reach their full potential as marketable items.

"So, how do I fit in with Gobitek?" Shelby said, thinking about Chicago deep-dish pizza as he sat across from Bern Brindlestickler in a high-ceilinged conference room. They both sipped coffee from mugs lettered with We Are Gobitek!

Bern, a blond Teutonic giant at six-foot ten, was from Bremen. Without glasses, he could easily be taken for a basketball player, which he had never been, but his black-framed glasses, reminiscent of safety glasses, gave him an air of the intellectual, a hint of the academic, which helped soften his imposing stature. He had inherited a sum of money short of a fortune, but far beyond a pittance, and he had parlayed it into a minor software company that made money, and he parlayed that into Gobitek, with the help of investors and his aura of self-confidence. People gave Bern money, even against any initial misgivings, because invariably and almost immediately they felt he was someone to look up to, and, when they first met him, most people certainly had no choice but to look up. Even Shelby, at almost six-foot three, was glad they were sitting down.

"You are unique, Shelby," Bern said as he brought his hands together as though about to pray. It sounded to Shelby like the start of a sermon.

"No," Shelby said quietly. "I'm just a man, Bern. Just a man from Boise, Idaho."

A smile unshackled itself across Bern's face, but slowly, haltingly, like a balky zipper needing some coaxing.

"Once—yes," Bern said. "Once—just a man, I agree. As I was once just a man. But now—now you have become like gold. Or like diamonds, Shelby. Things in short supply and thus of great value. Except you are in even shorter supply than gold, or diamonds. There is much gold, and many diamonds—but only one Shelby Albert Goddard, and thus, even more valuable."

Horseshit was the first word that popped into Shelby's head, but he decided to be patient and listen because he felt a free private jet trip to Chicago and deep dish pizza justified it.

"Do go on, Bern."

Bern leaned forward, but still seemed about to pray.

"I envision Gobitek ascending, Shelby. Growing even greater with the help—the association with—something in shorter supply even than gold and diamonds. I envision the man who saved the world—who made it possible for Gobitek to even have this opportunity to ascend higher, to now be part of an even greater Gobitek."

Shelby glanced up at the crystal chandelier above the table.

"How much greater does Gobitek really need to be, Bern?"

"Oh—there's always room for more, for ascending to greater heights."

More money, Shelby thought.

"Sort of like climbing Mt. Everest?" Shelby said.

"An apt example—exactly, Shelby. You are quite perceptive."

"And tell me, Bern—what exactly does Gobitek do?"

"We do it all, my friend," Bern said smugly. "We are everywhere. In everything."

"You're not in Parsons Grove."

Bern nodded gravely, appeared to ponder it a moment.

"True enough. But with your association, Shelby, perhaps something might be accomplished in your Parsons Grove as well."

"A swank office like this overlooking the river?"

Bern smiled. He leaned back slightly, pursing his lips. He appeared to regard Shelby with a mix of curiosity and indecision.

"Certainly, if Gobitek were to establish a presence in Parsons Grove, we would want offices—swank offices, to be sure—appropriate to who we are. Appropriate to *what* we are."

"We are Gobitek!" Shelby exclaimed.

"Indeed, we are," Bern said, looking quite pleased.

"But what would Gobitek do in Parsons Grove?"

"Why, what we do everywhere, Shelby."

"And what is that—exactly?"

"We help people, Shelby."

Shelby nodded enthusiastically, shifted in his seat and got more comfortable. He cleared his throat.

"Awesome, Bern. But how do you help them, and what do you help them do?"

"Why, we help them become better at what they do, Shelby."

"And how do they become better—at what they do?"

"By allowing us to *help* them become better, of course."

Bern smiled broadly as though he had just brilliantly solved a math equation.

"I'm hearing that helping is big around here," Shelby said.

"It's essential. Vital. It's who we *are*."

Bern absently smoothed his silk tie. Even sitting down he was gargantuan.

"We are Gobitek!" Shelby said again.

Bern nodded, but still looked quite pleased.

"And how does that work again—helping people?" Shelby said.

"We *enable* people, Shelby."

"And how does *that* work?"

"Through visions, Shelby. And synergies. And realignment."

"I see. And all these visions and synergies and realignments would be possible with my help?"

"Indeed, they would. Even more so—with *your* help."

"And what would I actually *do*?"

Bern leaned forward.

"You would do what you *can*, of course," Bern said as though it was quite obvious. Then he slowly eased his considerable frame back into the chair and smoothed his silk tie again.

"Of course I would," Shelby said. "And I would do so happily. But, when I would do what I *can*, what would that actually *be*?"

"It would be exactly what you *are*, Shelby."

"Of course—goes without saying. Clearly we think alike on this. But, when I'm being what I *am*, how would I be doing what I *do*?"

"Why, by just being *you*, Shelby. Do you see how that works?"

Shelby nodded tentatively, wished there were windows and a view of Lake Michigan—and deep-dish pizza.

"I think I do, but it's sort of like looking out a window into fog."

"I see," Bern said. "How can I make the fog go away?"

"Would I have an office here in Chicago, for example?"

Bern opened his arms wide, toward Shelby.

"But of course, Shelby. Here, in Chicago. Or Bremen. Or London. Or Shanghai or Hong Kong or Paris or New York or Los Angeles."

"Even Parsons Grove?" Shelby said.

"Certainly that is something to discuss. You could have an office in every Gobitek location, Shelby."

"Awesome. Would it be asking too much for, like, a different theme in each office? Maybe a safari thing going on in one of them. Is there an office in Africa?"

"Of course—Nairobi."

"Bingo," Shelby said. "Nairobi sounds perfect for a safari look. Tailor made. And then I'm thinking maybe a Victorian look at another office– the London office, for example."

Bern smiled even wider and extended his hands again, palms up. They were very large hands connected to a very large man. Shelby vaguely thought of a painting he had seen of Jesus.

"You can have it all—and more, Shelby."

"Sweet, Bern. I could jot down my thoughts for each office, if that's helpful. Sort of a guide for the decorators."

"A wise suggestion," Bern said. "Very helpful indeed. Quite thoughtful. It speaks well of you. The decorators will serve to execute your visions, Shelby."

The word execute, coming from a giant German, troubled Shelby, but the thought evaporated quickly enough. Still, Shelby fidgeted in his seat.

"Now, Bern—all this is exciting, for sure. But if I can just trouble you on one thing."

"Ask and you shall receive, Shelby."

To Shelby, Bern sort of sounded like a minister.

"What exactly would I *do* in all of those offices, Bern?"

"You would do what Gobitek does—help people."

"Awesome. Truly. And help them—*how*?"

"You would help them, of course, as Gobitek always helps people—with synergies, visions, and realignments."

In his mind, Shelby heard thingamabobs, thingamajigs, and doohickeys, which, of course, he now knew, thanks to further amplification by Bern, came from a company within a company supplied by yet another company with a relationship to Gobitek, which no one so far had adequately described or defined, and which didn't actually make those items or know who *did*—which was okay, Shelby decided, because he didn't actually know what thingamajigs, thingamabobs, and doohickeys were, or what they might look like, or what they did. And apparently there were no photos of them. Not that Roger's agency would ever allow photos to see the light of day. If there were photos, had Roger seen them? Would Roger even tell him the truth on that?

"Not a one?" Shelby said. "Not even one little, grainy, fuzzy cell phone photo?"

"None, Shelby. Because none are *needed*."

"Why is that, Bern?"

"The people who need and use those items know what they are and what they do, and how they are made, and how to acquire them, which we help with, of course—*acquiring* and not *making*."

"Of course," Shelby said. "And you're pretty familiar with my experience with thingamabobs, thingamajigs, and doohickeys."

"But of course—the famous process by which you saved the world."

"And it doesn't sound vague to you?"

"Not at all, Shelby. I understand perfectly."

"You do? Really?"

"Certainly," Bern said. "Yes, yes, yes. Synergies, thingamabobs—aren't they all really the same thing in the end?"

Shelby squinted at Bern.

"How so?"

"Details, specifics—all trivialities, Shelby."

"Really?"

"It's faith and vision that count most," Bern said. "Whether it's your thingamabobs, or my synergies, it's a belief that something *is* happening that's essential."

"But don't we need those trivialities—details, specifics?"

"Often they just get in the way, Shelby. Details and specifics hamper the process of success. They slow down the vision process. They can hinder creativity. They can restrict realignment. Don't you agree?"

Shelby rubbed his upper lip with a finger, though it didn't really itch.

"I'm sort of processing your visions on realignment, Bern. Give me a minute."

"Take all the time you need, of course."

"I know a guy named Roger you should meet," Shelby said. "He believes truth can be improved, for example. And it can be extended, whatever that means."

"A very astute man, this Roger. His theory on extending truth—fascinating. When I say that details and specifics, for example, can get in the way, I might add that this Roger makes me remember that we can't always allow truth to get in the way either."

Shelby leaned forward and cocked an ear toward Bern.

"We should shun truth?"

"Not at all," Bern said, putting his hands together in his praying gesture once again. "Truth is truth, of course. But perhaps your Roger would agree that a successful vision can depend on which truth you choose to allow as your guiding principle."

Tea Party, Shelby thought.

"He just might agree with you on that one, Bern."

"Excellent. I am so very happy we cleared all that up, Shelby."

"The clarity is blinding, Bern. Truly blinding. I can barely see because I'm so full of it. It's overflowing."

"And we have your friend Roger to thank."

"We sure do. And I'll be doing that soon. So, when would I start with Gobitek?"

"Right now, Shelby. Immediately. As we speak you are part of the Gobitek family. I have an office ready for you down the hall. Of course, you will want to decorate it as you see fit—and clearly you already have many ideas."

"Can I have a teakwood desk and ergonomic chair—and a sofa?"

"Of course."

"A really ugly red paisley sofa?" Shelby said. "And ridiculously thick white shag carpeting?"

"If that is your vision, it must be so."

"I think I'm getting the hang of this vision thing," Shelby said.

"I have the utmost confidence in you, Shelby."

"Could I also get a Chicago Bears banner for the wall behind my desk?"

"You can get anything you want, Shelby. Perhaps it can be arranged for an actual Chicago Bear to drop by."

"Jay Cutler?"

"I will look into it," Bern said.

"Because I saved the world," Shelby said.

"You certainly did."

"We Are Gobitek!" Shelby exclaimed.

"Indeed. We Are Gobitek! "

Gobitek put Shelby up in a lavish suite at The Drake. A tailor was dispatched to measure Shelby for new suits to come from Milan. Expensive Italian shoes arrived from Michigan Avenue shops. On a wall in his suite there was a huge We Are Gobitek! banner. Flower arrangements were delivered—yellow roses arranged to spell out Gobitek! On Shelby's pillows were chocolates in We Are Gobitek! wrappers. His towels and bathrobes and washcloths—even the damn soap all had Gobitek! printed on them.

And as Bern had suggested might be arranged, Jay Cutler, quarterback for the Chicago Bears, dropped by and they shared deep dish pizza at a Lou Malnati's. Cutler conceded that Shelby had had a better year than he had.

"But you played well before you got hurt," Shelby said.

"But *you* saved the world, dude," Jay said. "And I couldn't even save the season. And believe me, I heard plenty about it."

"People can be ungrateful no matter how hard you try to help them."

"Tell me about it," Jay said. "But what can we do?"

"Eat deep-dish pizza and smile, Jay. Buy deep-dish pizza for everyone at those press conferences. That's what I'd do."

"Think that'll work?"

"Sure," Shelby said. "Wear them down. Make them call you a jerk who smiles and buys them deep-dish pizza. Pretty soon that'll backfire on them."

"I'm going to do it," Jay said. "Thanks, dude."

"And maybe stop throwing off your back foot."

"That's old news, Shelby. I got that under control—but you're priceless, my friend."

"I've been hearing that lately."

"So, Shel—what do you make of this Gobitek outfit?"

"Utter nonsense. But it pays for the deep-dish pizza. And the suite at The Drake."

"And how about that Bern dude," Jay said. "I felt like a shrimp when I met him. But maybe he'd be a decent tight end."

"He believes in visions, synergies, realignment, and avoiding truth."

"He'd make a fine coach," Jay said.

Shelby's office was decorated just as he had specified—an ugly red paisley sofa, ridiculously thick white shag carpeting, a garish Bears banner behind the teakwood desk, and an ergonomic chair. But days went by with nothing to do and no word from Bern, who had flown to Bremen on business.

Shelby's secretary, Ethel Mermelstein, a well-preserved lady of sixty-four who colored her hair raven black, was pleasant, but told Shelby almost nothing and had to admit she knew almost nothing about why Bern had left and what he was doing or when he would be back. She had been hired just the week before Shelby had come on board. Since she was Shelby's secretary, it was obvious to him that she had nothing to do either and spent much time on the phone with her sister, Imelda, out in Oak Park. And he and Ethel were the only employees at Gobitek-Chicago.

Sometimes Ethel disappeared for hours at a time but always reappeared smiling, pleasant, but with nothing to tell Shelby other than the latest scoop from Imelda out in Oak Park. Sometimes Ethel would come into Shelby's office to check on him and they would put their feet up on his teakwood desk at his invitation and Ethel would regale him with the latest Mermelstein family news from out in Oak Park. Apparently a third sister, Margaret, had begun a torrid affair with a married man, a dentist. Shelby heard about all the Mermelstein marriages and divorces and listened attentively because there was nothing else to do.

Soon Shelby started taking two-hour lunches, and then four-hour lunches, and on some days he didn't go to the office until afternoon. He ate deep-dish pizza at all the good places and pretty soon had visited just about every store on Michigan Avenue. He bought gifts for all members of The Exalted Church of the Intergalactic Moment and had them shipped to Parsons Grove. He located a first-edition *Catch-22* for Oceanna. He sort of missed the kookiness of the group—especially Viola Atteberry's own special brand of nutty.

He also missed having a snort of Old Crow on Ray Spurlock's porch. He missed the meandering river full of rapids snaking through town. Fall had truly set in and it was brisk and breezy along Michigan Avenue and the lakeshore. He truly liked Chicago, though, and its colorful, friendly people. He attended several Bears games with tickets courtesy of Jay. The tickets always came gift-wrapped and with a We Are Gobitek! label. That was apparently the only work Ethel had done as his secretary other than to maintain constant communications with the Oak Park wing of the Mermelstein clan.

There was still no word from Bern. So, in addition to four-hour lunches, Shelby often walked across Michigan Avenue to the Billy Goat Tavern and got a little drunk before heading back to the office for the latest update on Margaret Mermelstein's torrid affair, which apparently was losing steam. Sometimes people recognized him at the Billy Goat and bought him drinks, but mostly he was left alone. It was a place used to celebrities. After all, the Rolling Stones were known to frequent. One of the bartenders made a half-hearted attempt to create a specialty drink called Shelby Saved the World on the Rocks, but it was just scotch on the rocks.

Then one day Ethel came into his office while Shelby, still sobering up from an afternoon at the Billy Goat, was half asleep on his ugly red paisley sofa. She got him on his feet, water splashed on his face, and some steaming black coffee in him because finally, amazingly, clients were coming to call and they were coming to call on Shelby. Bern had sent particulars from Nairobi before leaving for Shanghai.

"Me?" Shelby said. "They're coming to see *me*?"

"It's your name on the door, Shelby," she said.

"Is there time to change it?"

"I'm afraid you're stuck," she said.

"Is Bern coming?"

"Mr. Brindlestickler is off to Shanghai."

Shelby allowed the ringing finality of that statement to resonate in his head a moment.

"Really? Shanghai? What do they want with *me*?"

"How should I know? Mr. Brindlestickler sent a packet for you to read before you meet them."

Ethel straightened a crooked picture on the wall, an oil seascape, the waves threatening to crash into a small sailboat.

"When do they arrive?" Shelby said.

"In about an hour."

"An hour? You're sure Bern isn't coming?"

"As sure as my sister Margaret is playing with fire."

"How's that going?"

"It's all over but the fat lady singing—thank God."

She handed him the packet, which of course had We Are Gobitek! in large letters on its cover.

"Tell Margaret hello from me," Shelby said as he opened the packet and sat on his ugly red paisley sofa.

"Already have, Shel. She sends her best. I'll get you more coffee."

"Make it a gallon."

Shelby pulled the contents from the packet, which consisted of a photo of two middle-aged men in expensive suits and in an expensive office. There was also a handwritten note from Bern:

> Shelby—take good care of Mr. Fiddler and Mr. Bass. They're important people. Just be who you are and all will be well. Remember—visions, synergies, and realignments.
>
> —Bern

"What?" Shelby said. "That's it?"

He looked at the back of the photo but there was nothing there. Ethel came back and re-filled his coffee cup.

"Who are Mr. Fiddler and Mr. Bass, Ethel?"

"Sorry—never heard of them."

Shelby held up the photo."

"Well, this is them."

"Nice suits," Ethel said. "How's the coffee?"

"Keep it coming."

Shelby splashed more water on his face and drank another cup of coffee. Then Ethel announced that Mr. Fiddler and Mr. Bass had arrived and were having a cup of coffee. Shelby slipped on his suit coat and knotted his tie.

"Send them in," he told Ethel through the intercom. He met them at the door and offered a hand. They all shook vigorously and smiled moronically and Shelby directed them to the ugly red paisley sofa and he pulled his ergonomic chair over.

Shelby smiled even more and thought—what the fuck am I doing with these two grinning stiffs?

"A grand pleasure to finally meet you, Mr. Goddard," Mr. Fiddler said.

"Oh yes, indeed," echoed Mr. Bass. "Quite nice I should say."

They had English accents and so Shelby at least knew where they were from.

"And thank you ever so much," Mr. Fiddler and Mr. Bass said in unison. A third stiff in a suit would have made them a dandy choir.

"For what?" Shelby said.

"Why, for saving the world, of course," Mr. Fiddler said.

"Oh, that. Well, think nothing of it, guys."

Shelby glanced down at his pants and wasn't sure where to place his hands. He finally clasped them together in his lap, reminiscent of Bern appearing ready to pray.

"So modest," Mr. Bass said to Mr. Fiddler.

"As we expected, of course," Mr. Fiddler told Mr. Bass. "Mr. Brindlestickler speaks ever so highly of you, Mr. Goddard."

Well, at least someone has heard from the guy, he thought.

"Does he now?" Shelby said.

"Oh my word yes," Mr. Bass said. "He reveres you, Mr. Goddard."

"Call me Shelby."

"As you wish, of course—Shelby," Mr. Fiddler said.

"An honor to call you Shelby," Mr. Bass said.

"How is Mr. Brindlestickler?" Shelby said.

"Very well, we assume," Mr. Fiddler said. "Mr. Bass, when did we last see Mr. Brindlestickler?"

"Rome, perhaps," Mr. Bass said.

"And not Zurich?" Mr. Fiddler said.

"We may have seen Mr. Brindlestickler in Zurich at some point," Mr. Bass said. "He is often in Zurich, as we are, too. But I believe most recently we had the pleasure of Mr. Brindlestickler's company in Rome."

"Rome it is," Mr. Fiddler said, looking quite pleased.

Shelby wondered whether the two of them would like a scotch over at the Billy Goat. It certainly sounded good to him. Feeling a rare moment of duty and obligation to Gobitek, which was keeping him well-supplied with deep dish pizza at The Drake, Shelby said, "So, what can I do for you gents today?"

They beamed at each other. Mr. Bass rubbed his hands together expectantly, perhaps like a child at Christmas preparing to open a present.

"Of course," Mr. Bass began, "you have already done more for us than we could ever repay—by saving the world."

"Yes—that must be established," Mr. Fiddler interjected solemnly, nodding his head up and down vigorously.

Shelby really wanted a scotch over at the Billy Goat.

"Well, guys—I did my best. That's all I can say."

"And your best was supreme," Mr. Fiddler said.

"Oh indeed it was," Mr. Bass said. "Quite supreme."

Ethel stuck her head in to check their coffees and re-fill them. Shelby suddenly longed to hear the latest on the Mermelstein clan over a scotch at the Billy Goat.

"But, repayment must be attempted," Mr. Fiddler said. "Which is why we find ourselves at Gobitek."

"Of course," Shelby said, though he had no idea what they were talking about. "And here at Gobitek, we're, we're—we're happy to host you gents. You're very welcome about that whole saving the world thing." Shelby figured to try and wrap it up in a few minutes and head on over to the Billy Goat for a scotch.

"I'm curious," Mr. Fiddler said. "*How* did you save the world?"

Shelby shifted awkwardly in his ergonomic chair.

"Thingamabobs, thingamajigs, and doohickeys," he said, adding a nervous smile and recalling that those items were made by a company within a company and supplied by yet another company with a relationship to Gobitek, which no one so far had adequately described or defined, and which didn't actually make those items, or know who *did*.

Mr. Fiddler and Mr. Bass nodded gravely to each other.

"So we have often heard," Mr. Fiddler said reverentially.

"And very much like visions, synergies, and realignments," Mr. Bass said. "Don't you agree, Shelby?"

"Oh, sure. I absolutely do. They're really pretty much the same thing when you get right down to it. Don't you gents agree?"

"Oh, we do indeed," Mr. Fiddler and Mr. Bass exclaimed.

Shelby snuck a peek at his watch, wondered who was tending bar over at the Billy Goat. If it was Mark Czakowski, his first scotch was always free because he had saved the world.

"So," Shelby said. "What else can I do for you gents?"

"You've just done it," Mr. Fiddler said.

"Oh indeed you have," Mr. Bass said. "Amazingly so."

"And perfectly so, I might add," Mr. Fiddler added.

"I have?" Shelby said.

"Of course," Mr. Fiddler said.

"Until right this very moment," Mr. Bass said, "we had not decided whether to let Gobitek help us, whether we must become Gobitek clients."

And right up to this very moment, Shelby was thinking, he still had no idea what Gobitek did or had done or could do or wanted to do, and why it did whatever it was it did, which apparently it did quite splendidly and made scads of dough.

"But now we know that we must," Mr. Fiddler said. "Mr. Brindlestickler assured us that we would know what to decide once we met you, Shelby."

"He did?"

"Mr. Brindlestickler knew what we have now realized," Mr. Bass said. "We shall put ourselves in Gobitek's capable hands."

"Cool," Shelby said. "But what do you gents do? What do you want Gobitek to do for you?"

"We have companies, Shelby," Mr. Fiddler said.

"What kind of companies?"

"All sorts, really," Mr. Bass said.

"What do these companies do?" He thought again of thingamajigs, thingamabobs, and doohickeys, mysterious items somehow part of the of the Gobitek corporate structure and made by a company within a company and supplied by yet another company with a vague, murky relationship to Gobitek, which no one so far had adequately described or defined, and which didn't actually make those items, or know who *did*.

"All sorts of things, Shelby," Mr. Fiddler said. "We're quite diversified."

"And how can Gobitek help?" Shelby said.

"The usual ways," Mr. Fiddler said.

"Oh yes indeed," Mr. Bass said. "The usual ways."

"But, we did not know with any certainty that we wanted those usual ways that Gobitek has perfected until we had met you, Shelby," Mr. Fiddler said.

"And now we have," Mr. Bass said.

"And so a deal is struck," Mr. Fiddler said, extending his hand.

And that broke the tension, lifted the spell, and dispersed the Gobitek Fog. Shelby shook hands with both of them and they got up to leave, faces beaming, shiny, expectant. Shelby gestured toward the door and good-naturedly shepherded them through it.

"Such a pleasure to meet you, Shelby," Mr. Fiddler said.

"A grand moment in my life," Mr. Bass said.

"And a grand moment for me as well, "Mr. Fiddler said, not to be outdone.

"Mr. Brindlestickler will hear from us," Mr. Bass said. "We can assure you."

"And the credit is yours, Shelby," Mr. Fiddler said.

"We are Gobitek!" Shelby exclaimed as he watched them step into the elevator and the door closed on their pudgy, smiling faces.

Several days later, Shelby received a check for $1 million from Bern, who was in Stockholm but headed to Madrid. A note soon followed:

> Shelby—you were sensational with Mr. Fiddler and Mr. Bass. They were absolutely captivated by you. And now they are part of the Gobitek family as we ascend even higher. Keep up the good work. More to come!
>
> —Bern

Shelby read the note over a double Shelby Saved the World on the Rocks scotch on the rocks at the Billy Goat. Ethel joined him and drank a rusty nail. She caught him up on sister Margaret, who had gotten over her affair with the horny dentist in Oak Park, but had since taken up with a horny orthopedist in River Forest. She did seem to gravitate toward horny men in the medical fields. Shelby didn't want to pry into Ethel's financial affairs, but he wanted to make sure she was compensated for her part in landing Mr. Fiddler and Mr. Bass—whatever that meant—and so he gave her gift certificates in large amounts at Sak's and Gucci. He had no idea what to do with his $1 million.

Ethel had mentioned wanting to start an online dating site with sister Margaret, who certainly seemed to know much about dating, especially dating horny men in the medical fields, and Shelby agreed to give it some thought from an investor standpoint.

"We are Gobitek!" Shelby and Ethel exclaimed as they clinked their drinks together.

After a moment, when the scotch had warmed his stomach, Shelby said, "What does Gobitek mean? What does it even stand for—besides nonsense?"

"Don't ask me," Ethel said. "Ask Mr. Brindlestickler."

"The famous Bern Brindlestickler—who never shows up."

"Where is he now?"

"Stockholm," Shelby said. "But soon headed to Madrid."

"Quite a life," Ethel said. "What does Gobitek do—besides nonsense?"

"He didn't tell you?"

"Not a word. I was hired through a service. They said you'd tell me everything I needed to know. What do I need to know, Shel?"

"You already know it."

"Good to know. And thanks very much, dear, for Sak's and Gucci. Is that a regular part of the deal?"

"I have no idea."

"But when you do know, you'll tell me?"

"Absolutely, Ethel. As soon as I know something, which currently I don't, you'll be the first to know whatever it is that's no longer what I don't know."

"Sounds pretty clear to me," she said.

"Really?"

"No, but I'm sort of getting the hang of the place, I guess. Do *you* actually know what Gobitek does?"

As best as Shelby could reckon, Gobitek was in the smoke and mirrors business of helping already mega-rich people shuffle their mega-millions around through the guise of providing money-making services that very few people really understood in order to help the mega-rich become the mega, mega-rich, and the bottom line was to convince the mega-rich to invest with Bern instead of someone with another name, who was essentially the same as Bern, so as to keep Bern in yachts and expensive suits, and a couple steps ahead of anyone who might figure out it was all capitalist nonsense, a house built on a swamp with no roof. And then, of course, there were thingamajigs, thingamabobs, and doohickeys, items made by a company within a company and supplied by yet another company with a relationship to Gobitek, which no one so far had adequately described or defined, and which didn't actually make those items, or know who *did*.

"Gobitek helps people, Ethel."

"Who?"

"Well, clearly it helps rich people."

"Why?" she said.

"Because Bern probably doesn't have much interest in helping poor people."

"Why?"

"Poor people can't afford visions, synergies, and realignments," Shelby said.

"And what are those?"

Shelby thought a moment, and naturally the first thing that popped into his scotch-depleted head was thingamajigs, thingamabobs, and doohickeys, which were made by a company within a company and supplied by yet another company with a relationship to Gobitek, which no one so far had adequately described or defined, and which didn't actually make those items, or know who *did*.

"Those are the things I don't know, but that I just promised to tell you what they really are if they ever become things I no longer don't know."

"Clear as a bell, Shel."

"We are Gobitek!" he exclaimed.

"We are Gobitek!" she exclaimed.

"Gobitek even seems to have its own language," she said.

"And it all starts with helping people."

"Rich people."

"That's where the money *is*," he said. "And so that's where the help *goes*."

After a second round of drinks arrived, Ethel said, "How did we help Mr. Fiddler and Mr. Bass?"

"I have no idea."

"But they're rich people, right?"

"Fabulously rich," Shelby said. "Or they wouldn't need Bern's help."

She nodded, sipped her rusty nail. Shelby raised his glass of scotch, Laphroaig, and admired the rich amber color.

"But if they're already fabulously rich," she said, "why do they need Gobitek's help?"

"To be even more fabulously rich," Shelby said.

"Even though they already are?"

"That makes it even more urgent to help them, Ethel."

"The more someone succeeds, the more they need help succeeding?"

"Exactly," Shelby said. "For Bern, helping folks to succeed who aren't already succeeding doesn't make sense."

"Now, let me see if I get this, Shel. The rich are rich and don't need help, but because they're rich they get help anyway. Is that about it?"

"They get *all* the help. You hit the nail smack on the head, Ethel. That's the American way—that's the Gobitek way. Ever read *Catch-22*?"

"What's that?"

"A novel," Shelby said. "I'll get you a copy."

"Will it shed light on Gobitek?"

"Not at all."

"I look forward to it."

Shelby raised his glass.

"We are Gobitek!" they exclaimed.

WE ARE KETIBOG!

For the next week, Shelby alternated between pie-eyed soused at the Billy Goat, sleeping it off on his ugly red paisley sofa, and eating deep dish pizza with Ethel and helping her explore everything Michigan Avenue had to offer. Shelby also carried money from the $1 million Bern had sent him and routinely gave some to anyone on the streets that looked like they might be down on their luck.

But soon the Tribune ran a story about someone giving away money on the streets to anyone who looked down on their luck, and so he stopped doing that and instead created a foundation, with Ethel as its head, to discreetly find people who could use some assistance. He also funded the online dating service, which sister Margaret assisted with, and soon Margaret had plenty of men to date, and even more of them horny men in the medical fields, but Ethel and the whole Mermelstein clan of Oak Park were relieved to know that mostly they were single men.

Shelby enjoyed the irony of funding the foundation with Bern's money. Bern periodically emailed enthusiastically from Oslo or Dublin or Singapore or Rio de Janeiro to ask how it was going, and Shelby always assured him he stood ready to help Gobitek ascend to even greater heights.

Shelby's foundation was called The Ketibog Foundation and he had We Are Ketibog! banners made so that when Ethel entertained a foundation client in the Gobitek suite, they could just take down the Gobitek banner and replace it with the Ketibog banner. Shelby understood that while he had saved the world, he couldn't actually save everyone in it who might be in need, and so he and Ethel elected to be satisfied with helping who they could, when they could, and how they could. We are Ketibog! And the foundation and online dating serve commingled: Ethel could refer foundation clients to sister Margaret, who found them dates.

"We are Ketibog!" Shelby exclaimed.

"We are Ketibog!" Ethel exclaimed.

"But what does Ketibog mean?" Ethel said.

"Isn't it obvious?"

"Not to me, Shel. And it's a funny sounding name."

Shelby pointed at the Ketibog banner.

"Look at the word. What do you see?"

Ethel looked closely. She stepped closer for a better look and placed her hands on her hips. Shelby chuckled while she scanned the banner.

"I see, Ketibog. It's a weird word, Shel."

"Yeah, but now *reverse* Ketibog."

"Reverse it?" She looked again for a long moment. "Oh, lordy. I see it now—Gobitek! Ketibog is Gobitek in reverse."

"Exactly. Which is what we do—put Gobitek in reverse. A small part of it, anyway."

"It's genius, Shel. Brilliant."

"And pretty ironic, too," he said. "The rich shovel money into rich Gobitek and we shovel some of it out the other side to Ketibog and people who actually need help."

Ethel nodded, folded her arms across her chest.

"But I'm guessing Mr. Brindlestickler wouldn't approve."

"Oh, no," Shelby said. "He'd pop a gasket, I suspect. The poor can't afford Bern's visions, synergies, and realignments, and so his carefully-developed utter nonsense would be wasted."

"Is this legal?"

Shelby shrugged. "Once he gives me money, it becomes *my* money. It's not up to him how it gets spent."

Shelby was fairly sure that was true, but figured if he had to, he could pay the money back.

"What about the banners?" Ethel said.

"We make sure we have the right banner up when someone comes calling. As long as we do, no one knows the difference. If necessary, I can rent another office."

"What would Mr. Brindlestickler say if he knew we were running a charity out of his corporate offices?" Ethel said.

"If it came out, Bern would just take credit. He'd call it a PR coup."

"Works for me, Shel. And I can buy banners with removable letters so we can just rearrange the letters back and forth between Ketibog to Gobitek."

"Brilliant," Shelby said. "You're thinking like a true Ketibogger."

"But is all this going to get me fired, Shel?"

"Absolutely. I'd be surprised if it doesn't. But by then you can take over the foundation completely. And you've got the dating service, too."

"We are Ketibog!" Ethel exclaimed.

"We are Ketibog!" Shelby exclaimed

But before Ketibog could really get into full swing, Bern sent another note announcing the arrival of new clients, a Mr. Fracker and a Ms. Pottermeier. In the accompanying photo, Mr. Fracker was a jowly, sluggish-looking man in his fifties, Ms. Pottermeier a fortyish, bookish-looking woman with an icy stare and short blond hair. As usual, the note gave almost no notice and no information on who was arriving:

> Shelby—you were so splendid with Mr. Fiddler and Mr. Bass that I am now sending along Mr. Fracker and Ms. Pottermeier. More important people. Work the old Shelby magic! In Shelby we trust! Gobitek continues to ascend! And more to come!
> —Bern

Shelby and Ethel quickly rearranged the letters converting Ketibog banners to Gobitek banners and Ethel made a pot of coffee. Shelby selected a jacket and cinched his tie and the both of them stood waiting and smiling as Mr. Fracker and Ms. Pottermeier stepped off the private Gobitek elevator into the suite. They were Americans and from California—San Francisco. Shelby guided them to his ugly red paisley sofa and pulled his ergonomic chair over. Ethel brought coffee.

"Such an incredible honor to meet you, Mr. Goddard," Ms. Pottermeier said.

"Agreed," Mr. Fracker said. "Thanks so much for saving the world."

Shelby waved a hand regally, dismissively, and felt quite moronic as he did it. Had he become a Roman emperor? He made a mental note to tone the pretension factor back down to something resembling normal. A conversation soon with Roger would help nicely with that.

"Just another day at the office, folks. And call me Shelby."

"Shelby," they both exclaimed. "So modest."

Shelby shrugged. "But it's all just—old news. Am I right?"

Mr. Fracker and Ms. Pottermeier glanced at each other.

"From a marketing standpoint, it could certainly be utilized for a lot longer," Ms. Pottermeier said stiffly. "That is, saving the world creates an obligation and thus a product—and many buyers."

"I think Ms. Pottermeier is saying that gratitude to you, Shelby, could be milked a lot more," Mr. Fracker said.

"Yes," she said, glancing at Mr. Fracker.

"Milked," Shelby said flatly.

"A coarse term," Mr. Fracker said. "I apologize."

"And obligation becomes a product?" Shelby said.

"Oh, yes," Ms. Pottermeier said, smiling for the first time. "Saving the world creates the ultimate obligation, and thus, the ultimate product."

Shelby felt he knew a thing or two about ultimate obligations.

"Which can be milked," Shelby said.

"Like a fat cow in summer," Mr. Fracker said, grinning. Clearly it was an expression he loved to express.

Shelby sensed that under the slick suit and sweet smile, Mr. Fracker could be a bit of a brute who had acquired the genteel language and manners of high finance, but remained at true nature merely a hayseed who somehow tripped and fell into some sort of money pit that just kept filling up with money.

"Do you have any cows, Mr. Fracker?" Shelby said.

"Oh, sure I do, Shelby. Cows, horses, chickens, roosters, peacocks, alpacas, hogs, sheep, cars, trucks, planes, ships, buildings, and even skyscrapers."

"But we're not here to market gratitude," Ms. Pottermeier said. "That's your product, Shelby. And we admire your good fortune so much."

Saving the world, apparently, was just a prelude to a nifty marketing opportunity.

"We really do, Shelby," Mr. Fracker said. "Talk about falling into the river and coming up coated in gold."

"And pockets full of silver and diamonds," Ms. Pottermeier added hopefully.

"Sounds like it would be hard to swim with all that stuff," Shelby said.

Mr. Fracker and Ms. Pottermeier nodded feebly.

Ms. Pottermeier finally said, "What an attractive sofa," as she ran a hand across the fabric of the ugly red paisley sofa.

"And your chair there, sure looks comfy," Mr. Fracker said.

"It's ergonomic," Shelby said. "It's called The Miromack."

"Is that French?" Mr. Fracker said.

"I think it's Serbian," Ms. Pottermeier said. "I think I recall that from my studies at Vassar."

"Ms. Pottermeier's a solid Vassar woman, Shelby. Apparently she studied chairs there."

Mr. Fracker chuckled.

"I studied languages there—at Vassar," she sniffed.

"Cool," Shelby said. "And where did *you* go to school, Mr. Fracker?"

"I'm a Harvard man, Shelby."

"Sweet. I went to Stanford."

"A mighty fine school," Mr. Fracker said. "The Harvard of the west."

"But," Shelby said, "some might say that Harvard is the Stanford of the east, Mr. Fracker."

"I suppose *some* might say that," Mr. Fracker said quietly.

Ms. Pottermeier nervously brushed an imaginary bang from her face.

Shelby sensed that he wasn't quite wielding The Old Shelby Magic, as Bern called it, like a Jedi master with a trusty light saber, and that things were lurching south for Gobitek, which meant things were actually lurching south for Ketibog, which was what really mattered. A quick fix was in order.

"When I saved the world," Shelby said, "I utilized thingamabobs, thingamajigs, and doohickeys. Perhaps you've heard about them." And he very nearly added that they were items made by a company within a company and supplied by yet another company with a relationship to Gobitek, which no one so far had adequately described or defined, and which didn't actually make those items, or know who *did*.

Mr. Fracker and Ms. Pottermeier appeared to snap out of their Harvard-induced and Vassar-induced trances and their faces lit up nicely.

"Indeed," Mr. Fracker and Ms. Pottermeier exclaimed.

"The ultimate product," Ms. Pottermeier gushed.

"A river of gold," Mr. Fracker gushed.

Shelby frowned.

"Now, which is the ultimate product—the obligation created, or thingamabobs, thingamajigs, and doohickeys?"

"The obligation, of course," Ms. Pottermeier said. "Thingamabobs, thingamajigs, and doohickeys are, how we might say—the means of production."

"Ah," Shelby said. "Yes—the means of production. Did you learn that at Vassar, too, Ms. Pottermeier?"

"Among many other things," she said smugly.

Shelby eased back in his ergonomic chair, The Miromack, which was neither French nor Serbian and was in fact a word he had made up on the spot, and he felt things were now lurching north again for

Gobitek, which was to actually say they were lurching north quite handsomely for Ketibog, which was what mattered.

To seal the deal, he suddenly leaned forward, elbows on knees, his brow furrowed, and said, "Do you agree that thingamabobs, thingamajigs, and doohickeys are actually visions, synergies, and re-alignments merely by other names?"

Mr. Fracker arched his eyebrows.

Ms. Pottermeier appeared stunned.

"Yes, I do indeed," Mr. Fracker said. "You Stanford men are certainly quick."

"How amazing," Ms. Pottermeier gushed, "that you so easily—and I might say, adeptly—connect the parallel concepts of your means of production with that of Mr. Brindlestickler's revolutionary process."

"Agreed—amazing," Mr. Fracker said.

"Not bad for a Stanford man, eh?" Shelby said.

"My son is considering Stanford!" Mr. Fracker ejaculated, though Shelby thought he also looked green around the gills.

"So is my daughter," said Ms. Pottermeier, who didn't have a daughter.

Shelby eased back in The Miromack again, confident his grin was at least as good as a Cheshire Grin.

Shelby waited.

Ms. Pottermeier finally looked at Mr. Fracker, who looked back earnestly. Shelby speculated that the two were sleeping together, though the actual sex sounded like it had its tortuous moments and was more about punishment than pleasure.

"Well," Mr. Fracker said, rising. "I think we have found what we came looking for."

Mr. Fracker glanced, though, at Ms. Pottermeier, who merely nodded serenely.

Yes, Shelby thought—they were likely sleeping together, and although Mr. Fracker likely held the higher position business-wise, he needed her approval because of all the positions she put him through bedroom-wise.

Satisfied with Ms. Pottermeier's serene look, Mr. Fracker said, "I believe we have a deal here, Shelby. I'll alert Mr. Brindlestickler."

"You do that," Shelby said.

"I shall at my first opportunity," Mr. Fracker said.

Mr. Fracker offered a hand and Shelby accepted it. Shelby shook with Ms. Pottermeier, who had a cold, limp hand.

"We are Gobitek!" Shelby exclaimed.

Mr. Fracker smiled.

Ms. Pottermeier sniffed.

Ethel came in.

"More coffee?"

As usual, as expected, a note from Bern in Tokyo (with Caracas up next) and a check for $1.5 million to Shelby arrived several days later while Shelby and Ethel had resumed their Billy Goat and deep dish pizza routine:

> Shelby—more incredible magic from you, my friend. Mr. Fracker and Ms. Pottermeier have joined the Gobitek family because of you. Gobitek ascends even higher. Prepare more of that Shelby Magic. More clients to come!
> —Bern

"Where's Mr. Brindlestickler now?" Ethel said, sipping a rusty nail at the Billy Goat.

"Tokyo," Shelby said, staring into his drink. "But headed to Caracas."

Shelby had the usual, a Shelby Saved the World on the Rocks scotch on the rocks.

"As long as he stays out of our hair, Shelby."

"And the foundation money keeps flowing."

"It's flowing pretty nicely so far."

"Oh, yeah," Shelby said. "We're milking it like a fat cow in summer."

"I never heard that one before, Shelby."

"That's Mr. Fracker wisdom. He's a Harvard man who owns cows, and just about everything else."

"How long can we keep this going?" Ethel said.

"As long as we can, but perhaps not as long as we would like, Ethel."

"Is that Gobitek dialect, or Ketibog?"

"A little of both, maybe?"

"We're Ketibog!" Ethel exclaimed.

"We *are* Ketibog!" Shelby exclaimed.

"But some days we're Gobitek!" Ethel exclaimed.

"But only as a means of production!" Shelby exclaimed.

"Whatever that is," Ethel exclaimed.

For several weeks there was no word at all from Bern, and so Shelby and Ethel focused on the foundation and the online dating service. Shelby even made the trek out to Oak Park to have dinner with the Mermelstein clan. With help from sisters Margaret and Imelda, Ethel identified people who had lost a job, for example, because it had been sent overseas by CEOs who made anonymous large Republican donations so that they could pretend to be "job creators," who actually created lower-paying jobs in other countries, because after all, most American employees seemed to be immoral Democrats—and even worse, members of Stalinist unions—that expected an actual living wage, and who voted for people who actually believed in honest elections, and so that had to be nipped in the bud to make the American Dream a nightmare for the ungrateful masses, and a wet dream for the American rich, who controlled the American dream by right of birth and inheritance.

Shelby hosted a potluck dinner in the Gobitek office that mixed some of the foundation clients with subscribers to the online dating service, of which some were horny men in the medical fields who had dated Margaret Mermelstein. But several promising matches emerged from the evening and from people with average libidos.

The foundation's coffers grew unexpectedly when Bern sent another $1 million on a Monday to Shelby as a sort of advance on coming commerce—"the expected greater heights for Gobitek!" Shelby knew that it signaled new clients would show up soon enough—no later than Friday—to experience the old Shelby Magic.

Overall, though, Shelby was pleased with legally fleecing Gobitek to feed Ketibog. He cut his four-hour lunches at the Billy Goat and various deep-dish pizza joints down to two hours and walked more and even joined a health club. His goal was to lose ten pounds of scotch and deep-dish pizza weight. He and Ethel slowed down all their activities for the week, anticipating the day coming at any time when the inevitable note from Bern would arrive, giving them almost no time to receive clients. Margaret Mermelstein temporarily took over the online dating service. To save time, Ethel re-arranged Ketibog banner letters back to Gobitek and double-checked to make sure nothing linked to Ketibog was in the offices. Shelby and Ethel took turns staffing the offices when the other was out. They restricted their activities to luminous Michigan Avenue.

A light snow fell at mid-week, the first snow of the young winter, as Shelby strolled along Michigan Avenue. It was not terribly cold and there was no wind and so the day was still pleasant enough after he bought a nice Italian wool coat at a discount place instead of Saks. He enjoyed the soft flakes falling on his head and shoulders as he walked but bought a Bears cap to keep his head dry. He walked down to the Billy Goat, but decided instead to watch people hustle by from the bridge over the Chicago River.

Shelby looked down into the green river and wondered how life was going in Parsons Grove. He thought of all the members of The Exalted Church of the Intergalactic Moment, even Viola Atteberry and her obsession with robbing banks. By now, he hoped, Parsons Grove had gotten over Mob Day and viewed it as just another odd historical occurrence, like Porter Newhouse having a bridge named after him even though he never won a Civil War battle.

Shelby had gotten an email from Oceanna thanking him for the first-edition *Catch-22*. It was a dandy gift, he knew, not cheap, but he figured she took it as pretty much routine from someone with Shelby's money and so she probably didn't read too much into it. And, he owed her a favor from hiding him out when the town had temporarily imploded and went off the reservation.

Oceanna, he knew, was a little older than he, about five or six years, he figured, but that wasn't so much. She was smart, pretty—fast on her feet. He liked her wit. It had edge, but didn't seem to cut too deep, or shed too much blood. Despite her inheritance, he saw her as nonetheless rather self-reliant, capable, and authentic in her own right. She could take care of herself. But while he was in Chicago plotting the overthrow of the worldwide corporate structure he figured he should avoid romantic speculations. And Ethel had assured him the online dating service could easily find a date for someone who saved the world. Women often bought him drinks at the Billy Goat, but he avoided entanglements, knowing his time in Chicago would not be permanent.

Shelby called Ethel to check in, but no word had come from Bern. It was Thursday and almost lunch time. Shelby calculated that if nothing arrived by noon, then it would come Friday. It was a snowy lull and he was enjoying it.

Impulsively, he called Roger Valkyrie.

"Hola, Shel," Roger said. "Been drunk on any bridges lately?"

"I'm standing on one right now, Roger."

"Good Lord, kid—not again."

"Don't worry—I'm not drunk."

"But is there a helicopter hovering next to you?"

Shelby glanced around just to make sure. He was, after all, in Chicago.

"Nope. I'm on the Michigan Avenue Bridge, in Chicago. No choppers, no media, no Dixie beers—just Chicagoans walking by in the snow."

"Thank God and General Jackson," Roger said. "Hold on while I command impressive agency resources to locate you, kid."

"Google away, Roger."

"Ah," Roger said a few seconds later. "That bridge is a dandy. I remember it now. The wife and I were in Chicago a few years back. There's a dandy bar there just downstairs from the bridge."

"The Billy Goat Tavern."

"That's the one, kid."

"They make a drink named for me, Roger."

"Yeah? What's it called?"

"Shelby Saved the World on the Rocks."

"Awesome, Shel. A cosmonaut name. What's in it?"

"Scotch. And ice."

"Very imaginative, kid. I think I could make one of those."

"Any snow in Maryland, Roger?"

"A light dusting, kid. But the good news—the lawn is kaput. Mowing is kaput. Paying my wife's nephew is kaput. That albatross is nicely removed from my neck for a while."

"And you earned points big-time with the wife in Aruba."

"Big-time, believe you me, Shel. Enough points to coast on for some time."

"Cosmonaut."

"Very tres cosomonaut, kid. What are you doing in Chicago? Not enough excitement down in Dogpatch?"

Shelby hesitated. He thought of Bern, and Bern's money flowing into his own pockets. He remembered Mr. Fracker and Ms. Pottermeier and Mr. Bass and Mr. Fieldler.

"Still there, kid?" Roger said.

"I'm overthrowing the worldwide corporate structure."

"A worthy goal, Shel. And about time. How's that going?"

"It's actually going pretty well. Very cosmonaut."

"Are you doing anything illegal, or affecting national security, kid?"

Shelby thought a moment.

"I don't think so. Definitely no national security issues."

"Then I don't need the details, Shel. I probably don't want to know."

"You aren't worried I might actually topple corporations worldwide?"

"I'd still have my job, kid. What do I care?"

"Really?"

"Fucking with you. I would care, of course. But I'd still have my job."

"What form would you need if I did topple corporations?"

"There isn't one. We'd have to design that sucker in a hurry and what a booger it would be. I can just imagine—so try and limit the damage to one country or so. Preferably a small country no one gives a bug's ass about—a small Caribbean nation, for example. But not Jamaica. I'm thinking of taking the wife there in the spring."

"I'll cross Jamaica off my list, Roger. How about Aruba?"

"Go ahead, kid—been there, done that."

"So, Roger—you're not going to ask me for more specifics?"

"Such as?"

"You don't want to know what toppling the worldwide corporate structure means?"

"I'm your vaunted and capable secret agent slash government contact, kid—not your father. But I'm glad you called. We're due for a sit-down, a pow-wow—the old six-month in-person interview. In fact, we're past due on that, and much longer and—"

"Some crazy form?"

"Not just any form, Shel. The mother of all agency forms. The dreaded 1050D-2000A1, which is basically a Spanish Inquisition into why I didn't do a 1050D-2000."

"What's a 1050D-2000?"

"The standard form for a six-month check-in. I got an extension because I had vacation time scheduled—and you were busy inciting riots in Parsons Grove. But we can't put it off any longer."

"How much time do we have?"

"None, Shel. I'll need to come see you right away. Like, tomorrow. I'll be on a Chicago flight this afternoon or early in the morning."

"Tomorrow's Friday," Shelby said, reminding himself it was likely also showtime for Gobitek.

"Glad to hear you know what day it is, kid."

"Friday's good," Shelby said. "I think I can squeeze you in."

"That's highly cosmonaut of you, kid."

Shelby watched several boats pass under the Michigan Avenue Bridge toward the lake. The snow had stopped and the sun was even peeking out from behind clouds. He walked back to the offices and learned that nothing had arrived from Bern and so he treated Ethel to deep-dish pizza at a Lou Malnati's.

The next morning, after a hearty breakfast at The Drake, and after checking in with Ethel and hearing the coast was still clear at Gobitek, Shelby met Roger at the Billy Goat. They sat at the bar.

"Do we dare drink some whiskey at this ungodly hour, Shel?"

"It's almost eleven, Roger. I think we're a few hours past ungodly and approaching godly, whatever that means."

"And it's noon somewhere in the world, kid."

They ordered Shelby Saved the World on the Rocks scotch on the rocks, which of course was merely Laphroaig on the rocks.

"Breakfast of champions," Roger said, making a face after his first sip. "In Aruba, the wife and I sometimes had a Mimosa with breakfast. Or a Piña Colada."

"Very hedonistic, Roger. Are you still on Aruba time?"

"No, I've been to Mexico since then. Hola! I love that word."

"Hola!" Shelby said, raising his glass. "So, how does this interview go?"

"Informally. The agency requires it and it's a chance to get away and not really be on assignment. Next time, maybe I should bring the wife."

"You should. What's her name?"

"Mrs. Roger Valkyrie."

"I see. Confidentiality and all that?"

"Best to keep her out of the business, Shel. You understand."

Shelby nodded. "No problem."

Roger produced a pen and small notebook from inside his jacket.

"Anyway, kid—there's a protocol. I have to assess how you're doing. You know, make sure you aren't depressed and all that."

"But I'm not."

"Well, if you were, we'd get you help pronto. Like, same day. Immediately. On the spot. No waiting at the head doctor clinic. But you look good. And gained a few pounds, I'd say—good."

"Deep-dish pizza and scotch," Shelby said.

"That'll do it, kid. I aim to get some of that deep-dish while I'm here."

"How long are you here"

"As long as it takes."

"Then I'll take you to Lou Malnati's, Roger, for deep-dish."

"Deal," Roger said. "So, let's get business out of the way—why are you in Chicago?"

That was the question first on Shelby's mind every time he got out of bed at The Drake. He knew that eventually he would want to be able to articulate an answer at its basest level.

"I'm stealing from the rich and giving to the poor."

Roger nodded approvingly.

"The old Robin Hood gambit. Excellent, kid. I know folks like the Russell Crowe movie version, and he's pretty good, don't get me wrong. Sort of a Jason Bourne in tights. And he seems like one of the few actors who could actually kick someone's ass. I wouldn't turn my back on him and *I* know all sorts of ninja crap. But I'm kind of partial to the Errol Flynn version. I'm an old movies buff, I guess."

"What about the Kevin Costner version?" Shelby said.

"Please, kid. He should ditch the tights and stick to baseball movies. He's damn good in baseball movies. But he's not a tough guy."

"I see your point—on Costner. But don't you want to know how I steal from the rich and give to the poor?"

"Anything illegal, Shel?"

"I don't think so. I set up a foundation and fund it. Pretty straightforward. Nothing complicated at all."

"With your own money, kid?"

"Absolutely. It definitely does touch my hands on the way to the foundation."

Roger cocked his head to a side and grinned slightly. He swiveled on his stool to face Shelby.

"Do I hear the potential for a gray area in there? Do I hear possible business ethics from the Tony Soprano School of Commerce?"

Shelby's cell phone rang and it was Ethel. He listened, smiled slowly.

"Okay—on the way," he said. "Fifteen minutes."

Shelby put his phone in his pocket and finished his drink.

"Just how adventurous are you, Roger?"

"I'm a secret agent, kid. Remember? Adventure is our middle name."

"That must be confusing—everyone with the same middle name."

"There's that growing Shelby wit, kid."

"How's *your* sense of humor, Roger?" Shelby said as he got up and slipped on his coat.

"Will I need it?'

"Can't hurt, Roger. Can't hurt at all."

As they waited for the light to cross Michigan Avenue, Shelby filled Roger in as a light snow fell again. As Shelby told the tale, Roger surprisingly didn't interrupt and merely nodded from time to time when they made eye contact. A cab honked at them when they were a little slow reaching the other side of the street.

"Gobitek, Shel? I've heard of those monkeys."

"What have you heard?"

"That they're one of those fat-ass multi-nationals that does some sort of tap dance no one quite understands," Roger said. "And they do it all over the world."

"That's Gobitek alright. And somehow they're involved in thing-amajigs, thingamabobs, and doohickeys."

Shelby stared at Roger expectantly.

"Why are you staring at me, kid?"

"Does Gobitek really have something to do with thingamajigs, thingamabobs, and doohickeys?"

"What makes you think they do?"

"Because the head cheese of Gobitek said basically they're made by a company within a company and supplied by yet another company with a relationship to Gobitek, which no one so far has adequately described or defined, and which didn't actually make those items, or know who *did.*"

"Above my pay grade, kid."

"No fooling?"

Roger shrugged, swatted accumulating snowflakes off his shoulder.

"Would I kid you, kid?"

"Yeah, Roger—you would."

Roger wiped more snowflakes off his coat and rubbed his wet hands on his pants, which were forest green corduroy.

"There's stuff we're all better off not knowing, Shel."

"So, forget about it is what you're saying?"

Roger looked up at the nearest tall building.

"What good will it do to know?"

"Do you actually *know*, Roger?"

"I know that your description of how thingamajigs, thingama-bobs, and doohickeys, originate is a pretty good one."

"It's accurate?"

"Well, kid—what *is* accuracy but an accepted version of something that we all agree works best to define something that needs to remain undefined?"

"For the greater good?"

"Exactly."

"For *my* greater good?"

"Even better, kid."

"Well, I don't suppose it would change much of anything if I knew stuff that clearly people don't want me to know because it's better that I don't know what I already don't know."

"Now, you're talking, Shel. Welcome to *my* world."

On the way up to the Gobitek offices, Roger asked Shelby to explain just how he had gotten in bed with Gobitek and its byzantine corporate structure, and what he had to do for vampire industrialists who didn't make anything at all—"without actually telling me more that I'd want to know, or need to know."

"As best as I can tell—I'm their mascot."

"Mascot?"

"They parade me in front of their potential customers, who thank me for saving the world. I mention thingamabobs, thingamajigs, and doohickeys, and then a big check comes to me a few days later. That goes into the foundation."

Roger whistled.

"Damn, kid—that sure beats government work all to hell. What's your foundation called?"

"Ketibog."

"Ketibog?" Roger mulled it a moment and repeated the name several times to himself. "Shit—that's Gobitek in reverse."

"You're quick, Roger."

"I'm a secret agent, kid. We're trained to be quick. And quick to be trained."

"You like the name?"

"It's a humdinger. Where's your office?"

Shelby pointed up at the tall building and grinned.

Roger stared up, and then grinned, too.

"You're running Ketibog out of Gobitek, kid?"

"Or we could call it running Gobitek out of Ketibog."

"Slick as snot, my friend. Slick as snot. This is like Newman and Redford in The Sting. I like it."

In the private Gobitek elevator, Shelby glanced at his watch, stared at the door a moment, and then turned to Roger.

"Can you actually be a party to this?"

"I'm not a party to anything, kid. I'm an observer. I'm the eyes of the agency."

"But I'd have to pass you off as a Gobitek employee, Roger. Would that kick some special form into action?"

"This action's off the books, Shel. No forms."

"Really?"

"It's undercover shit. I have secret agent latitude."

"You're undercover now?"

"Anytime I want."

"Wait—not Joe LeFors again."

"Why not, Shel?"

"Because you can't be an accountant from Memphis. And because Joe LeFors chased Butch and The Kid, for God's sake. You can't say y'all and howdy. This is Chicago. You have to be a Gobitek employee."

"Okay," Roger said. "No sweat. I'll be Joe LeFors, your administrative assistant."

"Are you sure?"

"You'd prefer Jason Bourne?"

"No."

"James Bond?"

"Really?" Shelby said. "You would pose as James Bond?"

"How about, Bond James? It sounds cool."

"The scotch went to your head, Roger."

"How about Eric Clapton?"

"Sorry—no."

"Jimi Hendrix?"

"No and no. And please, only speak when they speak to you, Roger."

"Joe. Joe LeFors."

Ethel made coffee and Shelby slipped into a suit and tie. Roger still looked like Agent Smith from *The Matrix*, but that actually worked pretty well as a corporate costume for a corporate scene in the corporate theater of the absurd. After he was dressed, Shelby nervously looked out a window at the lake. He saw a few whitecaps and a small power boat slowly riding the swells.

"Love the sofa," Roger said, pointing at the ugly red paisley sofa. Can I sit in the ergonomic chair?"

"The Miromack?" Shelby said. "No way. That's a perk of being Gobitek's mascot."

"Miromack?" Roger said. "What's that—French, Serbian?"

"It's nonsense, like Gobitek. I made the chair's name up."

"Why?"

"In these encounters there's not much that's real."

"Sounds fun."

"It's mostly sort of *surreal*."

"Even better, kid."

Ethel handed Shelby the note and packet from Bern. Shelby took the photo out and frowned. He looked up at Ethel and grimaced, then handed her the photo.

"My word," Ethel said, handing it back. "I'll make more coffee."

"What's up?" Roger said.

"Looks like we're conducting a seminar today," Shelby said, handing the photo to Roger.

There were six people in the photo, three men and three women. All impeccably dressed corporate masters of the universe. In a crowd, none of the six faces would stand out.

"Awesome," Roger said.

The private Gobitek elevator opened and out oozed thousands of dollars in expensive clothes and expensive shoes from expensive stores adorning expensive masters of the universe, whose combined net worths and annual salaries and stock holdings, not to mention their egos, were larger than the worth of some island nations.

Mr. Lubeler hailed from New York.

Ms. Hackerton—Los Angeles.

Mr. Kiggenhooper—Miami.

Ms. Klaggenthorpe—Dallas.

Mr. Gildenklack—Atlanta.

Ms. Thickler—Charlotte.

Stiff, laconic introductions were made. The atmosphere was thick, soupy. All eyes were on Shelby, who smiled serenely and gestured toward the conference room. Once all were seated, Ethel poured coffee. Shelby sat at the head of the table with Roger at his left. Shelby fleetingly wondered if any of the six masters had seen *The Matrix* and noticed that Roger resembled Agent Smith.

"This is my administrative assistant, Joe LeFors," Shelby said, gesturing toward Roger.

"Not to be confused with the Joe LeFors who chased Butch Cassidy and the Sundance Kid," Joe LeFors said.

Shelby kicked Roger's leg under the table.

The six masters of the universe nodded slightly, as though grudgingly conceding that there could be views other than their own, and there were no smiles. An administrative assistant was too far down the food chain for more than a nod. Like Ethel with the coffee, necessary accoutrements. But there was an air about the six masters of the universe, like an unseen gas slowly enveloping a room. A growing, sluggish realization. Not used to being outranked, certainly not used to being overshadowed, their curiosity about Shelby finally swamped their diffidence and corporate veneers, and their faces,

Shelby thought, began to soften tentatively, and the meager makings of smiles teased playfully in the corners of their mouths.

The problem, though, was that none of them quite knew who should speak first because as individual masters at the gilded helms of their own empires, they always spoke first and always had the last word. But here, away from their palaces and attendant courtiers, in another's empire, in the presence of the man who had saved the world—a common man at that, from Boise, Idaho—they chafed at being subordinate, and now, demoted to six magnificent viceroys of equal rank, none could decide whose voice went first or commanded the most weight.

It was quite a pickle.

Shelby, eager to get the meeting in his wake on the way to a scotch and treating Roger at Lou Malnati's, sensed that something was needed, an icebreaker—a verbal laxative—to break the logjam. He glanced at Roger, who arched his eyebrows slightly. Then Shelby leaned forward and clasped his hands on the table, as he had seen Bern do.

"Thingamabobs, thingamajigs, and doohickeys," Shelby said lightheartedly, adding a big, confident grin, and then easing back in his chair.

The words were like a sudden and cooling fine mist countering humidity to the six masters of the universe, who visibly relaxed. A collective exhaling. The tentative smiles teasing from the corners of their mouths threatened to swamp the corners and become actual smiles. Several masters had twinkles in their eyes. Ethel circled the table, refreshing their coffees.

Ms. Klaggenthorpe, the Texan heir to oodles of Texas oil and scads of Texas precious metals, had gleams in her eyes and she spoke up:

"Forgive our silence, Mr. Goddard. We—"

"Shelby. Just call me Shelby, Ms. Klaggenthorpe."

"Shelby," Ms. Klaggenthorpe said warmly, though not offering Clara instead of Ms. Klaggenthorpe. "I think we all may have underestimated the gravity of meeting you."

"Yes," Mr. Lubeler said, nodding.

"Exactly," Ms. Hacker said, blinking her eyes.

"Indeed," Mr. Kiggenhooper agreed, fidgeting with his hands.

"Well said," Mr. Gildenklack said, adjusting the knot of his tie.

"My sentiments on this exactly," Ms. Thickler said, fingering a button on her blouse.

The dam had burst, the pressure relieved.

"Excuse me," Joe LeFors said, getting up. "I have duties."

"Yes—I'm sure you do," Shelby said as Joe left the room. "Be sure to attend to those duties—as we discussed, Joe."

"Cosmonaut," Joe said quietly as he closed the door.

"Your man seems a—a spirited sort," Mr. Gildenklack said.

"He's a former accountant," Shelby said. "From Memphis."

"With a mind of his own," Ms. Hacker said, as though that might be an oddity.

"But he does good work," Shelby said. "Very devoted."

"But did he just say cosmonaut?" Ms. Klaggenthorpe said.

"I thought I heard that, too," Mr. Kiggenhooper said.

"Yes," Shelby said. "It's just something we use to signal a specific—duty. A task needing attention."

"Code names for duties?" Ms. Klaggenthorpe said.

Shelby smiled. "It spices up things around here."

"Did Mr. Brindlestickler develop that approach?" Mr. Gildenklack said.

"No—no, that's my own contribution," Shelby said. "I thought that one up all by myself."

"Fascinating," Ms. Thickler said. "And what effect does it have on productivity?"

"On productivity?" Shelby said. "Well, it increases productivity. Massively. You can't imagine."

"Really," Ms. Klaggenthorpe said. "How massively?"

Shelby tapped his fingers on the table for a moment and looked into Ms. Klaggenthorpe's expectant face.

"Oh, in the usual ways," Shelby said. "It massively increases in the usual ways—the *expected* ways."

"And what are those?" Mr. Kiggenhooper said.

"The ones we see," Shelby said. "The ones we *experience*."

"I see," Ms. Hacker said. "Fascinating."

"Is this something new?" Ms. Klaggenthorpe said.

"No," Shelby said, easing back in his chair. "It's rather old, really—but we pumped new life into it, so to speak—gave it new meaning. Visions, synergies, and realignments, if you get my drift."

"Ah," the six masters of the universe uttered collectively, nodding to each other approvingly.

"Now you're talking," Mr. Kiggenhooper said.

"I'm liking the sound of it," Mr. Lubeler said emphatically.

"And is this new approach something to be introduced system wide by Gobitek?" Ms. Klaggenthorpe said. "Something for us all?"

"Yes!" Shelby said too loudly and pointing at her. "That's what I've been meaning to say. Exactly. It's the new, uh, Gobitek—thingie."

"Amazing," Ms. Klagenthorpe said.

"A game changer," Mr. Lubeler said.

"This may be the new new," Ms. Thickler said.

"Who knew?" Mr. Lubeler said.

"An entirely new way of seeing things," Mr. Gildenklack said.

"Perhaps the tip of a new iceberg," Ms. Hackler said.

"A new paradigm," Mr. Higgenhooper said.

"Maybe the ultimate paradigm," Ms. Hackler said.

"How was it formulated?" Ms. Klaggenthorpe said.

"Formulated?" Shelby said. "Well, the usual way."

"What way is that," Ms. Thickler said.

"The Gobitek way, of course," Shelby said. "With visions, synergies and realignments."

Ms. Klaggenthorpe nodded attentively.

"And what is the delivery system for all this?" she said.

"Indeed," Mr. Lubeler said. "We must know."

"Delivery system?" Shelby said. He looked around the table into the six expectant faces of the masters of the universe.

"Yes, Shelby," Mr. Lubeler said. "How do we get in on the ground floor of this?"

"How does this make us the sharp end of the spear?" Mr. Gildenklack said.

Shelby rubbed his lip absently for a moment.

"Thingamabobs, thingamajigs, and doohickeys," Shelby said as though it was as obvious as his face whispering into Lincoln's ear on Mt. Rushmore.

"Ah," the masters collectively cooed.

The six masters of the universe filed quietly out of the room toward the elevator. An electric glow seemed to emanate off them. The wheels turned and the gears interlocked in their brains.

Mr. Lubeler turned to Shelby. The other five masters clutched their coats and looked on eagerly. Anticipation dripped. Shelby suddenly had to pee.

"The thing that just transpired in that room," Mr. Lubeler said, his voice trailing off as he seemed to momentarily compose himself. "What just happened in there, I have to say, was—illuminating!"

"Revolutionary, I think," Ms. Klaggenthorpe said. "Certainly evolutionary."

All the masters nodded their heads.

Relieved, Shelby exhaled as quietly as he could. But soon he would really have to pee.

"And what do I tell Mr. Brindlestickler?" Shelby said.

"Why, tell him we're on board, of course," Mr. Lubeler said. "All of us."

It took Shelby a few seconds to get the words out of his mouth, as though it was filled with pebbles, but finally he said, "We are Gobitek!"

Shelby shook each master's hand. The need to pee had put a grimace on his face.

In a far corner of the hallway, just out of earshot, Ethel quietly said to Joe LeFors, "We are Ketibog."

"Cosmonaut," Joe said.

The six masters of the universe left and Shelby sprinted to the men's room.

Shelby and Ethel sagged into his ugly red paisley sofa. Shelby unbuttoned his jacket and exhaled loudly. He loosened his tie and then just slipped it off altogether and tossed it on the coffee table. Roger eased into The Miromack and played with the settings. Shelby sighed and glanced at Ethel, who rolled her eyes. Shelby was ready for scotch at the Billy Goat.

"We pulled it off," Shelby said. "But it was touch and go there for a while."

"That was a tough-looking bunch," Ethel said. "At first, they all looked constipated."

"Love this chair," Roger said. "I have to get one of these."

"Take it," Shelby said. "I don't spend that much time in it. I was thinking of rolling it over to the Billy Goat."

"It's better if I order one," Roger said. "Not that this one isn't dandy, kid. And I appreciate the offer."

"But an agency form comes into play?" Shelby said.

"Sure as shit, Shel. It's all about the lesser of two evils. Accepting a gift from outside the agency is permissible if an agent is willing to slog through 1050D-12A, which is worse than closing on a house. But if I order a chair, it's plain old uncomplicated 1050D-12, which is as easy as falling off a dock."

"Cosmonaut," Shelby said.

"Ultra cosmonaut, kid."

"Why do you guys say cosmonaut?" Ethel said.

"I don't know. Why do we do it, Roger?"

"Because we can."

"There you go," Shelby said.

"Are you really a secret agent?" Ethel said.

"He's an accountant," Shelby said.

"From Memphis," Roger said.

"And who is Joe LeFors?" Ethel said.

"The sheriff who chased Butch Cassidy and The Sundance Kid," Shelby said.

"Okay," Ethel said skeptically. "But you *are* a secret agent, right?"

"Well, it doesn't seem to be a secret anymore. Just think of me as a government employee who happened to be in the neighborhood."

"And so you're *not* an accountant?"

"And I'm not from Memphis, Ethel. But I do like Elvis."

"Clear as a Gobitek bell," Ethel said. "I need a drink."

"We are Gobitek—and Ketibog!" Shelby said abruptly.

"We are Gobitek—and Ketibog!" Ethel said.

"Love this chair," Roger said as he monkeyed some more with the settings.

After a drink with Ethel at the Billy Goat, Shelby and Roger went for deep dish pizza at Lou Malnati's on North Wells.

"An awesome pie," Roger said through a mouthful of it. "New York's good, but I like this stuff better."

"This town's chock full of great pizza joints," Shelby said. "You can't swing a dead cat without hitting deep-dish pizza."

"And this town is apparently knee deep in bullshit, kid. At least today."

"Is that why you left the conference room?"

"Absolutely—before form 1050D-147 kicked in, Shel."

"Which one is that?"

"That's the so-much-bullshit-a-guy-needs-waders, form, kid."

"You're fucking with me."

"I am. But I guess I didn't want to witness you wrestling in so much muck with so many assholes. And I didn't want to know the particulars—though, it sounded like particulars are in short supply in these little soirees."

"You should have heard the shit fly after you left. The vaguer things are, the more they seem to like it. But otherwise, you approve?"

"I don't *disapprove*, Shel. Not up to me. It's your gig."

"We do good, Roger."

"I don't doubt it, Shel."

"And the dating service is humming along, too." Shelby said. "It's making money, which goes into Ketibog."

"But just watch out for that Brindlestickler dude, Shel. Guys like that are so rich they don't have to be forgiving. Or moral. And they don't just rent lawyers, they own them. Politicians, too."

Shelby finished his pizza.

"So, I passed the interview, Roger? I'm good to go for another six months?"

"Oh, sure, kid. Certified and official. Actually, we could have just done it by phone."

"Really? Why didn't we?"

"I wanted some deep-dish pizza."

"Cosmonaut," Shelby said.

A few days after Roger left, the expected note arrived from Bern in Hong Kong:

> Shelby—amazing, my friend! What a coup! Gobitek has ascended in one leap as it has on no other day. Keep up that Shelby Magic. More to come, more to experience. Greater heights to ascend to. We are Gobitek!
> —Bern

A check for $5 million arrived and Shelby stared at the amount in disbelief for a few seconds and then gave it to Ethel as they had a drink at the Billy Goat. Ethel held the check up and stared at it while sipping from her drink. Then she dropped it onto the bar like it was just a napkin.

"We are Ketibog," Shelby said quietly, but pleased for the foundation.

"Damned if we aren't," Ethel said. "Wow! I've never held a check like this before."

"And more to come, Ethel."

"And greater heights to, uh, do, and to—what does Mr. Brindlestickler always call it?"

"To ascend. He's big on ascension. Maybe he thinks he's Jesus. Money changes people."

"Has it changed you?"

Shelby looked at her and shrugged.

"Probably. But I don't think I'm an asshole."

She nodded.

"Am I, Ethel?"

"No way, Shel. You help people. You could just keep the money and live like a king, but you don't."

He shrugged again.

"Maybe some folks would think that makes me stupid."

"They'd be the stupid ones, Shel." She sipped her rusty nail. "So, Roger's gone back to being James Bond?"

"He prefers Jason Bourne."

"Bourne's good, have to admit. Matt Damon's a cutie—a hottie cutie."

"To Matt Damon," Shelby said and they clinked their glasses together.

They had another drink and then another. Finally Ethel set off to take the "L" home to Oak Park, but she was a bit tipsy and walking a straight line was a challenge. Shelby poured her into a cab and gave the driver plenty of cash. He judged himself still nimble on his pins and donned his Bears cap and watched the cab's tail-lights until they disappeared down Michigan Avenue into traffic. Then he pulled up the lapels of his new wool coat and walked back to The Drake through throngs of strangers. Thick snowflakes fluttered silently onto the sidewalk and frosted his shoulders.

Part Three

"Before you can *save* the world, you have to *live* in the world."
—SHELBY ALBERT GODDARD

WE ARE GOBIBOG!

Gobitek clients continued to arrive regally and depart humbly, suitably dazzled by Shelby's presence and spouting the appropriate utter and surreal nonsense before ponying up serious cash to Gobitek. More money poured from Gobitek into Ketibog. It was like running a hose and siphoning cash from Bank A to Bank B.

Shelby and Ethel had taken to calling it Gobibog.

The online dating service continued to do very well, too. Ethel and her sisters had it cruising in high gear and were attracting subscribers from all over the country and not just local horny men in the medical fields. The next step was to make it global. Ethel and Shelby joked over drinks at the Billy Goat that the dating service was "ascending." But Shelby felt he no longer *personally* ascended. There was a vague but persistent feeling of having leveled off. Perhaps even a feeling of slowly losing altitude. Deep-dish pizza still held its allure, but fleecing Gobitek and its clients no longer was exciting or daring and had become routine. Business as usual. Like Bern perpetuating utter nonsense, and Gobitek clients eagerly abandoning reality to spoon it up, Shelby had become equally as proficient at refereeing the corporate mud-wrestling match.

Shelby was mortified to realize he was actually earning his Gobitek pay, which was actually Ketibog pay, but that distinction didn't entirely salve the wound. It was as if Gobitek and Ketibog were merging.

We Are Gobibog!

But something had to give.

Once again, it was quite a pickle he found himself in—a whole barrel of pickles.

Shelby pondered it one day as he walked along Michigan Avenue, glancing in store windows, but not really focused on what he saw. His eyes performed their functions, but neglected to get the images to the brain to be converted into anything. The snow had let up and it was not terribly cold, though a winter storm was brewing to the west and would arrive soon enough and that was always a sort of unifying thought in a city like Chicago. As usual he wore his Bears cap and warm wool coat and sunglasses for some privacy and anonymity. No one seemed to recognize him. Or perhaps no one cared anymore about Shelby Albert Goddard, who had once saved the world.

He didn't regret the lack of attention. He got way more of that than he ever wanted during the corporate mud-wrestling with Gobitek converts. Perhaps he was now invisible on the streets, or suffered the delusion of invisibility, like T.E. Lawrence on the streets of Deraa. He had watched *Lawrence of Arabia* one late night at The Drake. Or, if not invisible, he was now sufficiently out of focus, and thus sufficiently anonymous, the way individual members of a crowd on a street appear to be when no one is looking closely because they have no overriding reason to look closely.

But he was no Lawrence, had no desire to be even remotely equated with Lawrence, even though it was a dandy film and he could not imagine anyone but Peter O'Toole as Lawrence. And maybe what Lawrence meant by invisible, Shelby thought, was that Lawrence had finally blended in and wasn't actually invisible in a way requiring the disappearance or masking of molecules, but in a way requiring the absence of suspicion. The task, then, had never really been about how he looked but how others *thought* he looked—or didn't look at all. Maybe all Lawrence had meant, and fairly innocently so, was that he had achieved a lack of focus in the eyes of everyone on Deraa's streets, which was sort of the same thing as invisible and pretty much had the same desired results—except he was dead wrong about that, of course, and got his ass pounded. But, for Lawrence, was it all about perception as truth? Something to run by Roger next time. He also wondered whether Lawrence had actually said he was invisible or it was just a movie manufacturing its own history. Working with Bern had taught him that reality could be manufactured. Was this the extending of truth that Roger had mentioned?

All the Lawrence crap made his head hurt and he stopped at the Billy Goat for a snort of scotch to wash the thoughts away. But he didn't feel like drinking after one Shelby Saved the World on the Rocks scotch on the rocks. The scotch invigorated him and that was enough and he went out and stood on the Michigan Avenue Bridge to watch people trudge by, some of them monitoring the sky occasionally for the storm expected from the west.

What was the truth about all this, he wondered as an army of people marched by. Why did humanity continue to trek by as solitary figures, and some in pairs, and some in groups, and even in legions along a city street? What was the purpose? *Was* there an actual purpose? Where was Lawrence going on the streets of Deraa? Shelby couldn't remember enough about that part of the film. But why do we trek by, he thought. And for centuries. Why is humanity an endless trek, an endless parade? Where did it want to be? What were we marching *toward?* Or were we marching *away* from something? And what should we happily find at the end of our trek? Or better yet, since the end of a trek implied the end of everything, what should we happily discover *during* our trek?

The human race trekking by on Michigan Avenue was good and bad, old and young, tall and short, pretty and ugly, clean and dirty, handsome and grizzled, thin and fat, colorful and drab, stylish and oblivious, rich and poor, and any other economic level between having it all and having almost none of it. There were people with purpose and aimless people, too. All going *somewhere.* Where was Shelby going? Toward truth? What was truth? He thought hard and at first could not articulate it even in fragments in his mind. But he finally suspected that truth might have something to do with the ability to see what was around us as it truly was, warts and all, and not as we wished it to *seem.*

What we see all around us, Shelby knew, could be changed, altered, improved, replaced with concrete effort, but merely claiming a reality didn't make it so—like conservative propaganda claiming that helping the rich actually helped the poor. That was greed and not truth. That was Bern and his Gobitek clients. That was not truth. That was not—sanity.

"Not sanity," Shelby said, and several people looked at him without emotion as they went by.

"We need more sanity," Shelby said, louder.

Two teenage girls strolled by in parkas and ski caps pulled down over their long blond hair and Shelby heard one say, "Yeah—more sanity, dude."

"How much more?" Shelby called.

"All you've got, dude," she said, smiling and waving goodbye.

A growing feeling bloated inside Shelby. It was not yet a realization. But it was the start of *something*. He looked up, at the building housing Gobitek. The building housing Ketibog.

The Gobibog building.

It wasn't sanity.

But it could be.

Something was needed.

Action was necessary.

"More sanity!" he yelled as he stared up at the building. He stared so long that people stopped and cupped hands over eyes to stare with him.

"What are you looking for?" a young man said.

"Sanity, brother," Shelby said.

"Let's go," the man's wife said as she pulled on his arm. "He's drunk."

"Not at all," Shelby said. "I'm not drunk at all."

"Maybe he's crazy," a middle-aged man said from the small crowd that had gathered, and Shelby knew a thing or two about crowds on bridges.

"That's right," an elderly woman said. "Maybe he needs help—maybe he ought to be institutionalized."

The sudden and as yet vague notion of institution dropped into Shelby's gut and rattled around noisily before settling heavily, and he suspected it could not be long ignored.

"It's a free country," a young woman said. "Let him speak."

"What are you preaching, preacher?" a young man said and the crowd laughed.

Shelby smiled. "Sanity. But I'm not preaching, brother."

"Are you crazy?" a middle-aged man said

Shelby shrugged. "No more than you, my friend. No more than any of you—unless you've actually escaped a mental hospital."

The crowd laughed.

"Hey—aren't you Shelby?" a young woman said.

"That's right," a middle-aged man said. "That's Shelby."

"Shelby who?" a young man said.

"*The* Shelby, dickhead," another young man said.

"I saw him on Oprah," a young woman said.

"What was Oprah like?" another young woman said.

"He saved the world," a dozen people of all ages exclaimed, as though members of a choir that practiced every Wednesday night.

"How'd you do it, Shelby?" a young man called out.

"Thingamabobs, thingamajigs, and doohickeys," the Wednesday night choir sang.

The crowd laughed again. Shelby smiled benevolently.

"Can't you tell us how you did it, Shelby?" a young woman said.

"Does that really matter?" Shelby said quietly. "The result would be the same."

"Why'd you do it?" a young man said.

Shelby shrugged, sighed. "Because I could, I guess."

"Are you a god, Shelby?" a teenager said.

"God, no!" Shelby said, and the crowd laughed again.

"What *are* you?" a young man said.

"Just, Shelby. Just—me." He moved his arms by his sides as though they were the fins of a waddling penguin unsure as to which direction was best.

"What's next, Shelby?" a young woman said.

Shelby scanned the crowd and looked into expectant faces. They all had been headed somewhere, were stopped now, momentarily, tenuously, skeptically, in this odd and rare moment of community among strangers, yet he felt most people nonetheless were lost and merely wandering, more like hamsters in wheels, even though they had daily routines and obligations and destinations and even goals. He looked up again, at the Gobibog building, and back into the faces in the crowd. Snow began to fall again, lightly. People were hamsters in wheels and the wheels were provided by masters, oiled by masters, insisted upon by masters. It was an institution. A global institution.

"Are you okay, Shelby?" a young woman said.

"Never better."

"What should we do?" a middle-aged woman said.

"Live," Shelby said. "I mean it, folks—live!"

"What do you mean?" a young woman said. "How?"

"Do something unexpected. Take a chance. Do something differently. Embrace sanity."

"Embrace sanity?" a young man said.

"Yes—what do you mean, embrace sanity?" a young woman said.

Shelby wiped snowflakes from his cheeks. Spurts of breath ejaculated from their mouths. He could see he had them, had the crowd focused on him and nothing else.

"Insist on truth," he said. "Insist on sanity—on truth. Not the pretend truth, not the corporate truth, and not the truth that politicians mangle for their own purposes."

"How?" a young man said.

"Ask questions," Shelby said. "And insist on answers—insist on specific answers. Challenge what corporations say. Challenge what politicians say."

"Then what?" a middle-aged woman said.

"Talk to each other," Shelby said. "Talk to strangers. And turn off Fox News. Turn off TV altogether. Read newspapers."

"What should we say?" a middle-aged woman said.

Shelby took a deep breath, focused.

"Anything—at first. You'll just know what to say as you go—talk about what really matters."

"What really matters?" an elderly woman said.

"Truth matters," Shelby said after a pause. "Shut off your TVs and talk to each other. Go out into the streets as often as you can and talk to people, to strangers. And when politicians speak, show up and demand the truth!"

"Damn right," several people said.

"Don't accept vague promises," Shelby said.

"We can do it," a young woman said.

"You can!" Shelby yelled. "And you must! It's all riding on you."

"What's riding on us?" a young man said.

"Is this a revolution?" a young woman said.

"I hope so," Shelby said, smiling. "The Michigan Avenue Bridge Revolution. How does that sound?"

"Awesome," several people yelled.

"But what are we revolting against?" a middle-aged man said.

"Being lied to," Shelby said. "That's as good a place to start as any."

"For sure," the middle-aged man said. "And long overdue."

"Who's lying to us?" another middle-aged man said.

Shelby pointed up.

"The people who own these buildings," he said. "And the people that own the people who own these buildings."

"What are *you* going to do, Shelby?" a young woman said.

The whole crowd stared at him, their eyes boring in, and it warmed him, thawed him. The fog lifted inside Shelby. Clarity settled in. He would do something. Something awesome. He felt something coming, something on the verge of revealing itself, something his gut had worked over and was now ready to launch to his brain and out his mouth as words—ideas.

"I'm going to create something," Shelby said. "Something that needs to be created. That must be created."

"What are you going to create, Shelby?" a young man said.

Shelby looked at the young man, then into the faces of many in the crowd. He waited for words to come, felt sure they would. The pause was long and awkward, snow falling, people stomping feet to keep warm.

"I'm going to create sanity," Shelby said. "I'm going to create a place to make it."

"You're going to *make* sanity?" a middle-aged man said.

"No—not make it," Shelby said, emboldened. "But I'll encourage it. Insist on it—demand it!"

People in the crowd arched eyebrows and glanced nervously at each other. But some smiled and nodded approval.

"What's all this going to be called, Shelby?" a young man said.

Shelby glanced up at the Gobibog building.

"I'll call it," he said, his voice trailing off for a moment. "I'll call it—The Institute."

"Awesome," a teen-aged girl said.

"*Most* awesome," a teen-aged boy said.

"Cool," a young man said. "But not very snazzy."

"You're right," Shelby said, nodding. "It needs more. It needs a name that stands out, that reaches out and grabs—something snazzy. I'll call it, The Most Awesome Institute. The Most Awesome Institute—of Truth."

"What happened to sanity?" a young woman said.

"Truth sounds better."

The crowd cheered.

Shelby wasn't sure what else to say.

The crowd fell apart.

Shelby still couldn't think of anything to add.

The crowd drifted away.

But Shelby felt energized all the way back to The Drake.

Shelby barely slept the night of the Michigan Avenue Bridge Revolution. His brain declined to stop working, the wheels turning, gears meshing, except for an hour or two here and there in the night. The next morning he showered early, skipped breakfast at The Drake, and hurried to the Gobibog building and revealed to Ethel his plans for the Most Awesome Institute of Truth, which he had to concede was as yet mostly awesome concept instead of awesome reality.

"What about Gobibog?" Ethel said.

"Kaput," Shelby said. "Finito. We're done here—don't you think?"

She nodded tentatively.

"I suppose we are, Shel," she said, handing him a cup of coffee. "I guess we had a good run. And we didn't get arrested."

"There's that," he said. "And you still have the dating service, Ethel. And that last Gobitek check goes to you and the Mermelstein clan."

"Oh my God, Shel—that's too much. Really."

"Nonsense. You and your sisters earned it."

"But, it's—all the money in the world. Even Bern would agree."

"Not even close," Shelby said, smiling.

"But it is, Shel. It's—overwhelming. Are you really sure?"

"I insist."

Ethel hugged him. She smelled like lemons.

"Find a date for every single person in the world, Ethel. That's a worthy cause. And start that line of shoes Imelda keeps talking about. Just do it. But always treat customers like people—treat them as the reasons you made it. Never take people for granted."

"We will, Shel. I promise. You know us."

"I do. I know you'll do it right."

They hugged again.

"When do you leave?" she said, wiping tears from her cheeks.

He sipped his coffee.

"Right away, I guess. Today. This afternoon, maybe. There's nothing to stop me."

"Where will you go? Where will this institute be?"

"I thought about that all last night. I barely slept. I'm going to do it in Arkansas—in Parsons Grove."

"Why there?"

"Because nothing much *is* there. It's perfect."

"What do I tell Mr. Brindlestickler?"

"Nothing, Ethel. Nothing at all."

"We just disappear?"

Shelby gestured toward the conference room.

"We were never part of this, Ethel. It was a means to an end. That's all. A charade, a game. Time to go."

"Well, I knew it couldn't last."

"And we wouldn't have wanted it to," Shelby said. "Let the service know you're quitting and just go home. Take your sisters out and drink some rusty nails. Have some fun. Live."

"You're a good man, Shelby," she said. "And I have always wanted to ask—did you really save the world?"

"That's what they keep telling me. It must be true."

"Do you believe it?"

"I don't *disbelieve* it. It is what it is. And it's old news."

Tears ran down her cheeks and she dabbed at them with a tissue.

"So, this is really it?" she said. "We just leave?"

Shelby nodded, grinned. "We just walk out and follow our paths, Ethel."

"Just like that?"

"Just like that," he said, snapping his fingers. "But, before you go, will you do one last thing for me, Ethel?"

"Of course. Anything."

"Have a new banner made, to hang in the conference room. The biggest you can find."

"Okay, Shel. What do you want it to say?"

Shelby wrote it on a sticky note and handed it to her:

Dear Bern—We Are Gobibog!

Shelby and Ethel hugged one more time on the sidewalk outside the Gobibog building and he put her into a cab for Oak Park. Neither could stem the tide of tears racing along their cheeks. She waved through the cab's back window as it slipped into a sea of cabs. After a moment, he couldn't tell which cab was hers. He stood there a few minutes, just looking at faces going by. Shelby glanced south and then north. But Parsons Grove was south. The institute was south. And so he walked south.

The sun was out and the snow had stopped. Shelby had just the clothes on his back under his new wool coat, and his Bears cap, and that was enough to get started. He walked and smiled often at oncoming people until he reached Union Station and caught a train south to Memphis.

The Most Awesome Institute of Truth

Shelby hired a limo in Memphis—not because he wanted luxury, and certainly not because he wanted to be seen in one, but because he wanted time to think without distractions on the way to Parsons Grove. He persuaded the driver, a young man with a ponytail and tenuous understanding of who Elvis was, to swing by Graceland for a few minutes.

They both got out and examined the guitar-playing figures flanking musical notes embedded in the gates. In a way, though vaguely, Shelby felt like he had some idea of what Elvis's life had been like, and he felt rather sorry for The King. On the way to Parsons Grove, as the limo crossed the Mississippi, he called Roger.

"Merhaba, Shel."

"Merhaba, Roger—but I don't know the language."

"That's Turkish for hello."

"Are you in Turkey?"

"Nope. Home. On the sofa. Wearing pants. But I was in Cyprus just the other day. They speak Turkish and Greek there."

"Was it fun?"

"It was business, kid. But one night we did get into the ouzo pretty good. Don't drink too much ouzo, kid. That's rocket fuel and fire *will* come out your butt. Avoid open flames."

"Duly noted, Roger. Fire and butts don't mix."

"Not unless you like flamethrowers. So, where are you, Shel?"

"Memphis. But crossing the river into Arkansas—any second now."

"Memphis—the home of Joe LeFors," Roger said.

"The one and only," Shelby said. "The famous Memphis accountant. We went by his house."

"Really? And how did you do that?"

"We went by Graceland," Shelby said.

"There you go, kid. That's Joe LeFors's house, for sure. Whose this *we*?"

"The driver. I'm in a limo."

"Headed back to Dogpatch, are you?"

For now, Dogpatch seemed as good a destination as any. He wasn't actually doubting the decision. Parsons Grove had its charms. He liked Chicago very much, but maybe it wasn't the place for someone who wanted a quieter life. It was a place to visit often, but Chicago would always remind him too much of Bern Brindlestickler and Gobitek.

"I guess so, Roger. But I'll miss deep-dish pizza."

"Me, too, Shel. We'll have to meet there again sometime. Are you being chased out of Chicago, or leaving voluntarily?"

"Voluntarily. It was time to go."

"What's with the limo?"

"I need some time to think. I took the train down here and caught up on my sleep."

"How's Ethel, Shel?"

"Rich."

"Good. And what about Gobitek, kid?"

"Been there, done that."

"What's waiting in Dogpatch?"

"I'll know it when I see it."

"Sounds like a lot of bumper sticker philosophy, kid."

"Maybe. I'm taking it a day at a time."

"Slap that one on the limo bumper, too, Shel."

Shelby took a last glance at the muddy brown river. It was quite a sight. They had crossed into Arkansas, into West Memphis, a poor and violent town. Shelby was looking forward to leaving it behind and reaching Parsons Grove.

"How do you feel about sanity, Roger?"

"I'm pretty damn glad to have it. Without it—we're insane. Get my drift?"

"How many people do you suppose really have it?"

"All the ones who know they do, kid. The ones who don't know— they don't have it."

"Is sanity the same as truth?"

"Reality is truth," Roger said. "And truth is reality. Take your pick. Sanity is knowing you have reality. Something like that."

"Are you sure?"

"Of course not, kid. But it sounds good."

"So, as long as truth *sounds* good, it *is* good?"

"Goes without saying, Shel. But why the twenty questions?"

"Nothing specific. I'm just—grabbing at perspective, I suppose."

Shelby knew that he was practically grabbing at straws to help understand where he was going, and why, and what he hoped he would get from it all. But doubt could become a good motivator. It could keep him in the hunt for perspective.

"Ah, good old perspective, Shel. With perspective, we don't need to pursue truth."

"How can there be perspective without truth?"

"I'm not saying you don't *need* truth, kid. I'm saying if you have perspective, truth is a given. Perspective has to be based on something existing. Perspective means you have a product to speculate *on*."

"Truth is like a product, Roger?"

"Of course. Truth has to be sold, or it's not truth at all."

"What is it if it's not sold?"

"Desire."

"I see," Shelby said. "And like truth, can perspective be improved on?"

"Oh, yeah, Shel. For sure. You see, once you know you've got the right truth, perspective is just the process of deciding how you feel about it."

"Does truth change, depending on how we feel about it?"

"Exactly. If you don't feel good about the truth—"

"Change it?"

"You're quick, kid. But then, you saved the world."

"That's the rumor."

"A rumor is just a stage before truth, kid."

"I'll file that one away, Roger. For a rainy day."

"Feel free to have it made into a bumper sticker, too," Roger said. "Now that we have all that out of the way, Shel—you're sure there's no warrant out for you on that Gobitek nonsense? No mess for me to mediate? No need for a presidential pardon?"

"Reasonably sure, Roger. I think that's pretty much run its course."

"Cosmonaut, kid. Have fun in Dogpatch—and stay off that damn bridge."

"Maybe I should just buy that bridge, Roger."

"You buy that bridge, kid, and I'll come down there and sit on top of it with you."

"And drink Dixie beer?"

"God no—that's foul stuff. But, maybe some ouzo, kid. We'll sit on top, drink ouzo, and have fire shoot out our butts."

"But avoid open flames."

"You're sharp today, kid. Cosmonaut sharp."

"I could maybe go into orbit, Roger."

Shelby bought a roomy A-frame house with a hot tub and lots of skylights on a gentle rise overlooking the river. A winding lane guarded by tall, thick pines led up to the house. Over the front door a simple, hand-carved wooden sign was erected: The Most Awesome Institute of Truth. He had Truth! painted in red on his mailbox down at the end of the lane. It was only 3.2 miles into Parsons Grove across the Porter Newhouse Bridge. This would be his Fortress of Solitude, except that he hoped he didn't end up being solitary.

It had turned cold, but no snow had fallen, and at night sometimes wind whistled through the pines as Shelby enjoyed a fire in the massive stone fireplace. It was definitely winter but felt more like a late fall compared to winter in Chicago. Often Shelby wandered down to the river in his warm wool coat and Bears cap and enjoyed the sound of the rapids and water cascading over falls. He saw circling hawks and river otters and one day a shy red fox slipped out of the woods and drank from the river. A large yellow cat wandered into his yard one day, looking lost but in good shape, and Shelby fed it tuna from a can and then opened a can for himself. The cat settled into a nap on his sofa overlooking the deck and river and showed no signs of leaving, which was fine with Shelby, who named it Joe LeFors.

On mornings when Shelby chopped wood for the fireplace, the cat sat on a tree stump and watched him swing the axe and the cat would monitor the flights of chips and shavings from each axe strike. Then they would breakfast together, the cat picking at bacon and toast on the edge of Shelby's plate. Shelby was not ready yet for people, but also not trying to be a hermit, felt quite gregarious, actually, and the cat was good company until it was time for wider society. Sometimes wind whistled eerily up and down the chimney and the cat's ears would pick up at the sound and Shelby would reassure it. At bedtime, the cat would eagerly leap onto the bed and curl up at his feet with its bushy tail flicking lazily.

Shelby decided to learn all there was to learn about the truth which, truthfully, seemed like an overwhelming task and so he opted to find some sort of a Cliff's Notes version of the truth and learn as much as was truthful. But the internet wasn't very truthful because it was an endless digital parade of what different groups with warring agendas wanted people to believe was true, and mostly it was about politics and religion. On the internet, truth was what people emotionally said it was, and if someone didn't like another group's truth, they offered counter truth, or claimed the first group's truth wasn't truth at all, or that their—the second group's truth—was better truth than the first group's. Or, they merely posted insults. Homophobia was often part of the insults.

Conservatives, he noticed, were especially fond of insults—and homophobia—and not fond of facts in the pursuit of truth, and preferred to question a rival group's integrity or sanity or faith, and even its patriotism—and definitely its sexual persuasion—if the other group would not allow itself to be force-fed conservative truth with no recourse to analyze said conservative truth. Conservative truth, he learned, seemed to revolve around never questioning the 227-year-old Constitution, which was written at a time when slavery was okay and flintlock muskets were high-tech. Conservative truth especially depended on blindly believing anything claimed by Rush Limbaugh and Fox News, and virtually anything uttered by anyone with a divinity degree, especially if it was aimed at gay people and Muslims, or the first black president, who was a Muslim socialist who no doubt yearned to also be a French communist.

Shelby noted that liberals could be as snarky as conservatives, but seemed much more comfortable basing truth on verifiable facts rather than making truth conform to a rigid ideology, which conservatives clung to. Instead, Shelby read Breakfast of Champions by Kurt Vonnegut and laughed out loud a lot and afterwards felt he understood truth better than anything he saw on the internet, though not by so much, and then he fell into a deep sleep and woke refreshed with the cat sitting on his stomach.

Oceanna Cooper got wind that Shelby was back and where he lived. She showed up one day and stood outside his house in a blue parka and a white knit hat pulled down over her ears and hollered down to him and the cat as they sat by the river.

"It's too cold to sit down there, you doofus," she said as he and the cat eased up the gentle slope to her. "And who is *this* little monkey?"

She kneeled down and stroked the cat behind the ears and it sprawled at her feet.

"That's Joe LeFors," Shelby said.

"Another accountant from Memphis," she said. "How nice. Does he own a helicopter and act like a lunatic?"

Shelby shrugged. "He hasn't mentioned one yet. But maybe he keeps it out in the woods."

"A tiny little cat helicopter?"

"It would be easy to hide, you have to admit."

"Speaking of lunatics," she said, "have you seen the other Joe LeFors lately?"

"In Chicago. A few weeks ago."

"So, that's where you've been."

"Keeping track?"

"Don't flatter yourself," she said. "Thanks for *Catch-22*, by the way. A signed first edition all the way from New York—very cool. But then, you can afford it, so I won't feel guilty."

Shelby was reasonably sure that she rarely felt very guilty about anything she said or did, and he found that comforting—appealing.

"Thought you might like it," he said. "I sent a gift to everybody in the group."

"So I hear," she said. "And I wouldn't want to feel special or anything."

"We couldn't have that—no," he said.

"Unless you *wanted* me to feel special."

"I'll give it some thought."

"*Because,* after all, I hid you when the town went squirrelly."

"Hence, the gift," he said.

"But everybody got a gift."

"Not everyone got a signed first edition *Catch-22*. I sent Viola Atteberry a book about Jesse James and all the banks he robbed."

She rolled her eyes.

"Maybe you can sell that explanation to Joe LeFors."

"Which Joe LeFors?" he said.

"Both."

She looked up into the sky and shaded her eyes with her hands.

"What are you looking for?" he said, looking up.

"That lunatic and his chopper. You sure he isn't about to parachute into town again?"

"I would have heard by now. I'm sure he's pretty busy."

"Busy spinning fairy tales and undermining governments, maybe," she said. "Look—is that a parachute?"

"That's a white cloud. It's not even moving."

"Clouds are always moving," she said. "We just don't notice."

Shelby gazed up at the cloud a moment.

"I just saw it move, but it's not *falling*."

"Maybe it's a stealth cloud, Shel. And Lunatic LeFors is hiding inside it."

"He'd probably like that," he said. "But they'd just use a satellite if they wanted to check on someone. I asked about that once."

She looked up again.

"That didn't stop LeFors from blowing up the town square with his chopper," she said.

"He admitted that that should have been re-considered."

"Maybe there's hope for him after all," she said.

"There's always hope," Shelby said quietly. "Let's hope for hope."

"I hope you're right," she said, getting into the spirit of it.

They walked to the front porch and Oceanna spied the sign over the door. She stared at it, hands on her hips.

"Okay—I know there has to be a really good story behind *that*, Mr. Shelby," she said with a smirk.

Shelby paused, stared at the sign, and realized he really wasn't quite prepared to explain it to anyone, but that now was as good a time as any.

"How does it sound?" he said.

"Well, don't go by me, Shel. But it does seem sort of pretentious. What are you going for here?"

"The truth."

"The truth about what?"

"The truth about—life, I guess. The universe. Planet Earth. Living and dying. Our reason for being and all that. I'm making the house an institute of truth *and* my home."

"Most folks around here are content with a Baby Jesus scene on the lawn, Shel. But you do still see some lawn jockeys."

The next day, Shelby took the sign down.

A literary agent in New York, Sara Tonin, contacted Shelby to see if he wanted to tell his life story, which she was certain would be a mega-bestseller and thrilling and make more money than a forklift could lift. He told her it had been a fairly dull life so far, except for the one day, of course, when he saved the world, though his time with Gobitek in Chicago had been pretty lively, he had to admit, which he definitely did *not* admit to Sara Tonin on the phone.

"It's been a pretty dull life so far," he told her. "Except for the one day, of course."

"But that one day is everything," she said.

"And that's why you called? Is that enough for a book—one day? How did you get my number?"

"I got it from Oprah's people," she said. "They owed me a favor. And yes, saving the world is a book, Shelby."

"I'd thought of writing about enlightenment, but lately I'm more focused on truth," he said. "Say—don't writers usually contact agents instead of the other way around?"

"Oh, sure," she said. "Writers contact us all the time. They never stop contacting us."

"That's good, right?"

"It's awful," she said. "As soon as we say no to one, a dozen more descend on us like a flock of crows. Or swarms of locusts. I can't decide which I prefer. But none of them have saved the world."

"So you don't listen to what they have to say?"

"It's not that we don't listen, Shelby. But we really don't have *time* to listen."

"So, you don't actually know what they have to offer and you reject them anyway?"

"Oh, sure—we reject them all the time. We reject them left and right. We reject them as soon as we open an email from them, or shortly after, because we really don't have time to listen. We challenge ourselves to see how quickly we can reject them—to save time."

"Like that TV show," he said. "*Name that Tune*."

"I think I've heard of it," she said. "My memory's slow on that one."

"They try to see how fast they can name a song. They see if they can name it by hearing just three or four notes at most. Sometimes just one note. Maybe two."

"Exactly, Shel. We're sort of like that show, except we're not a show, of course, Shel—may I call you Shel?"

"You just did. But do you ever actually listen to writers before rejecting them? You know, to know what their book would be about?"

"That would take time—actually listening to them, Shelby. It's better to end the relationship before it gets started. A clean break before entanglement is kind to all parties."

"But how do you know whether a writer might have something, if you don't find out?"

"We just know, Shel. Call it a sixth sense. Or a crap detector."

"A crap detector?"

"Sure. Supposedly Hemingway said writers need crap detectors. Well, agents need them, too, and have them if they're any good at all."

"So they can reject writers."

"Exactly," she said. "And to save time. We glance at the email query, or the letter, and we just know. And the sooner we can go to the next email query, or next letter, and *feel* it, we can say no."

"Is it bad to say yes?" Shelby said.

"It's risky to say yes."

"And so the emails, or letters, don't actually get read?" Shelby said.

"Often they don't, I admit."

"Really?"

"Actually—never," she said. "I no longer write back that I read their work and considered it, because I probably didn't actually read any of their work, just a few words in their pitch. But certainly we *glance* at it—the pitch. See, reading the whole thing takes time. Reading chapters takes time. We go by *feel*. If we don't *feel* we might have a winner, we have to move on—to save time."

"Even though it might be a really good book?"

"We can't get bogged down in what *might* be good," she said.

"And so, after glancing at the query, you just thank them and reject them?"

"We certainly do thank them for taking the time to query us. That's good manners."

"Even though you don't take the time to read the entire query, or their actual work, right?"

"Time is money, Shel, and only money can create time."

"Don't you want to discover good new writers?" he said.

"New can be disconcerting, Shel. Change upsets people. It's really easier if the same writers get the ink."

"But doesn't that create—sameness?"

"Don't sell sameness short, Shel. People tend to like sameness, crave sameness, are comforted by sameness. You go to Arby's and maybe there's a new sandwich from time to time. But mostly, it's the same old trusted and proven lineup. That's comforting—familiar."

"But if the writer is someone famous—like me," he said, "you'd actually read the pitch and their work?"

"Oh, sure—of course we would, Shel. We would definitely read what you sent. And if a famous writer sent us something, of course we'd read it."

"But, don't famous writers start off as not famous writers?" he said. "If you don't read the work of not-famous writers, how can they become famous writers?"

"Like I said, we go by *feel,* Shel."

"Then, why not issue notice that no writer should send a pitch?"

"That would make us seem unapproachable."

"We wouldn't want that," he said.

"It wouldn't be polite," she said. "After all, we're all about people. And dreams."

"No doubt," Shelby said.

Shelby agreed to let Sara send him a contract, but he only glanced at it, didn't actually read it—to save time—and sent an email to her thanking her for the query, but expressing sorrow that he could not sign it because it really didn't *feel* right.

Time is money, and only money can create time.

A few days after declining the book deal, Shelby was invited to visit the Willow Oaks Country Club over in Shady Glen. Presumably, he supposed, to bask in the glow of self-righteous exclusivity. There weren't any willows or oaks at Willow Oaks that Shelby could see, mostly just short, lonely-looking bony trees that had been trucked in from a nursery and planted randomly. Josiah Grizzard, a charter member of the country club, gave Shelby a tour of the grounds, which consisted of short, lonely-looking bony trees planted randomly, and so the tour only took a few minutes.

Josiah, fiftyish, had a thin leathery face baked from too much time in the sun. He wore white golf shoes, a crisp white polo shirt under his jacket, and khaki pants with razor-sharp creases.

"As you can see," Josiah said, "we're pretty proud of what we've created here."

Shelby looked around at the short, lonely-looking bony trees planted randomly.

"I can really see that," Shelby said. "It jumps out at you. It's practically an oasis."

"Indeed, indeed," Josiah said. "A good way to think of it. We certainly see it that way, too. And it's a refuge for us."

"From what?"

Josiah frowned.

"Well, from the rigors of life, I suppose, Shelby."

"What rigors are those? Just so I don't get confused."

Josiah pursed his lips and sniffed.

"Well, I suppose we see it as a refuge from things we can't control."

"Such as?"

"Well, for instance—for instance, from events we find hard to understand."

"Like saving the world?" Shelby said.

"Oh, no, my boy. That one we understand. We embrace that one. We celebrate that event. That one's clear as a bell."

"Really?" Shelby said. "What do you understand about it?"

"Why, thingamabobs, thingamajigs, and doohickeys, of course."

Shelby noted that Josiah appeared to be sober and said it with a straight face.

"You understand those things?"

"Well, Shelby—it's not really necessary that we actually understand what they are, or what you did with them. That could be—counterproductive. It's only necessary that we believe in them as an explanation."

"We should believe, but not question?"

"If we question it, we could erode the truth in it, my boy. Truth is the explanation, and so the explanation is truth."

Josiah looked quite pleased with what he'd said.

"I see," Shelby said, not seeing at all. "And what are these other events—the ones you can't control?"

Josiah lowered his voice conspiratorially, glanced around quickly. Only a groundskeeper was around, and he was yards away examining the branches of a short, lonely-looking bony tree planted randomly.

"You see, my boy, there are things in life that require refuge. Many things. A deluge of things—hence, the need for refuge."

"What things?" Shelby said, lowering his voice, too.

Josiah glanced over at the groundskeeper, who had moved on to another short, lonely-looking bony tree planted randomly.

"There are winners and losers, in life, Shelby. It's just how the universe works. I'm sure you have come to see that."

"Like in a football game?"

"Exactly. Like a football game. And to the winner go the spoils. That's natural. That's inevitable. That's—American. It's—uniquely American."

Shelby looked around, at several short, lonely-looking bony trees planted randomly.

"Is Willow Oaks the spoils?"

"Yes," Josiah said excitedly, gesturing toward the nearest short, lonely-looking bony tree planted randomly. "You're seeing it, Shelby. I felt you would be like-minded."

Shelby nodded.

"How do we know who should get the spoils, though?" Shelby said. "How's that determined? How do people get to be members of Willow Oaks?"

Josiah shifted from one foot to the other and glanced at the ground a moment.

"That's income-based, Shelby. It takes a certain income threshold, to be blunt."

"And a fee to join, and annual dues, right?"

Josiah smiled, looked relieved.

"You know the drill—good," he said. "The fee to join—that's sort of good faith money. And it helps to provide some of the club's services, of course."

"Of course," Shelby said, glancing at the nearest short, lonely-looking bony tree planted randomly. "May I call you Joe?"

"Of course, my boy. After all, you saved the world."

"Thanks, Joe. So, I could join Willow Oaks?"

"Of course, my boy, of course. That's why we brought you over."

"Because I saved the world?"

"Doesn't hurt," Joe said, chuckling and tapping Shelby's elbow lightly. "Willow Oaks is still here because of you. And you do meet the income threshold—you're richer than sin now, I hear."

Shelby nodded pleasantly.

"And I'm white."

Joe frowned, then quickly grinned.

"Well, we'd certainly still be grateful if you weren't and had saved the world."

"It would be foolish not to at least be grateful," Shelby said.

"Exactly, my boy. Of course it would. It would have been the end of us all."

"But, the club remains—exclusive."

Joe arched his eyebrows very slightly.

"Don't regard it as exclusive, Shelby."

"How *should* I regard it?"

"Regard it as—orderly."

"How is it orderly?"

"Everyone is most comfortable among their own, Shelby. That's been true since the dawn of time. There's an order to things. It's not natural to force people together. And there's truth in order. Order is truth."

"And you preserve it, here at Willow Oaks—order, that is."

"Exactly. But truth is preserved as well. Willow Oaks is all about order. The order of things is truth. It's just how things are. And how they were meant to be."

"Meant by who?" Shelby said.

"God, of course," Joe said.

"God wants country clubs?"

Joe blinked rapidly several times and coughed.

"God wants righteous people to exert their influence, Shelby. To preserve order. A country club is merely a part of the apparatus of order. A symbol, really— call it a symbol of that order."

"So," Shelby said, pointing at several short, tired-looking bony trees planted randomly, "all this is mostly symbolic?"

"Sure—pretty much," Joe said. "We could look at it that way. Now, would you like to play a round of golf on our championship course?"

"Could I play in reverse?" Shelby said.

"Reverse? I don't understand."

"Instead of starting at the first hole, could I start at the eighteenth and work my way back?"

Joe Grizzard looked awfully perplexed. He wiggled his nose several times and sighed.

"Why would anyone do that, Shelby?"

Shelby shrugged.

"To change the order of things?"

A black limousine rolled ominously up the lane to Shelby's house the day after his visit to the Willow Oaks Country Club. He watched it climb the lane slowly, the cat sitting on the back of a chair by the window and flicking its tail as if to signal danger. A tall, slender man in a white suit and white loafers unpacked himself from the limo and looked around a moment, taking in Shelby's property.

The man had a nice head of short, jet black hair. To Shelby, he seemed faintly Mediterranean or, like Joe Grizzard, maybe just over-tanned. The man stretched his arms and arched his back, likely to get relief from a long limo ride. Then he approached Shelby's front door and rang the bell.

Shelby decided to open the door out of pure curiosity as to who needed a limo to come a knocking.

"Shelby Albert Goddard, as I live and breathe and have hope for the future," the man said, grinning and extending a massive hand.

Shelby took the hand and the man shook Shelby's vigorously, Shelby's hand a captive in the maneuver.

"Well, we already know who *I* am," Shelby said. "Who are you?"

"I'm Witt Boguson," the man said as though it ought to be obvious.

"How's life, Witt Boguson?"

"Dandy as piles of flapjacks swimming in maple syrup, Shelby—can I call you Shelby?"

"Everyone else does—so go ahead. But what are you selling?"

"Well, I'm sure not selling flapjacks, though they're mighty easy to sell."

"Sales must be good," Shelby said, pointing to the black limo.

"Don't mind that," Witt said. "It's merely an object, a tool—a tool of the trade."

"And what trade are we talking about, Witt?"

"Optimism, Shelby. Good, old-fashioned optimism."

"You're selling optimism, Witt?"

"I surely am. And doing quite well at it. The limo sort of reflects success, if you get my drift. You see, I have an institute—the Institute for Optimism, if I may take credit for developing the name."

Witt fumbled for a card from his jacket pocket and gave it to Shelby.

"Sure enough," Shelby said. "It does say Institute for Optimism. And your name's just below it. Witt Boguson."

"Keep that one, Shelby. The limo is full of them."

"Full of it, you say?" Shelby said.

Witt placed his hands on his hips and arched his eyebrows.

"Oh, I know what you're thinking, Shelby. I do know, believe me—you're thinking, what sort of scam is this?"

"You must be clairvoyant, Witt. I was thinking that exact thing, and in those exact words."

Shelby placed *his* hands on his hips and the two of them looked a bit like two teenage boys about to have a scrap.

"Understandable, Shelby. Very understandable. Before I became an optimist, I was definitely a skeptic."

Shelby nodded.

"Seems pretty logical."

"And I'm betting you're an optimist, too, Shelby."

"Well, I'm certainly hopeful some days, Witt. But I've stopped expecting anything from Congress and the Chicago Cubs, just so you know I can still be skeptical."

"And you have a fine sense of humor, Shelby. That's actually one of the key steps toward optimism."

"Imagine that."

"I imagine it every single day, Shelby."

Shelby sensed that once Witt managed to get into the house, he would be a booger to dislodge, like a tick boring into a dog.

"I'd like to tell you some more about my institute, Shelby."

What Shelby heard was more like, I'd like to inflict more mental pain on you as I waste your time.

"That sounds—optimistic," Shelby said sweetly.

"I live optimism, Shelby. Every day."

"So you said. And I guess it wouldn't be as effective to live it only now and then."

"Not at all, Shelby. You make a fine point there."

"No offense, Witt, but why do you want to tell me about your institute?"

"You saved the world," Witt said. "What better example to reinforce the power of optimism?"

"I'm flattered, Witt—truly. And that's not just optimism talking. But that's over with, the whole saved the world shtick. It's sort of old news."

"But the hard work lies ahead of us, Shelby—the hard work of fostering and maintaining optimism."

Shelby wished for a sudden downpour, like the ones in the tropics.

"I'm optimistic you can create some more optimism, Witt, because you're pretty optimistic about it."

Witt gestured toward the limo.

"Come for a short ride with me, Shelby. Be my guest, listen to my story. Nothing ventured, nothing gained."

"To where, Witt?"

"Oh, just down the road, and here and there. Just for a few minutes. Where we actually go doesn't matter."

"Because you're optimistic, Witt?"

"Exactly."

Shelby glanced at the driver, a young, clean-cut man who appeared to be a sane person and not, for example, an accomplice in a kidnapping.

"So, just be—optimistic, Witt?"

"That's it, Shelby. You hit it right on the head."

"I do have hidden security cameras filming all this, Witt, so you know," Shelby lied, optimistic that a little lie was a useful thing from time to time.

"That's wise, Shelby. Prudent." Witt waved toward the front door and smiled. "But what does a man who saved the world have to fear?"

"You really are optimistic, Witt. Is there a bar in this limo?"

"There's a bar, a TV, a stereo—and on the way up here from Little Rock, I stood up in the sunroof and drank in the breezes of optimism, Shelby."

"That was pretty optimistic of you, Witt—but watch out for low-hanging wires."

"Your concern is noted, Shelby—and appreciated. And concern is one of the keys to optimism."

"I thought humor was the key to optimism."

"There are many keys to optimism, Shelby."

"Just how many keys are there, Witt?"

"Forty-two, at last count."

Shelby glanced at the sky, desperate for that tropical downpour. "When did you last count them?" Shelby said.

"Two weeks ago. So, I might yet identify some new ones."

"I'm optimistic that that's true, of course."

"If you're optimistic, Shelby, then it becomes true."

Witt and Shelby sipped Maker's Mark on the rocks from the limo bar and actually rode as far as Shady Glen and back, with Shelby pointing out the short, tired-looking bony trees planted randomly at the Willow Oaks Country Club as they passed by.

"There were no oaks or willows that I could see," Shelby said.

"But I'm optimistic those trees will grow and tower over us all some day, Shelby."

"A pretty safe bet, Witt."

"Agreed. But a skeptic might say a tornado will come knock them over. See what I mean?"

Shelby nodded happily. The Maker's Mark had certainly made him more agreeable. And at least Witt's horseshit was pleasant enough horseshit—optimistic horseshit. Witt had apparently made a career out of horseshit, which he chose instead to call optimism. He explained to Shelby that he got into real estate sales right out of Vanderbilt with a business degree, and then gave pharmaceutical sales a go for a while, too. He even sold cars—Cadillacs—and did fairly well at it. But there was something lacking, he said. All those things he did were commerce without a sense of ownership. Without *personal* ownership.

"So, I started the Institute for Optimism, Shelby."

"And that sure makes more sense than calling it The Institute for Negativity, Witt. But what does it do?"

"Anything I want it to, Shelby. Anything I can *make* it do."

"I see," he lied. "What have you made it do lately, Witt?"

"Well, for example, I now have a line of gourmet chili," Witt said. "It costs much more than regular chili in a can, but it's better—gourmet."

"And where does optimism come in on all that?"

"I sell people on the quality of the chili, Shelby. But really, they're buying optimism—that it *is* better chili—and so I'm really selling optimism and not chili."

"What do you call the chili?"

"Optimist's Blend," Witt said. "What do you think?"

"How much for a can?"

"Ten dollars."

"That's optimistic."

"But profitable," Witt said.

"How much more expensive is it to make gourmet chili than just cheap chili?"

"Well, if I revealed that, I'd be revealing business secrets, Shelby."

"And why again do you need an institute to sell chili?"

"So that investors believe they're investing in optimism, and not just chili."

"But they *are* investing in chili."

"But more than just chili, Shelby. I remind them that some of their money goes into the institute. So, they invest in making and selling chili, but also in spreading optimism."

"And that works—the spreading?"

"Oh, indeed it does. They begin to see themselves as humanitarians while also practicing capitalism. They become optimists—optimistic capitalists—which certainly makes it easier to get them to invest. I tell them that their money helps me spread optimism, which in turn helps solve world problems."

Shelby pondered it a moment. He vaguely wondered whether Witt was either related to, or actually knew, Bern Brindlestickler.

"So, some of the money goes to making and selling chili," Shelby said, "but some goes to your institute? Doesn't that mean it's *all* going to you?"

"Well, Shelby—if you choose to look at it that way."

"What other way is there to look at it?"

"There's always an optimistic way to look at anything, Shel."

Shelby frowned. He knew that his face was definitely not conveying any optimism to Witt.

"Isn't there an illusion there with your investors that some money goes off into Greenpeace or UNICEF or Habitat for Humanity?" Shelby said. "Or do you actually contribute to those things?"

"Oh, Lordy—no, Shelby. If I spent money that way there wouldn't be much at all for spreading optimism and creating gourmet chili, either. And since there's already a UNICEF, for example, I don't need to create redundancy. That would be counterproductive. Who would spread optimism?"

"And spreading it is what you're really good at, Witt."

"I like to think so."

"Do you tell your investors you don't actually invest the money in charities?" Shelby said.

"I tell them that anyone can invest in charities, Shelby. And many do. And many have. I even tell them that if they'd like to provide extra money, I'll invest it for them in charities. But I point out that what I do is *enhance* all those charities by providing something extra—optimism. You can fund charities, which are already funded, or you can develop an altogether new and additional service, which I chose to do."

"So you're overcharging them to develop the gourmet chili?"

"I choose to see it as charging what it takes to develop gourmet chili, plus money for the institute."

"Which is really just money for you since the institute doesn't really make anything," Shelby said.

"But it *does* create something, Shelby—optimism. There's a price for doing business, of course. Overhead, costs."

"And the cost of this limo—your suit."

"But they aren't really luxury items, Shelby. They're tools of the trade."

"You have swell tools, Witt."

"The best money can buy, Shelby."

"You mean, the best that *optimism* can buy."

"Exactly. Very nicely put."

When Witt let Shelby out back at the house, Shelby pleasantly agreed to read over a prospectus for investors and accepted a complimentary gift of a case of Optimist's Blend gourmet chili, which Witt got out of the limo's trunk. Then Shelby, the case of Optimist's Blend gourmet chili under one arm, thanked Witt for the ride and especially for the Maker's Mark. Shelby waved and smiled as Witt's limo rolled out of sight down the lane, Witt standing up in the sunroof, arms extended, head thrown back—drinking in the breezes of optimism.

Shelby stored his 24 cans of Optimist's Blend gourmet chili in a cabinet next to the refrigerator and for a moment admired such a generous supply. He looked forward to trying the chili. He was optimistic that it would be good. After all, it cost ten dollars a can and helped make the world more optimistic.

The next day, he had an electronic gate erected and security cameras installed over his front door.

Unable to manage a decisive grip on what truth really was, despite Joe Grizzard's earnest explanations, and Witt's undying optimism, and how truth could be recognized and expressed—sold, as Roger had suggested—Shelby decided to open his house to others who might have better luck at it than he. A symposium of sorts, he supposed. He named it The Search for Ultimate Truth Symposium. He had considered calling it The Most Awesome Search for Ultimate Truth, but went with the revised version, even though he felt that perhaps ultimate was a bit too definitive, and even a bit pretentious, but it sounded good, and after all, it was *his* symposium.

Oceanna, intrigued by how much potential the symposium suggested for becoming quite ludicrous, and even downright embarrassing, volunteered to handle the media and sent press releases. Legions of cameras and talking heads descended like vultures to a rotten carcass. Shelby invited six prominent authorities on truth—names he stumbled across on the internet—and all philosophers of different stripes. Shelby even got Lou Malnati's to send deep-dish pizza from Chicago for a fee and in exchange for being designated official pizza of the Search for Ultimate Truth Symposium.

Four invitees were able to accept on such short notice—Fernando Woody, Sayles Wilmott, Orzias Trulock, and Olivia Murker, and they enjoyed a generous honorarium, first class air to Memphis, a limo for each, and exquisite rooms with four-poster canopy beds at Viola Atteberry's bed and breakfast overlooking the river. And of course, Lou Malnati's deep dish-pizza waiting for them in their rooms, now equipped with microwave ovens to re-heat the pizza, a gift from Shelby to Viola Atteberry, who had finally given up on goading Shelby into robbing the Shady Glen Bank.

Quick as lightning and just as sudden, Shelby's property was transformed from bucolic and rustic to a high-tech media circus. Camera trucks festooned with satellite dishes filled the lane all the way to the house. Townspeople came out from Parsons Grove, cars and trucks streaming all the way back across the Porter Newhouse Bridge, as citizens jockeyed for a place to get a look at the commotion. Reporters/celebrities-in-waiting screeching from circling helicopters compared it to aerial footage of Woodstock. But there were no hippies in sight and no mob actions broke out, most residents remembering just how exhausted and confused they were after the last one. TV reporters/celebrities-in-waiting adjusted their hair and makeup in truck mirrors and strained to get a look at Shelby or anyone else.

Oceanna stepped outside and asked if any of the reporters/celebrities-in-waiting would like a margarita, but there were no takers.

Inside, Shelby welcomed his guests to the kitchen table, which had a dandy view of the river. The cat jumped up on the table on the way to a nearby counter, from which it elected to oversee the proceedings. Oceanna sipped a margarita in the living room, but positioned in a chair with a clear view of the kitchen table and the participants. She put her feet up on the ottoman and looked quite amused.

Before things could get under way, Shelby excused himself to take a call out on the deck. It was Roger.

"Hola, Roger."

"Hola, kid. I'm sitting here looking at your spiffy damn house on CNN."

"Yeah? How does it look?"

"Cosmonaut, Shel. I like A-frames. And I see you're by the river."

"The view's awesome, Roger. You at home?"

"Nope—at the office. We've got a little pool going on here to see how long it takes before you cause another riot in Parsons Grove."

"What'd you draw in the pool?" Shelby said.

"Six hours. We all kicked in twenty bucks and the winner takes $100."

"How do you like your chances, Roger?"

"I'm stoked, kid. The boys here say six hours is too low, but they don't know you like I do. My money's on you, kid."

"That sustains me in my time of need, Roger. What happens to the money if there's no riot?"

"It buys lunch for us all tomorrow. There's a new Chinese place just down the road. Noodles to die for, Shel."

"How about I arrange some Lou Malnati's deep-dish instead," Shelby said. "I don't think we'll have any riots today."

"What about tomorrow, kid? Should we switch the pool to tomorrow? With more time we can get more agents to pitch in."

"I wouldn't. The whole shebang'll be over tomorrow afternoon at the latest."

"Well, then send the Lou Malnati's," Roger said. "Listen, kid—protocol requires me to ask. Everything under control? Do I need to alert the president? Congress? Catch a flight and grab a chopper to Dogpatch?"

"Nope. And the town enacted an ordinance making chopper landings on the town square illegal, Roger. They still talk about that."

"Took it a little hard, did they?"

"They also banned anyone from having their taxes done by any accountant from Memphis."

"Ouch, kid! That one smarts. Oh, well. So—you're on top of this?"

"I've got it, Roger. We're aiming to get at the truth here."

"Well, you know that line from Jaws, right, Shel?"

"Which one?"

"The one about needing a bigger boat."

"We're in my kitchen, Roger. And I haven't seen any sharks in the river."

"But plenty out on your lawn with microphones in their hands."

"I noticed, Roger."

"Okay, Shel. I'll get out of your hair so you can locate the truth. And lots of luck with that. But are you sure six hours won't hold up? I'll bet if you shinnied up that bridge again with some Dixie beer, this $100 sitting on the table here would be mine."

Go have some noodles, Roger. And Lou Malnati's is on the way."

Shelby inaugurated the symposium with a private panel discussion in his kitchen, away from prying cameras and conniving TV reporters/celebrities-in-waiting. A press conference was tentatively scheduled to follow at some point, providing the reporters/celebrities-in-waiting could behave themselves and not become the spark somehow igniting another Mob Day. And Shelby had asked politely that they not peek in any of the windows or pee on the lawn. Some enterprising soul from town hauled out porta-pottys and charged to use them. Shelby figured that Witt Boguson would call that optimistic capitalism.

In advance of the event, Shelby had a website created so that people could email questions for the panel of experts. The first question came from Amanda Van Hoevanheusen of Grand Rapids, Michigan. Amanda wanted the panel's reaction to a thought about truth that came to her one night when she was washing dishes: But what is sleep, but death, and what is death, but sleep?

"Very poetic," panelist Olivia Murker said.

"Makes me think of Frost," panelist Sayles Wilmott said.

"It rather sings, I think," panelist Fernando Woody said.

Panelist Orzias Trulock nodded approvingly.

"But what does it mean?" Shelby said.

Sayles Wilmott pushed away from the table a little and crossed his arms across his chest. He glanced toward the ceiling a moment. Everyone else followed his glance—the cat momentarily too, and Oceanna raised her margarita in silent toast from her chair with a view from the living room.

"Well," Sayles Wilmott said. "We might begin to examine her admittedly poetic statement by first acknowledging that life is a transition—ever a transition. Her statement certainly signals that."

"I agree most strenuously," Orzias Trulock said, and Olivia Murker and Fernando Woody nodded approvingly. Oceanna raised her margarita again in silent toast from her chair with a view from the living room.

"What transition are we talking about?' Shelby said.

"Life to death, of course," Fernando Woody said. "The ultimate transition."

"Well said," Olivia Murker said, nodding approvingly.

"So, what's the truth in that, then?" Shelby said.

Orzias Trulock leaned forward to catch the eye of Olivia Murker.

"This would seem to be right up your alley, Olivia—Pergenics, your pioneering concept, of course."

Fernando Woody and Sayles Wilmott also leaned forward and nodded approvingly.

"What's Pergenics?" Shelby said.

"The title of her new book, of course," Fernando Woody said, casting an admiring glance at Olivia Murker, who was no beauty, but was curvy and attractive in a quiet librarian sort of way with her dull blonde hair pulled into a tight ponytail. The men were all middle-aged, a bit rumpled in appearance—Albert Einsteins without the wild hair and Groucho moustaches.

"The study of transitions," Olivia Murker said confidently.

Shelby caught a quick glance of Oceanna, sipping her margarita with the cat now in her lap from her chair with a view from the living room. She caught his glance and raised her glass, her face seeming to convey, let me know when to toss you a lifejacket.

"Are transitions the keys to truth?" Shelby ventured.

All four panelists arched their eyebrows.

"Ah," Fernando Woody said. "Intriguing."

"Your next book, Olivia," Orzias Trulock said.

"The gears are spinning as we speak," she said, smiling. "It's un-folding in my mind. I'll make notes tonight at the bed and breakfast."

"We can debate it at dinner, too," Fernando Woody said. "Over the local trout."

The other three panelists nodded approvingly.

Olivia Murker clapped her hands together.

"Well, we've made remarkable progress."

"Groundbreaking, perhaps," Fernando Woody said.

The other three panelists nodded approvingly.

Oceanna raised her margarita from her chair with a view from the living room.

"I move we adjourn the session," Orzias Trulock said.

"Seconded," Fernando Woody said.

"Done," Sayles Wilmott exclaimed.

"I think a margarita might be in order here," Fernando Woody said.

"We've certainly earned it," Olivia Murker said.

"I'll fire up the blender," Oceanna said as she walked by the table, the cat following her.

Shelby chewed his lip, even as he tried to smile politely. The cat stared at him.

After serving margaritas, Oceanna stepped outside and spoke to the reporters/celebrities-in-waiting. They surrounded her as effec-tively as Custer had been surrounded at Little Big Horn. Cameras bored in. A helicopter hovered directly above the house, its churning blades rattling tree limbs.

"The panel has made remarkable progress," she said. "Anyone want a margarita?"

There were no takers, though several videographers were tempted.

"Will there be a statement from Shelby?" a reporter/celebri-ty-in-waiting yelled.

"Not immediately," she said. "He's meeting with panelists."

"What are they talking about?" another reporter/celebrity-in-waiting hollered.

Oceanna pondered it a moment and smiled.

"Transitions," she said.

"What kind of transitions?" yet another reporter/celebrity-in-waiting hollered.

"I'll leave that to Shelby to explain," Oceanna said happily and she stepped back into the house.

"What's it like out there?" Shelby said.

"They're preparing to burn the house down," she said. "They're lighting torches and preparing the battering ram, too."

"Well, as long as it's nothing serious," he said.

"You mean like this symposium, Shel?"

He rolled his eyes.

"It did sound better as an idea."

"It's not too late to flee and climb the Porter Newhouse Bridge with some Dixie beer," she said. "Then at least all these talking heads would have something semi-newsworthy."

"The truth isn't newsworthy?"

"How much truth do you see lying around here, Shel?"

"Maybe we're just not looking hard enough. Or in the right place, I suppose."

"How about a margarita?" Oceanna said.

"And then we'll go rob the Shady Glen bank."

"Now, there's a thought," she said. "Viola would be ever so pleased."

"Maybe that's the truth," Shelby said. "Pleasing others."

Hurtling Through the Unknown Universe

"Ooooooommmaaaaaaaeeeeeeeeeeeeeeeee!"

Again, Shelby screeched, Ooooooommmaaaaaaaeeeeeeeeeeeeeeeee!"

As he was about to screech it again, he was also aware he was not actually screeching it—not actually saying it, not actually hearing it out loud in any conventional sense. It was implied, it was in his head, but also outside his head. It was—like background music.

Like elevator music.

It was his voice but more like a voiceover.

Was it the voice of God?

No, he was sure it was the voice of Shelby.

How would he know the voice of God?

Was he, Shelby, actually God, and just discovering it?

What an odd thought.

But then, what an odd experience.

He looked around.

There was no horizon.

Only a black endless field and pinpoints.

Stars?

"Ooooooommmaaaaaaaeeeeeeeeeeeeeeeee!"

Where was he?

What was he?

There was movement.

No, not just movement—amazing movement. Dazzling movement—supersonic movement. Here-to-there-in-an-instant movement—here-to-there-in-a-flash movement, no feathers ruffled.

He was flying!

But without any sensation of flying. No sensation at all. His hair did not stream behind him. He didn't feel wind in his face or along his arms or body. He was just—suspended, but comfortably, happily.

Weightless.

In his peripheral vision he saw his arms, outstretched—outstretched as though he were Superman. Outstretched to form wings, because, after all, he was flying!

How?

But—incredible!

I'm—flying!

There were no engines, but he had propulsion.

And he could breathe, even though wherever he was, whatever he was, seemed not to be in an atmosphere or requiring one.

He was here, and he was there, and he was everywhere.

But he could breathe.

Or maybe he didn't need to and just thought he could.

And he discovered he could maneuver.

He could bank and roll.

Speed up and slow down.

Climb and descend.

He just had to think any maneuver.

But he was also naked!

He looked down along his body, his penis hanging straight down like a rudder.

Not a large rudder, mind you.

He was glad, in his present state, to still have a penis.

But not sure why.

"Ooooooommmmaaaaaaaeeeeeeeeeeeeeeeee!"

Was this heaven?

Was it hell?

It seemed too comfortable to be hell.

There was no heat, no cold.

It just *was*.

Where had he been before this—this odd place, this unknown universe he seemed to be hurtling through?

Shelby could not remember.

He knew his name—Shelby.

Shelby Albert Goddard.

That seemed to be all that he knew.

Other than that, his penis seemed to function like a small rudder.

And that it *didn't* function as a rudder.

It just looked that way.

Seemed that way.

What a thing to think of, at a time like this.

But what *was* this time?

What was this place?

Was it nowhere?

Was it everywhere?

Was it anywhere?

Was it all those things?

Was he dead?

If so, death wasn't so bad.

His ability to fly increased with his ability to accept that he merely had to think an action and it happened. If he wanted to fly as though he were standing, as though he were just casually walking—he could.

If he wanted to fly as though sitting—done!

And he did.

Such fun! Streaking through—streaking through something black and endless and starry, as though walking, as though standing, or sitting, no sense of aerodynamics or lift or anything of hard science.

And seemingly a place with no need to be understood.

He was even able to do somersaults as he flew.

And he flew upside down.

He flew with arms crossed over his chest.

He flew feet first.

He flew with his body sideways.

He flew with an erection.

And without one, too.
Just streaking through—the universe?
Or heaven?
Or hell?
Something in between?
And toward *what?*
Toward *whom?*
From *where?*
Should he care?
Would that help?
He didn't know.
And he didn't worry.
Worry seemed to have left him.
Odd words popped into his—consciousness:
Thingamabobs, thingamajigs, and doohickeys.
He had no idea what they meant.
He didn't care.
He could fly!

A planet was ahead.
Shelby sensed that it was quite close, within easy reach, and he could land there.
Or not.
He just had to think a decision.
How did he know that?
He just did.
Not knowing why, he chose to visit the planet. He changed course and then he was on the planet without any sense of time having been involved. As with his hurtling through the unknown universe, Shelby could breathe on the planet, though, as when flying, there was no real awareness of a need to breathe.
Where he descended onto the planet was a long and wide plain with distant mountains. Their peaks were white and snowy. The plain had many purple flowers and red trees and the few buildings were like blazing orange igloos. The sky above the planet was a dull yellow and rather sickly. He walked for a time, then looked down

and saw he was not actually walking, but suspended above the ground and appeared to be walking.

Up ahead he saw four figures—people?

They were encased in white from head to toe and did not have faces, though they had arms. They were not men or women, just vaguely humanoid figures encased in white. They seemed to be doing something, to something, but it was not clear to Shelby what they were doing or to what. As he got closer he could see there was a fifth figure, lying on the ground among the purple flowers.

Somehow, the thoughts inside the four figures were made available to Shelby. He didn't know how or understand it. There were no thoughts coming from the fifth figure encased in white. That figure did not move and seemed almost asleep among the purple flowers.

Shelby listened to the thoughts from the four figures encased in white and watched their actions. They told him they were trying to revive the fifth figure, but it was not clear to Shelby what had happened to it or how the others were trying to revive it. And what reviving it might mean—where it was now as an entity and where they wanted it to be.

Was it close to death, the fifth figure?

Or already dead?

Perhaps just asleep, Shelby hoped, and he conveyed that thought back to the others.

Shelby glanced around, to the distant mountains with snowy peaks, up at the sickly yellow sky.

Was *this* heaven?

Hell?

Did those things even exist?

He watched the four figures work on their comrade.

Was the fifth figure encased in white—God?

Or maybe a disciple?

Were all five of them intergalactic tourists?

He glanced at the distant mountains again. There were dark clouds now over them, obscuring the snowy peaks. Where had the clouds come from? They had not been there a moment before. But then, time was not time in any sense of events moving forward or backward, or at all, he sensed.

There was no time, just *here*.

Shelby sensed that whatever the four figures were doing to, or for, the fifth figure, would take some time and so he thought himself into movement toward the distant mountains for a closer look. As he increased velocity, he sensed that the dark clouds—black as coal—were moving toward him and had increased their velocity, too.

As he got closer to the clouds, he became aware of a thick fog snaking along the floor of the plain and shrouding everything. The blazing orange buildings that looked like igloos had disappeared, had become engulfed by the meandering fog—swallowed. He could not see the red trees or any more purple flowers.

Shelby looked back, at the four figures working feverishly, but could not see the fifth figure or the purple flowers it nested in. The black clouds were almost on him, their size now leviathan. He tried to think them away, think them into dissipation, but that would not work. He was close enough to the clouds to hear loud rolling thunder and even see flashes of crackling lightning within them. The clouds seemed likely to explode, seemed capable of destroying the planet.

Suddenly Shelby felt an unknown, gentle force pulling him—reeling him back toward the four figures on the plain, who were still hunched over the fifth figure. Their thoughts came into him again, entered him gently, easily, and filled him up. Their thoughts were compassionate and loving. He thought he even heard them say his name several times, not surprised that they might know his name, given just how weird the whole experience truly was.

The leviathan black clouds, as coarsely dark as raven feathers, crept even closer, a wall of black so high that Shelby could not see or imagine above it. It was a dark cloud tsunami and it kept rolling on, building strength. He sensed that the cloud tsunami was moving faster than whatever force it was that reeled him back, toward the group of white-encased figures. Their thoughts grew louder, conveyed alarm, despair.

The cloud tsunami seemed close enough to touch and Shelby did extend a hand to see if he could, and to know what might happen if he did. He was quite calm and even a little surprised at that. There was a moment, for lack of a better term, given that there seemed to be no time in service, in which Shelby's hand penetrated the surface of the cloud tsunami and disappeared into it. The hand and forearm, he felt, were still attached, just hidden as they protruded into the cloud. There was no real sensation. He did not really feel anything as he watched his arm disappear and the surface of the cloud slowly roll up his arm toward his shoulder.

As the cloud enveloped Shelby all the way to his shoulder, he felt something else, a tingling, a teasing, a caressing. A sense of lightness, of absolute calm, and a breeze of sweet, fragrant air—the smell of peaches, perhaps—shot into him and flowed within him, filling him to the brim. He managed a quick glance over his other shoulder and saw that the fifth figure, the one that had sprawled lifelessly in the purple flowers, was being helped to its feet, and then darkness clouded Shelby's thoughts and he felt himself pulled out of the cloud toward the figures encased in white, and then there was nothing but one last "Oooooommmmaaaaaaaaeeeeeeeeeeeeeeeeee!" escaping him from the deepest point of his being.

"Ooooooommmaaaaaaeeeeeeeeeeeeee!"

Shelby's eyes fluttered as though balky shutters resisting an attempt to open. And they were quite dry, the eyelids heavy. He could not be sure how long it took for them to finally stay open. His sense of time lacked something—context, a point of reference, something. And at first, his eyes would not focus and all he saw was what seemed to be a white ceiling. He supposed that meant he was lying down. Or maybe it was a wall and he was actually standing. But where? After more fluttering, the eyes focused and it was indeed a white ceiling.

His senses returned slowly and he became aware that he was in a bed. He could feel his arms and his legs and he wiggled his toes. He felt something attached to an arm. He discovered his head would swivel and he turned and saw that some sort of line, a tiny clear hose, was hooked to his arm. Fluid flowed from the hose into his arm. White sheets and blankets covered him to his chin.

Shelby slowly lowered his chin to his chest and as his gaze traversed from ceiling to wall he saw a shelf high on the wall with a TV on it. The TV was not on. Then he slowly traversed lower and saw four people, all wearing white coats, huddled at the foot of his bed. There were two men and two women. He guessed the men were in their 40s and the women in their 30s. One woman had long blonde hair and the other short dark hair. Both were pretty. One of the men was taller than the other. Both men were pleasant-looking. One had gray hair at his temples and the other, the shorter one, wore glasses.

One of the women, the blonde, turned to Shelby and pointed at him, a smile developing.

The other three turned and all grinned.

"Well," the taller man said. "He seems to finally be back with us."

Shelby blinked his eyes and digested the words. I'm back? Where have I been? Where am I now?

The four people surrounded his bed, a man and woman on each side, as though couples. The taller man shined a light into Shelby's eyes.

"We should get something into these eyes," the man said, glancing at the woman with long blonde hair. "They're quite dry."

Shelby was aware that the woman rummaged for something in a cabinet beside the bed. The man continued to shine a light in his eyes. Shelby considered speaking, wondered if he had the ability, decided not to rush things. As the man shined the light in each eye several more times, Shelby studied his face, saw the nameplate on the coat— Morrissey. Dr. Morrissey. So—he was apparently in a hospital. That was something to build on. Promising, he figured. He didn't imagine he was dead and that heaven was a hospital room with pretty women, but maybe he was wrong about that, and if he was, then heaven didn't seem too bad so far.

Or, was hell a hospital with pretty women?

Unlikely, he decided—the temperature was quite pleasant.

He looked at the other three people and saw that the women were nurses—Thompson and Atteberry on their nameplates. The other man, the shorter one, was Dr. Mermelstein.

After Dr. Morrissey had finished examining his eyes, Nurse Atteberry squeezed drops of something into his eyes and he could see even better than before. Her face had been very close to his and he thought she had lovely skin.

"There," Nurse Atteberry said. "That should put you right."

Still not sure of his ability to speak, Shelby nodded feebly, grinned slowly, thinly.

"We've been expecting you back at any moment," Dr. Mermelstein said.

Back? From where? Shelby grinned feebly at him, too.

"But we had to give you some help for that," Dr. Morrissey said.

Shelby nodded again.

Dr. Mermelstein leaned close to Shelby's face.

"Can you speak?" the doctor said, a bit too loudly, and it caused Shelby to blink rapidly. He grinned weakly.

"He seems—overcome," Nurse Thompson said.

"But he looks rather happy," Nurse Atteberry said.

Shelby wondered if he felt happy, looked happy, and wasn't sure. He felt—neutral—no, cautiously expectant, hopeful.

He was pretty confused, actually.

"That's to be expected," Dr. Morrissey said. "He's been gone for some time."

Gone? Where did I go? He tried to raise his arms and draw up his legs but they were sluggish, heavy.

"I often wonder, in cases like this," Dr. Mermelstein said, "just where they go, and what it's like. Whether they can hear us—do they dream?"

"I'm certain they hear us," Nurse Atteberry said.

"Perhaps," Dr. Morrissey said. "I guess I won't discount it."

"Well, I always talked to him," Nurse Atteberry said. "Just small talk."

"I did, too," Nurse Thompson said. "I told him what the weather was every day."

"Even housekeeping talked to him," Dr. Mermelstein said. "So I heard."

"And his family, too," Nurse Atteberry said.

"I saw them all the time," Nurse Thompson said. "Where are they today?"

"I don't know," Nurse Atteberry said.

"Families can become sort of eccentric in cases like this," Dr. Mermelstein said.

"Well, now he's back," Dr. Morrissey said. "That's what matters. The family will show up presently, I'm sure."

"How do you feel, Shelby?" Dr. Mermelstein said, leaning close again.

Shelby concentrated, opened his lips:

"Oooooommmaaaaaaaeeeeeeeeeeeeeeee!"

The circumstances of the coma were explained to Shelby by Dr. Morrissey.

"You were in an accident, Shelby. You wrecked your car. Do you understand?"

Shelby nodded.

"But thankfully, no one was killed. Do you understand, Shelby?"

Shelby nodded again. His ability to nod and swivel his head improved daily.

"It happened almost two months ago," Dr. Morrissey said. "Out on Chinden Road. It was raining, and I guess you lost control. You smacked a utility pole—knocked it clean over. Do you understand, Shelby?"

Shelby nodded, tried to recall a scene like the doctor described, but could not.

"Do you know what city you're in, Shelby? Do you know where you live?"

Shelby wasn't sure and frowned.

"Boise," Dr. Morrissey said. "Boise, Idaho. I was here the afternoon they brought you in. We weren't sure you'd make it. Do you understand, Shelby?"

Shelby nodded

"Your old noggin got battered around there," Dr. Morrisey said. "But I think you'll do just fine. Do you understand, Shelby?"

Shelby nodded.

"Soon you'll be up and about. Do you understand, Shelby?"

Shelby nodded.

"Do you remember what you do for a living, Shelby?"

Shelby frowned, chewed on his lower lip.

"You're a math teacher," Dr. Morrissey said. "At one of the high schools. Do you understand, Shelby?"

"Oooooooommmaaaaaaaeeeeeeeeeeeeeeeee!"

After a few days, Shelby was judged fit to sit in a wheelchair and Nurse Atteberry rolled him outside to a patio with several plastic tables and chairs under a tree, a short, tired-looking bony tree. It was early summer, but not yet hot. The sun slow-baked his face and felt exquisite. Getting into the chair had been difficult and required the help of three people. Shelby's muscles had atrophied just enough that he sort of felt like a helpless baby.

"You were in a coma for nearly two months," Nurse Atteberry said. "That's a long time. Okay if I smoke?"

Shelby nodded.

"Do you remember anything, Shelby?" she said as she lit the cigarette and exhaled blue smoke.

Shelby watched the blue smoke rise and dissipate.

"Did you dream, Shelby?"

He felt that something—memories?—*were* trying to come to him, so he nodded yes.

"Did you hear me talking to you?" she said.

Shelby frowned.

"Did you hear other people?" she said.

That perplexed him. He felt there had been voices in his head, but he wasn't sure what to make of them. So, instead of nodding either way, he shrugged—his first shrug, and he felt rather proud of it. He looked up, into the sun, and closed his eyes a moment, the sun warming him, a slight breeze caressing his face.

"Ooooooommmmaaaaaaaeeeeeeeeeeeeeeee!"

His voice was growing stronger.

His family showed up. They had stopped coming every day a few weeks before Shelby woke up. They peeked in the doorway to his room, tentatively at first, as though unsure they had the right room, or should even be there. Shelby recognized Louise and George Goddard as his parents, but at the same time, it was as if he was meeting them for the first time after hearing about them for years. He could not muster any images of growing up with them. His father was tall, more than six-four, a strong jaw, thinning blond hair, and his mother was only five-five, thin but still pretty, her hair short and dark. Shelby thought she seemed like a tiny bird.

His mother rubbed one of his arms lightly. His father patted one of Shelby's thighs. They didn't quite know what to say or do.

George Goddard glanced around the room, at machines, at walls, at the floor, even though he'd seen it all many times.

"There, there," his mother cooed.

"Hang in there, son," his father said resolutely.

Shelby said, "Oooooommmmaaaaaaaeeeeeeeeeeeeeeeee!"

Nurse Atteberry walked in at that moment.

"I'm afraid he does that from time to time. You'll get used to it."

"I'm not so sure," George Goddard said quietly.

"What does it mean?" Louise Goddard said.

"Probably nothing," George Goddard said.

"We don't know," Nnurse Atteberry said. "But it's surely a good sign—maybe he's warming up his vocal chords."

"It's downright primal," George Goddard said, remembering to once again pat Shelby's thigh. "Like something I might have heard in the army."

"Do we know that he can actually talk, though?" Louise Goddard said.

Nurse Atteberry nodded.

"Dr. Morrissey says there's no reason to believe he can't. But give him time—he's had an amazing shock."

"Can he move?" Louise Goddard said.

"Oh, sure," Nurse Atteberry said. "He can swivel his head, nod, frown, smile—move his arms and legs. He's all there."

"What about his mind?" George Goddard said.

"These things take time," Nurse Atteberry said.

"Can he sit up?" Louise Goddard said.

"Not quite yet," Nurse Atteberry said. "His muscles are still learning how to work—remembering how to work. But I took him outside yesterday, in a wheelchair."

"Really?" Louise Goddard said. "How'd that go?"

"He really enjoyed the sun on his face," Nurse Atteberry said.

"I'll bring sunglasses next time," Louise Goddard said.

"Oooooommmmaaaaaaaeeeeeeeeeeeeeeeee!"

After a week, Shelby began to have sensations in his head that he decided were memories warming up—percolating, trying to start, attempting to form. He would hear voices and they became clearer, but the words were still a bit fuzzy. Images would come and go in a flash, too quickly to see clearly what was in them, but he was encouraged that they came at all. He felt he was on the verge of something.

He spoke his first word one day when no one was in the room.

"Swellby."

His mouth felt as though filled with pebbles and so he worked it some with a hand and then worked it with mouth and facial muscles. He opened his mouth as far as he could and held it open as long as he could.

"Shelby," came out clearly.

Then, "Goddard."

Then, "Boise."

Then, "Idaho."

He was so pleased he spent the next half hour listening to the words reverberate in his head.

When Nurse Atteberry came in, Shelby said, "Nurse."

She placed her hands on her hips and smiled.

"Talking, are we?"

"Shelby."

"That's right, honey—you're Shelby."

"Nurse."

"And I'm a nurse—that's right. Nurse Atteberry."

"Atteberry," Shelby said with the biggest grin Nurse Atteberry had seen on his face so far.

"TV," Shelby said, pointing at it, his arm still weak, but working better than the previous day.

"You're becoming a regular songbird," she said.

"Window," he said, pointing.

"Very good, Shelby."

"Bed."

She squeezed his hand. "What else can you say, honey?

"Oooooooommmaaaaaaaeeeeeeeeeeeeeeeee!"

One day while Nurse Atteberry checked Shelby's blood pressure, Dr. Mermelstein shined a light in his eyes.

"Merstein," Shelby said happily.

"Pretty close, Shelby," Dr. Mermelstein said. "You just need to toss a few more letters in there."

Shelby concentrated on the name, saw it in his head like a little billboard. He focused.

"Mermelstain."

"Stein—Mermelstein," Dr. Mermelstein said as he shined the light some more.

"Mermelstein," Shelby finally said.

"Good work," Dr. Mermelstein said. "That's not an easy one. How's his pressure?"

"Splendid," Nurse Atteberry said. "One-ten over seventy."

"We do good work here," Dr. Mermelstein said. "Has he been outside lately?"

"Yesterday, but I can take him now," she said.

"That sound good, Shelby?" Dr. Mermelstein said.

"Good," Shelby said. He managed to do a thumbs up with both hands.

"Awesome," Dr. Mermelstein said and he high-fived with Shelby. "How are the memories coming along, Shelby? Can you remember anything?"

Shelby thought hard. Images again flowed throughout his brain. One image popped into view fairly clearly, but fleetingly.

"Roger Valkyrie," he said.

"Who's that?" Dr. Mermelstein said.

Nurse Atteberry looked at the doctor and shrugged.

Shelby just grinned, remembering something unclear but promising.

One day after his parents had gone for the evening, and nurses had made rounds, a man from housekeeping came into Shelby's room to spruce it up. Nameplates were the first things Shelby tended to notice about people. This man's nameplate said Roger Valko. The name sounded vaguely familiar. Shelby noticed that the man seemed athletic, light on his feet—graceful—and he was a good six-three if a day. His hair was blond and fine, but not thinning like his father's.

The man appeared to be fortyish, not much younger than his father, really, but seemed younger, acted younger—moved younger.

"Howdy pardner," Roger Valko said when he saw that Shelby was awake. Good to see you're back in the world."

"Howdy," Shelby said, enjoying a new word so much he said it again—"Howdy."

Then, "Pardner."

Roger Valko grinned and swept the floor.

"I heard you were awake, kid," he said. "How you feeling?"

Kid? Shelby had to think about that a moment. Was he a kid?

"Ducky," Shelby finally said. He had heard someone say it on TV.

"Ducky?" Roger Valko said. "That's awesome. I guess after what you've been through, you're lucky to feel anything at all."

Shelby nodded.

"Ducky."

"Are you okay with me doing the room right now?" Roger Valko said. "Usually, it didn't matter if I was here."

Shelby nodded.

"Shelby."

"I know that's your name," Roger Valko said. "How about I call you Shel? Is that okay, to call you Shel?"

Shelby gave a thumbs up.

"Shel," Shelby said, pleased.

"Okay, Shel. Now we're loaded for bear."

"Bear," Shelby said.

"That's right, kid. That's just an expression—loaded for bear."

"Loaded for bear," Shelby said.

"Here's another expression, kid—cooking with gas. How do you like that one?"

"Cooking with gas," Shelby said.

"All right, Shel. We're making progress here. Soon you'll be reciting Shakespeare."

"Ooooooommmaaaaaaaeeeeeeeeeeeeeeeee!"

"And hola to you, too, kid," Roger Valko said. "It ain't quite Shakespeare, but it's a start."

When Nurse Atteberry checked on Shelby the next morning, he was already awake and watching TV. She glanced up at the TV.

"Daffy Duck, eh?" she said as she checked his blood pressure. "He's a funny little thing."

"Loaded for bear," Shelby said.

"Now where'd you hear that one?" she said. "TV?"

"Cooking with gas," Shelby said.

"My husband says that sometimes," she said absently. "You're sure getting an education from somewhere. Pressure's good, Shelby, as usual."

"Shakespeare."

"Shakespeare?" She looked up at the TV. Daffy Duck had just gotten his bill knocked off again. "I don't think that's quite Shakespeare, Shelby. But that little black duck sure is funny."

"He's damn funny," Shelby said, and they both looked at each other with arched eyebrows.

In the evenings after his parents left, Shelby looked forward to seeing Roger Valko. His parents meant well, but they were rather dull and never quite knew what to say. Roger taught him new expressions and made him laugh.

"Here's a new one for you kid—piss up a rope."

"Piss up a rope," Shelby said. "Cool."

"But maybe you avoid repeating that one when the nurses are around, kid."

"No good?" Shelby said.

"It's okay to say around men, but not women, I suspect," Roger said. "Don't say that to a nurse, or maybe she gives you the needle in the keester instead of the arm."

"Really?" Shelby said.

"Fucking with you, kid," Roger said.

"Fucking," Shelby said.

"But never ever ever say that one to the nurses, kid. Not ever. Promise?"

"Promise," Shelby said.

"I'm serious, Shel. You can't ever say that to anyone. They'd fire me if they heard you learned that from me."

"Okay, Roger. How about keester?"

"That one's okay, Shel. But when they show up with the needle—protect your keester, my friend."

One night, Roger finished sweeping the floor and cleaning the bathroom and then he pulled a chair over by Shelby's bed.

"Listen, kid. I need to talk—I have to make sort of a confession."

"Were you bad, Roger?"

Roger looked down at the floor

"No. Not really. Well, I don't think so."

"Then, what did you do, Roger?"

"Nothing bad, trust me."

"Then what's there to confess?"

"Because it affects you, kid, I guess. It's not so much a confession as sharing information."

"If it's not bad, then it's okay," Shelby said.

"Not always," Roger said. "But I hear what you're saying. Thing is, now I feel like I took advantage of you, Shel."

"When?"

Roger eased back in the chair.

"Sometimes I talked to you, when you were in the coma."

"Everybody did," Shelby said. "I heard everyone say so."

"Do you remember it, Shel?"

"No. Not really. But I guess I did hear it. They say I did."

"They do say folks in a coma can hear people talk," Roger said. "I think there's something to that. In a way, I even thought talking to you was helpful, was good for your recovery and all that. I believed it. Still do."

"Maybe it was, Roger. I don't know."

"You're not mad at me, are you, kid?"

"No. Why would I be mad?"

Roger got up and looked out the window.

"Well, you were a captive audience, so to speak. See, I'm an actor, Shel—trying to be anyway."

"An actor? Like Daffy Duck?"

"Yeah," Roger said, turning back to Shelby. "Like Daffy Duck. Only better, I hope—not that Daffy ain't pretty good for a little black duck. But I'm with the theater group at the community college. I take classes during the day. When I cleaned your room, I'd—I'd be various characters, and try them out on you. Because you couldn't react one way or another, I felt comfortable doing them."

"Okay by me," Shelby said. "I guess I was a silent critic."

"Sorry," Roger said.

"Well, it's not like I had anything to do, or anywhere to go."

One night, just before Shelby was released, and he could speak again as well as before—and after Roger Valko had appeared and gone—he woke up and there was a man sitting in the chair by his bed. But the lights were low and the man had maneuvered a lamp so that Shelby couldn't see his face, and even in the poor light, the man's face would have been shaded. Shelby was sure it was a man because he was dressed like a man from the neck down. Or, he supposed it *could* be a woman who liked suits and ties.

"You know I can see you there, right?" Shelby said.

"Of course," the man said, clearly a man because he had a deep man's voice. "But this light suits me."

"What about the lamp?" Shelby said.

"Here—I'll move it back. There. How's that?"

"I still can't see who you are."

"Good. That's the idea."

"What idea?"

"The idea behind our chat. My name's Jarvis."

"Really? Jarvis? I never met a Jarvis."

"Now you have."

"You're not a doctor, I know that much," Shelby said. "They don't sneak in, and they like to be seen and heard. Especially if pretty nurses are in the room."

"No, I'm not a doctor. And Jarvis is not really my name, but it will do for this little chat."

"What are we going to chat about, Jarvis?"

"Your future."

"Awesome. But who are you?"

"I'm with the government, Shelby."

"Oh."

Shelby didn't think he knew anyone in the local government, though he abruptly had a memory of standing next to a Boise mayor once, when he was about eleven. Maybe twelve. It was during a Fourth of July parade, but he couldn't recall the circumstances.

"Which one," Shelby added. "The Boise city council?"

Jarvis chuckled.

"No, my boy—a little higher than that."

"The mayor's office?"

"Higher."

"The governor?"

"Okay—this is not getting us anywhere, " Jarvis said. "*The* government, Shelby. An agency in the *federal* government."

"CIA?"

"No."

"FBI?"

"No."

"AARP?"

"The American Association of Retired Persons isn't part of the government, Shelby."

"AA?"

"And Alcoholics Anonymous isn't part of the government, either, Shelby."

Shelby realized he had a limited repertoire of government agencies, but he supposed, as his memory improved, he could eventually name them all. It seemed like a worthy goal.

"How about FAA?" Shelby said hopefully.

"Do I look like a pilot?"

"Some other acronym, then?" Shelby said.

"Yes."

"Okay by me," Shelby said. "What can I do for you, Jarvis? Is this about my taxes being late? I was in a coma, you know."

"I'm not with the IRS, Shelby. And you won't have to worry about taxes. I'm here to help you."

"Cool. I was also worried you might somehow be a hit man for Tony Soprano."

"I enjoyed that show, too," Jarvis said. "Did you like Tony?"

"Yes. That's what made it so creepy—liking a monster."

"Agreed. An astute assessment, Shelby. But I'm here to follow up on what Agent Valko told you."

"*Agent* Valko? Roger, the housekeeper? He's one of yours?"

"Indeed. What did he tell you?"

Shelby shrugged.

"Just that he talked to me all the time when I was in a coma. He said he tried acting roles out on me since I was pretty much a coma-tose audience and all that."

"Valko has caught the acting bug, I'm afraid," Jarvis said. "Though I did see him once in dinner theater and I must admit, he wasn't bad."

Shelby attempted to picture Roger Valko as an actual actor in a movie, up there on the big screen, maybe kissing a pretty actress. No actress names would come to him, though. All in all, he was sure Roger Valko would be better off in non-romantic roles.

"He seems a bit average to be a leading man," Shelby said. "But he'd make a dandy father, I suppose—or a bachelor uncle. A sergeant in a war movie, too."

"I can buy that," Jarvis said. "I can see that—yeah."

"So—why was Valko here? *Agent* Valko, that is. By the way, he does a crackerjack job of housecleaning. Really manages a spiffy bedpan."

"Good to know because bedpan experience might come in handy at his next assignment," Jarvis said.

"He's in deep shit, you're saying?"

"Knee deep. You see, Valko was here to look out for you, Shelby. We weren't sure you'd pull through."

"That's what everybody says. Why are you guys looking out for me?"

"Because you saved the world."

Shelby sniffed, wiggled his nose, and lips all at the same time. Jarvis cleared his throat.

"Hmmm," Shelby said. "How's that again? I thought I heard you say I saved the world. The acoustics in these rooms aren't too good."

"That's what I said, Shelby."

"How did I save the world—which part?"

"All of it."

"I saved the world? Planet Earth?"

"The whole damn enchilada," Jarvis said.

"Oh, sure."

"Scout's honor, Shelby."

How?"

"The details must always remain—murky," Jarvis said. "It involved thingamabobs, thingamajigs, and doohickeys, for lack of more specific terminology."

Shelby perked up, sat up a little.

"Damn," Shelby said. "I've heard those words before. In my head. What do they mean?"

"Nobody knows."

"Then how does it help to say them?"

"It helps because nobody knows what it means when you say them. That's the whole idea—to keep folks in the dark."

"Like you are now."

"Part of the job, Shelby. You see, we couldn't be sure you could handle the burden of saving the world. And we fretted about your safety, that someone might use you to access technology."

Shelby contemplated the notion of technology. All that would come to him was the image of a channel changer, a TV remote control.

"I know technology worth accessing?"

"At one time, Shel. But it sounds like you don't remember. If that continues—fine by us. Meantime, always say thingamabobs, thingamajigs, and doohickeys."

"This is pretty weird," Shelby said. "But pretty interesting."

"That's the spirit, Shel. So—to continue, we created a hero in your place, but an agent playing the part. Someone who could operate with the burden of it all. And then that very night, you had the accident."

"What are you telling me, Jarvis?"

"You saved the world. Two months ago."

Shelby sat all the way up, though he still couldn't see Jarvis' face clearly. Then Shelby slumped back into the bed.

"I didn't dream all this?"

"Yes, you did that, too," Jarvis said. "We arranged that. But, it's still true.

"How can I dream up something that's true?"

"With help, of course. It's complicated. But possible."

"Everything about this is complicated," Shelby said. "You're saying you induced dreams—into me?"

"Something like that—to protect you, of course. But agent Valko got a little—overzealous, creative."

"And so he went all Death of a Salesman on me while I was zonked out."

"See, Shel? You're remembering. And you know the theater, too."

"I remember a lot, actually. But only recently. Let me get this straight—you're saying Parsons Grove is a real place?"

"As real as Boise, or Kalamazoo, Michigan, or Wahoo, Nebraska."

"Ever been to Wahoo?"

"I was born there, Shelby."

"Is that true?"

"No."

Shelby began to wonder if he had actually been born in Boise, whether he might actually be from someplace he wasn't remembering yet, like Tupelo, Mississippi, but he didn't think he had a southern accent. No one had mentioned one, anyway.

"I see. And the people in my dreams?"

"Real."

"And Agent Valko put that into my head?"

"We thought you might die, Shel. Really sort of expected it. It became sort of an ethical issue. We decided, even though you were in a coma, to tell you that you saved the world. Since we expected you to die, it was certainly no skin off our noses."

"And all the rest?"

"That's you, Shelby. Your imagination ran with it."

"Why tell me about Parsons Grove?"

"A potential cover story, Shel. In case you recovered, didn't recall who you are. An identity, essentially, in case you needed it."

"Good Lord and General Jackson!"

"Where does that come from, Shel?"

Shelby thought hard. It was as if he could actually see what he'd just uttered in neon lights, like on a sign, but in his head.

"My dreams, I guess. Or maybe Valko. Who knows."

"Agent Valko has a lively imagination. He did do some summer stock in college, you know."

"Where is he?"

"Oh, he's around."

"Cleaning bedpans? You didn't make him vanish or anything, did you?"

"Not our style, Shel. But the bedpans—like I said, a very good idea. Valko will be reassigned to bedpan duty."

"You have bedpan duty?"

"We can certainly create it."

Shelby tugged at his covers and ran his other hand across the sheet-covered mattress. He looked all around the room and back at Jarvis.

"So, you're real, and all this is real?"

"Don't I look real and sound real?"

"You look—shadowy."

"Comes with the job."

"I can imagine. But c'mon—I'm just a math teacher."

"A good one, apparently."

"Where did it happen?" Shelby said.

"Out at the plutonium factory."

"I worked there?"

"That day you did."

Shelby tried very hard to imagine where he might have worked, or lived, or played, before this very odd notion of having worked in a plutonium factory, but his mind gave him no images, no clues.

"And before that day?" Shelby said.

"You'll remember it all—eventually."

"Or not at all?" Shelby said.

"That's possible, too. Maybe likely. And perhaps best."

"I see, though really I don't," Shelby said.

"It's better if you don't, really."

"I'm sensing that. So, I really saved the world?"

"You stopped a really big boom, that's for sure."

Shelby wondered just how *big* of a boom, and why there might have been a boom at all. But his mind on that topic was all cobwebs and darkness.

"But nobody knows I did it, right? This other guy gets the credit, your agent?"

"But you get the money, Shelby."

"Who *is* this other guy?"

"Just Google saved the world, Shel. But it will be a manufactured name and identity, of course. All part of the plan."

"The plan," Shelby said, nodding. "What does the other guy, your agent, get?"

"Satisfaction."

"Is he pretty thrilled with that?"

"He also got a bump in pay grade and the undying gratitude of the agency."

"Woo-hoo. But I got the money."

"You did," Jarvis said. "You will."

"Ooooooommmaaaaaaaeeeeeeeeeeeeeeee!" Shelby said. "Sorry. And what's this about not sweating taxes?"

"You don't have to pay them," Jarvis said. "Ever."

"Ooooooommmaaaaaaaeeeeeeeeeeeeeeee!" Shelby said again. "Okay, I lied—I had another one of those in me."

"Perfectly understandable."

Shelby was starting to cotton up to the idea. And the money sounded good, too. But what had he actually *done?*

"And all this is because I was, what—in the right place, at the right time?"

"Pretty much."

"Is that saving the world?"

"Close enough," Jarvis said. "And America needed a hero."

"Really? Why?"

"America always needs a hero."

"Why?"

"We are always in times requiring heroism."

"Why?"

"We just are. Trust me."

"And it's worth all the money I'm getting?"

"Having a hero is always worth the cost," Jarvis said.

It occurred to Shelby that he was being called a hero in private, but not in public. He was being bought off, essentially.

"Who decided we needed a hero?"

"That came down the food chain. Above my pay grade."

"The president?"

"Wouldn't surprise me at all, Shelby. It certainly wasn't the Boise city council."

"But I guess I didn't actually kiss his wife on the mouth—the first lady. That was in my dream."

"You have ambitious dreams, Shelby. We might arrange a little peck on the cheek—no promises, though."

"Thanks. That's mighty governmental of you. So, how much money are we talking here?"

"Enough, to be sure. Scads, really. But someone else will fill you in on all that."

"Roger Valko?"

"Are you requesting?"

"Does a hero get to do that?"

"Just this one time."

"Then I am—requesting," Shelby said. "Disappointed he'll miss bedpan duty?"

"A little. But I'm a patient man."

THE INTERGALACTIC
BOOK-OF-THE-MONTH CLUB

Shelby had spent a lot of time in Parsons Grove in his mind, in his dreams, and now he was visiting it for the first time in person, in reality. It was a sleepy hamlet nestled in the green hills straddling a Spring River valley. Swift, cold water rushed and created many rapids as the river meandered aggressively through town. Just outside the city limits a very large and very black crow picked at a carcass on the road and declined to move aside. Shelby had to swerve to avoid it. There was something familiar about that crow in the road, as though it had happened before. When he looked back, the crow puffed itself up and spread it wings menacingly.

But Parsons Grove wasn't a carbon copy of the Parsons Grove from his dreams. It wasn't the Porter Newhouse Bridge, for example, that he rolled across as he entered town. A sign pocked with bullet holes indicated it was the Jubal Patterson Bridge. And there was no town square, no Civil War cannon standing guard on the lawn of the courthouse. The main street—Cuppersmith Street—was lined by various businesses, many of them arts and crafts shops hawking Ozark treasures to northern tourists struggling to understand the local accent.

As Roger Valko had explained it, Parsons Grove was chosen rather randomly as a potential place to stash Shelby should it have become necessary to do so—if somehow it got out that he was actually the guy who had saved the world and needed to join a sort of witness protection program for saviors of humanity.

When the decision had been made to tell the comatose Shelby he had in fact saved the world, in case he would soon die and if there was a chance comatose people really could understand what was said to them, Roger also took the opportunity to talk about Parsons Grove to comatose Shelby—when he wasn't also trying out various characters he wanted to portray in plays and using Shelby as an audience that couldn't talk back. Shelby had absorbed everything, and it fueled his imagination, which activated his dreams. He remembered much of the dreams and they played in his head often like simply activating a video camera.

Within days Shelby had bought a rustic A-frame house overlooking the river and guarded by a lane of tall, thick pines similar to the one in his dreams. Roger Valko had given him a bank book indicating an amount of money that was staggering to Shelby, though perhaps trifling to Mitt Romney, and definitely pedestrian to the intrepid Koch Brothers. It was the government's thank-you for saving the world, with a bit, too, from other governments. One day a stray orange cat wandered into his yard but instead of naming it Joe LeFors, he named it Roger Valkyrie. The cat looked well-fed, took an immediate shine to Shelby, and signaled he was staying by curling up on a sofa near the fireplace.

Some of the characters from his dreams were actual people. Ray Spurlock was indeed a trucker who had started a church called The Exalted Church of the Intergalactic Moment, initially to sort of honor the man who saved the world, but also to locate other like-minded folks and fellow liberal Democrats. But after a while, the church members, who met over drinks to gossip at the American Legion Hall, felt it was a bit much to claim to be a church, seeing how all the members were rather progressive folks for a town as squeaky conservative as Parsons Grove, and they were all refugees from the local Baptist church. The Baptist church had chafed them considerably because the pastor, Rev. Artemis Huckley, was rumored to be cheating on his wife with a member of the choir. One rumor had the choir member as male, and another rumor asserted it was a female, and one rumor had him in a threesome with a male and female just to make sure all bases of sin were covered. Infidelity aside, it was the pious hypocrite of a pastor attempting to tell them what was moral and what was traitorous, and that the blame for a degenerate America ought to be laid at the feet of a Muslim president, that got Ray and his flock looking for the door and an antidote to willful ignorance.

So, by unanimous vote one night over many drinks at the American Legion Hall, the Exalted Church of the Intergalactic Moment morphed into The Intergalactic Book-of-the Month Club right about the time Shelby arrived in Parsons Grove. The first book the group took up was *Catch-22,* at the instigation of Ray, who had read it when he was in the Army and thought it a humdinger and sort of a manual for understanding the military.

Shelby heard about the book group at a downtown coffee shop—someone had tacked a flyer on to the bulletin board announcing the group's inaugural foray into literature. He showed up that night, happy that no one knew he had saved the world, and enjoying the irony that they didn't know he actually had, and yet there he was, joining a group that had once entertained notions of worshipping a messiah.

As had been the custom at the start of every evening for his former church, Ray began the book club with a reminder:

"My friends—let us never forget thingamabobs, thingamajigs, and doohickeys."

"Hallelujah," Don Harrison said, and they all raised their drinks.

"Here's mud in your eye," Bob Pickering said.

"Down the hatch," Rita Evermore said.

"Who's this new guy?" Sharlene Tompkins said, gesturing toward Shelby. Shelby shifted in his seat and smiled weakly.

"Everyone, welcome our newest member," Ray said. "Shelby Goddard."

Shelby stood and bowed, felt rather stupid as he did, and then sat down a little too hard, nearly missing his seat.

"Glad to be here," Shelby said self-consciously.

"Let's toast to Shelby," Ray said.

"And to thingamabobs, thingamajigs, and doohickeys," a pretty woman said as she raised her drink to the group.

"Thank you, Oceanna," Ray said.

"Oceanna?" Shelby blurted out.

"Oceanna Calhoun," the woman said, leaning forward for a better look at Shelby down the aisle from her. She looked around thirty and had long straight blond hair down well past her shoulders, and large, lively eyes—darting eyes.

"Have we met before?" she said to Shelby

"I don't think so," Shelby said. "I would remember."

Oceanna smiled pleasantly and sipped her drink, which was a margarita.

"You're new to town?" Rita said.

"Just a few weeks ago," Shelby said sheepishly.

"He bought the Sellers place," Don said.

"I did, yes," Shelby said quietly. "The good old Sellers place."

"I love that old A-Frame," Don said.

"There's a dandy view of the river," Rita said.

"How's that working out for you?" Don said. "How do you feel about the property taxes? Was it in good shape? I knew Old Man Sellers—he could be a funny old coot."

"Don't badger the man," Oceanna said. "He just moved here, for God's sake."

"I wasn't badgering him," Don said. "Just enquiring."

"More like a Spanish Inquisition," Oceanna said.

"I was just talking to the man, for Lord's sake."

"Probing," Oceanna said. "I'm hearing probing, probing, probing."

Shelby liked the sound of her voice. It was sweet, but not syrupy. When she said probing, it didn't come out like it was about a prostate examination.

"Where'd you move from, Shelby?" Anita Cassidy said.

"More probing," Oceanna said quietly.

"Memphis," Shelby lied.

"Funny," Anita said, "but you don't sound like you're from Memphis."

"You're badgering, Anita," Oceanna said.

"No I'm not. I'm just being—inquisitive."

"More like probing," Oceanna said.

"Inquisitive," Anita said.

"Probing," Oceanna repeated.

"It's okay," Shelby said. "Memphis is just where I lived for a while. I'm originally from North Dakota."

He wasn't at all sure why he said North Dakota instead of Idaho, instead of Boise. But one place of origin was as good as another, he supposed. In America, it was pretty much all interchangeable.

"What did you do in Memphis?" Anita said.

"I was an accountant," Shelby lied.

"You setting up shop here in Parsons Grove?" Bob said. "You figure to hang out a shingle? What do you charge for taxes, Shelby?"

"Shelby likely isn't here tonight to do any taxes," Oceanna said.

"I'm just asking, Oceanna," Bob said. "A good tax person is hard to find."

"That's certainly true," Anita said.

"I don't do taxes anymore," Shelby said. "I sort of transitioned away from that."

"Then what line of work are you in now?" Anita said.

"Badgering, Anita," Oceanna said. "Badgering, badgering, badgering."

"Well, who elected you queen of Sheba?" Bob said.

"That's right," Anita said. "We just like to know who someone new might be. What if a bank robber were to join our group?"

"An excellent point," Bob said.

"Shelby," Oceanna said, "are you a bank robber?"

Shelby wasn't sure he could definitively say no, given that some of his memory had yet to come back to him. But he couldn't imagine himself robbing a bank.

"I don't think so."

"See?" Anita said. "He isn't sure."

"Dearie," Oceanna said to Anita, patting her knee, "would you like another margarita?"

"I certainly would if we're to be invaded by Yankee bank robbers."

After the book club meeting broke up, and Oceanna had winked at Shelby with twinkles in her eyes, Shelby walked back to his house across the Jubal Patterson Bridge and just 2.1 miles from town. He was encouraged by her wink and filed it away as something to build on, an adventure for another day, and perhaps soon. Oceanna struck him as plucky, which he liked. He supposed there might even have been sort of an instant chemistry between them, electricity in the air, or maybe he was imagining that. But he was willing to find out. It was a warm night, no traffic on the road, and the sky was littered with glittering stars. He thought he saw something moving in the sky but thought nothing of it. Walking up his lane, he saw glowing eyes lurking among there trees, but figured they belonged raccoons, or maybe deer, was pretty sure it wasn't Roger, or some agent sent by Roger. Sometimes at night he saw raccoons climb up the steep slopes of the A-frame roof.

Instead of going inside, he opened the back door and the cat shot out into the yard. Shelby eased down the slope to the river. The cat joined him as he looked down at the water shimmering in the moonlight. He could hear the rapids and falls gurgling. Two deer emerged from the woods and drank. They looked up several times toward Shelby, their eyes glowing, and the cat's ears were bent back as he flicked his tail rapidly. Shelby leaned down and stroked the cat behind its ears.

"You're ambitious, boy," he said. "But go after them if you think you're up to it. Dream big. No point in dreaming small, I guess."

The cat instead elected to sprawl across Shelby's feet. And Shelby decided it was time for his first check-in call to Agent Valko. He retrieved his phone from a pocket and sat down on the river bank. The cat rubbed against his legs.

"Hola, Shel," Roger Valko said.

"Hola yourself," Shelby said. "Where are you?"

"Still in Boise, kid. But leaving soon."

"Leaving for where?"

"Greener pastures and broader horizons, I hope."

"What's keeping you in Boise, Roger?"

"Bedpans, Shel. The boss wasn't kidding about cleaning bedpans."

"Damn, Roger. Are you cleaning them, or emptying them?"

"Now I'm just shining them. Every damn one. A mountain of bedpans. It takes a hell of a lot of elbow grease, believe you me. But they look pretty damn good now. You can even see your face in them. I'll be done tonight and then my penance is over."

"Good to hear," Shelby said. "Sorry about that."

"That's okay, Shel. It builds character. And hand muscles, too. How are you doing down in Dogpatch?"

"I'm okay. I just got home from the book club."

"Nothing like exercising your mind, kid. What book you doing?"

"*Catch-22*. Ever read it?"

"Sure. In college. How'd the group go?"

"Oh, the actual book discussion is for next week. By the time all the drinking and gossiping was over, it was time to go home."

"Life is slower down there, kid."

"That's fine by me. I can stand some slow life for quite a while."

"You've earned it, Shel."

"Have I? What have I earned?"

Shelby couldn't quite imagine that he had earned anything at all. But could he just take it on faith that he had? Well, that was what faith was, he decided—believing in the improbable. It was about just taking the leap and not letting fear stop him.

"Whatever you want," Roger said. "That's what you've earned, kid."

"What if I don't know what I want?"

"Nothing wrong with that," Roger said. "Life's about figuring that out, and then getting there."

"Getting where, Roger?"

"Where you should be, kid, and then you'll understand life. But sometimes you have to shine a lot of bedpans to understand the meaning of life."

"It's the journey and not the destination, right?" Shelby said.

"That's why it's a bumper sticker, kid."

"Listen," Shelby said. "Got a request for you."

"Shoot, kid."

"Can I call you Roger Valkyrie?"

"Valkyrie? I don't see why not. It's got a nice ring to it. And besides, Valko isn't my real name. Neither is Roger."

"Figured that," Shelby said. "So I guess a name doesn't matter. But I like Valkyrie. It was the first name I recalled after the coma."

"Then it's the one we use, kid. But, that's just between us. To formally change my code name for a specific assignment means a form

1200A-121. And it's a booger, believe you me. The paperwork for a mortgage takes less time."

"I hear you," Shelby said. "If Jarvis shows up, I'll remember to call you Roger Valko."

"Bingo," Roger said. "If you don't, kid, we *both* might end up shining bedpans."

That night, Shelby had bedpan dreams bordering on becoming bedpan nightmares. Everywhere he went in the dream, there were bedpans. Great heaps and mounds and piles of them towering to the sky and disappearing into the clouds. He dreamt of bedpans small enough for a mouse and large enough for an elephant. Bedpans large enough to sail an ocean. Tiny bedpans that could slip into a pocket. Great silver bedpans so shiny he could see his face reflected in them. The bedpans were stacked to the roof of some building, a warehouse, perhaps—a building so vast it seemed like the Roman Colosseum to Shelby, or a football stadium. And it was chock full of bedpans. Bedpans on every square inch. Bedpans stuck to the ceiling. Stuck on walls.

Shelby tried to move among the bedpans but kept tripping over them and falling into piles of them, but he was thankful they all seemed to be empty. It was a universe of bedpans with the collective volume to contain a river of diarrhea. And then, to his horror, a river of diarrhea began to flow from somewhere and fill the immense building, and the vast field of bedpans, and Shelby woke up sweating, but relieved it was sweat and not diarrhea. He sat up for a few minutes, the moon peeking in the bedroom window and bathing it with soft light, the cat draped across his legs. His wits restored, he fell back into a sound sleep without bedpan dreams or diarrhea rivers.

The next morning, he slept late and lingered over a breakfast of eggs, bacon, toast and hash browns. He felt rested. Calm. Even serene. The cat devoured tuna on a plate and groomed itself at the edge of the table while Shelby sipped his orange juice, his mind nearly barren, thoughts spurting by like the occasional car along a lonely country road. The sun radiating through the kitchen window was bright and warm on his neck and the back of his head. He made tea with plenty of honey and sipped it, leaning against a counter. Through the kitchen window he watched a plump red cardinal ruffling its feathers on a bony tree branch. The cat sat expectantly at the sliding glass door and pawed at the glass.

The cat made eye contact with Shelby, who rolled his eyes, but took his cue: He slipped on a jacket and cap and eased down the gentle slope to the river, the cat fast on his heels. Shelby stood on the bank and looked far upriver, where it made a bend out of sight, and then downriver, where the glittering water flowed under the Jubal Patterson Bridge toward Parsons Grove. Above, an eagle soared, dipped, and banked lazily. He watched it until it disappeared over tall trees on a ridge, and then again when it returned minutes later.

Shelby had saved the world, so it was said, but not by many because it was a secret. Almost no one on the planet that still rotated on its axis thanks to him knew the secret. It was the secret of all secrets. But was something true only if everyone knew it? Did truth increase in volume as it grew in recognition? Couldn't truth be a speck of dust? Wasn't there undeniable truth in the tiny leaf of a plant so deep in a forest that no one might ever lay eyes on it? He was now that leaf. He had saved the world, for all the good and the bad in it. Those were the cards he'd been dealt. There were worse cards. Far worse. He was holding aces, but no one could see his hand, of course. And no one needed to see it. It didn't matter. As long as *he* knew the truth, it was *enough* truth for him. Shelby had his hopes. He was prepared to embrace a purpose, too, whenever it elected to show up. He sensed that he was becoming more patient, time slowing down for him and not a blur hurtling past. It was just a feeling, but he felt that patience might be the truth he sought—the truth that was possible.

Shelby squatted next to the river, in the sandy loam, the cat brushing up against him. He admired the perpetual foamy rapids, the bleached white froth from air bubbles and water colliding violently with exposed rocks, the river's sentinels. He looked into the shallow, transparent water—into the very rumbling soul of the river—at smooth, golden pebbles nestled in the river bed, chiseled into place. They sparkled like gold nuggets. Maybe even some of them were gold. Or fool's gold.

Gold or rock, for Shelby the simple smooth stones, worn and sanded by the endless flow of the river, were as valuable, as beautiful, as all the gold the river might conceal. He gingerly dipped a hand into the rushing, clear river. It was very cold. Numbing. But the electric roar of water cascading over boulders was comforting, insulating. A liquid cocoon.

About the Author

Michael Loyd Gray is the author of the novels, *Well Deserved*, *Exile on Kalamazoo Street*, *The Canary*, *King Biscuit*, and *Not Famous Anymore*. He earned a MFA from Western Michigan University, a bachelor's from the University of Illinois, and teaches Creative Writing and British/American literature at a college in South Carolina. He won the 2005 Alligator Juniper Fiction Prize, the 2008 Sol Books Prose Series Prize, and a novel support grant from The Elizabeth George Foundation. His volume of creative non-fiction, *Still Sort of Original in Unoriginal Times*, was released in 2016. Gray is a lifelong fan of the Rolling Stones, Chicago Bears, and Fender guitars.

For other titles available from redbat books, please visit:
www.redbatbooks.com

Also available through Ingram, Amazon.com,
Barnesandnoble.com, Powells.com and by special order
through your local bookstore.